Skylark

SKYLARK

THE DRAGON LADY

a novel

EMILY N. MADISON

NEW YORK

LONDON • NASHVILLE • MELBOURNE • VANCOUVER

SKYLARK

THE DRAGON LADY

Published in New York, New York, by Morgan James Publishing. Morgan James is a trademark of Morgan James, LLC. www.MorganJamesPublishing.com

Proudly distributed by Ingram Publisher Services.

ISBN 9781631958366 paperback
ISBN 9781631958373 ebook
Library of Congress Control Number: 2021951289

Cover Design by:
Karen Dimmick
ArcaneCovers.com

Interior Design by:
Chris Treccani
www.3dogcreative.net

To my dad, who craves the sea and all its beauty,
thank you for instilling your love of pirate adventures in me.

And to all the little girls who loved pirate tales more
than the princess tales, pirate princesses exist too.

CHAPTER 1
"HAIL, BELLADONNA! QUEEN OF ZODIAC!"

The *Zodiac* was at war, and Belladonna Skylark hid herself away from the fight. Cannon and musket fire pierced her ears with a deafening shrill. Splintered wood, small enough to break the skin and large enough to take off the head, sailed through the air. And the smoke was dense; a dark haze wafted through the air. Between these things, it was almost impossible to remember the vast depths of the sea that spread itself beneath the bow of the *Zodiac*.

Belladonna emerged from her hiding place in the sleeping quarters when she heard Starlene's name shouted above her. She knew who had declared war upon her captain. She ascended the steps, one by one, slowly but surely, avoiding any possibility of a quick movement that would result in her death. When she was eye-level with the main deck, she wished that she had never left her hiding place. Every member of Starlene's crew was engaged in combat with dark, wicked men. Swords clanked, bullets whizzed through the air, and the ship rocked with every blow of the opposing cannons and every cannon fire the *Zodiac* returned.

But then there was the blood. The blood had begun to seep through the cracks, slowly dripping into the sleeping quarters. Belladonna looked behind her at the stairs and noticed she had trailed some of it, leaving sticky footprints on each step. As she looked down at her hands and her gown, she noticed she was dotted with droplets. She felt her stomach lurch and had to place her hand over her mouth to keep from retching. She stumbled onto the deck, woozy from nausea. Among the blood was a mixture of limbs, severed heads, entrails, and the like. Belladonna stood among the mess, looking around her at faces she recognized, now twisted in agony during their final moments of breathing. Somehow, in the few seconds it took for her to take in her surroundings, she was kept safe. It was all too much. She heaved her guts out, no longer paying attention to the bloodshed still happening around her.

She stood up, wiping her mouth as she focused on Starlene's cabin, harsh wind wrapping her deep red hair across her face. The doors were open—not a good sign in the heat of battle. Before moving forward, she looked from side to side. Starlene, Snaggletooth, and Romulus were nowhere to be seen. She had to shield herself from the rigging that had torn free and was now falling to the deck. Not one of Starlene's crew paid her any mind. They were far too engaged in saving themselves and the ship. Far too many had already been lost.

Romulus appeared in Starlene's doorway and let out a low wail. He raised his snout in her direction, luring her toward the open doors. Belladonna moved toward the cabin, feeling as if she were floating above the deck and gore. Bloody footprints still followed her. It was obvious from Romulus's eyes that Starlene was in danger. How could a tiger's eyes look so sad?

The Lord's good graces protected Belladonna between the place where she had stood moments before and Starlene's doors. Romulus snorted at Belladonna, and she swore she could see his eyes watering. He turned and flicked his tail, beckoning her to follow behind.

"Belladonna?" She heard a hoarse rasp call quietly from deep within the dark quarters.

"Yes, Captain. It is I." Belladonna took a brief moment to prepare herself for what she might see.

"Come to me, my love." Starlene lay on her monstrous bed with her black pillows propped behind her. Snaggletooth, the *Zodiac's* quartermaster, leaned over the bed close to her body. His salt and pepper hair hung loosely in his eyes and his old, feeble hands worked in the dull candlelight. He pulled away rags that were red enough to have been torn from a gown, much like the color of the gowns that Starlene and Belladonna wore. It did not take long before Belladonna realized that the rags were dripping with Starlene's blood. Now that she'd seen what was happening, she realized the cabin reeked of blood and sweat. It was enough to make her sick all over again.

As she approached, she knew that Starlene's life would end shortly. Starlene's left hand was placed gently on the side of her stomach while her right hung limply from the bed. Belladonna noticed an ever-growing pool of blood on the floor under Starlene's dangling fingers. Large cannon splinter from the ship's wheel jutted grotesquely from the right side of Starlene's stomach like it had grown from her very skin and become part of her. Where the wood protruded from her skin was the same scarlet red of the rags and the pool on the floor.

Starlene's face was ashen and expressionless. With her left hand, she gestured for Belladonna to come to her.

"Captain, no! What happened?" Belladonna felt her face turn pale and the room began to spin. Her captain was the prize and love of her life. "You must make it. Please, you must."

"I have done all that I can do, Bella." Starlene was the only one that Belladonna ever allowed to call her by her short name. "But please, come down to me. Snaggletooth, can you try to put more pressure on it?"

"I don't want to hurt ye, Captain. Be still." Snaggletooth grunted at Romulus, who picked up another white rag in his teeth and placed it gently in Snaggletooth's hand. He folded it down the middle and pressed it to Starlene's side, first slowly then firmly. Starlene let out a scream, her body twisting in agony.

"Starlene, you need to be still. And why is the surgeon not here? Romulus, go fetch the surgeon!" Starlene grabbed Belladonna's wrist and squeezed tightly. She looked at her firmly and spoke through gritted teeth.

"No! There is nothing that can be done, child. This is the end of my fight. I have fought hard, but the blood has flowed out of me too quickly. There is nothing that dastardly surgeon Cromley can do to keep me from bleeding to death now."

"But perhaps there is something he *can* do. Some ointment he has, maybe. Please, Captain, please let him try." Belladonna felt a tear escape her eye and roll down to her chin. It landed on Starlene's chest. She looked down at it questioningly.

"Enough of that," Starlene demanded. "I don't want to hear any more about saving me. I had Romulus call you here because I wanted you to be with me. I don't know how much time is left." In the sixteen years that Belladonna had spent in Starlene's care and custody, this was perhaps the first time that she heard a slight twinge of fear in her captain's voice. The fear she heard willed her to thicken her own skin.

"I'm right here, Captain." Belladonna grabbed her captain's hand, not minding the blood that squelched between their fingers as they intertwined. This would be the first and last time that Belladonna would see Starlene shed a tear.

"I always thought I was too fearless to be afraid of the end, but here I am." Starlene attempted a small laugh but ended up coughing instead. Blood dripped from the corner of her mouth. Snaggletooth was quick to wipe it away with a fresh cloth. Romulus rested his chin on the thigh of her wooden leg and sat patiently by her side. With her other hand, she reached out to him, patting him slowly on the head. "They say that animals know when someone is about to die."

"Don't talk like that," Belladonna commanded.

"You have always been good to me. I thankee for that, my love." Starlene reached out and touched Belladonna's cheek, which was not far from her own now. Her chest fluttered, and she let out a gasp. Her fight was growing difficult.

"You know that you don't have to thank me. You know that I owe far more to you than I have been able to give. You have raised me, which is more than anyone has done for me."

Snaggletooth removed another rag from her side. The crimson flow did not cease. It poured forth with each beat of Starlene's pulsing heart.

"Need I remind ye, Captain, that while it is well 'n good to have Belladonna here with ye in yer last moments, ye arsked me to remind ye of what ye needed to tell her." Snaggletooth looked down at Starlene's face and then up at Belladonna's, his namesake tooth revealing itself from his lower lip. He appeared stern and sullen.

"Thankee, Snaggletooth. You have been just as good to me." She stroked his cheek and turned her face back to Belladonna's.

"Bella, my love. I have much to tell you and not much time to tell it. But you need to know it. Your parents made me promise to tell you if I ever ended up with a piece of the ship stuck in me." She tried to say this last bit in good humor, but Belladonna knew that she was still afraid of facing her end. Belladonna had not thought about her parents in years. She never knew them, so she gave up thinking about them and cleared the word *parents* from her vocabulary.

The word seemed to awaken a part of her that had been asleep for many, many years.

"Are they truly dead?" she asked.

"Yes, darling. That part remains true. But there is much more you will learn about them soon. I need only tell you what they asked me to relay should they pass prematurely." Starlene looked at Snaggletooth and issued a heavy, efforted sigh, gaining the strength needed to tell her tale. Belladonna's heart began to beat faster and louder in her ears.

"So what of them?" Belladonna asked. "What is it you need to tell me?"

"You know that I united with your parents many years ago as allies. Aye, they sailed the seas as part of my fleet. They always felt it was their destiny to be at sea, to take back what had already been taken. In those days, I had three ships in my fleet. They quickly became more to me than just allies in the name of piracy. Your father and mother were my confidants, my most trusted companions. But when Cornelius Blackfoot found out who they were and what they were doing, he found his way to them. To us. Blackfoot was their long-seated enemy, and so I became his enemy as well. One of the last things your father said to me was that he wanted me to make sure Blackfoot was cast to the bottom of the ocean in your mother's name. He is the demon of the seas. He deserves to be cast to the bottom of the ocean just as Satan himself was cast back to hell by Christ."

Belladonna knew who Blackfoot was. She knew that for as far back as she could remember, Blackfoot trailed the *Zodiac* wherever she sailed. She also knew that Blackfoot, in the very moment that she was sharing with Starlene, was doing all in his power to shred the *Zodiac* bit by bit, thus taking all the crew with her. However, she did not know that Blackfoot's anger did not lie exclusively with Starlene, that it started because of her association with the Skylark name. But why? And how? These were all things that Belladonna desperately wanted to ask but knew that if she simply listened, Starlene may give her the answers.

"Blackfoot is the enemy. He is my own enemy, and now, he will become yours as well. Even before you knew of him, he was your enemy. I have kept you hidden from him for your entire life. He does not know that you exist. He knows that your parents had a child, but he does not know about *you.* He is unaware that you live and breathe this very day. If you don't hold onto any of the things I have told you today, mark my words; you will want to hold on to these: Blackfoot is your enemy because he was first your parents' enemy.

"Your mother, Jade Skylark, outlived your father by mere moments. Just as you are now, I was by her side to witness her final breaths. She made me swear on my life and my ship that I would send you to finish what they started—what *we* started. To rid this wicked world of Cornelius Blackfoot. It is the prophecy."

The prophecy? Belladonna had never heard any mention of a prophecy in her life with Starlene. And a prophecy about her? What was she to fulfill that she knew nothing about? "Captain, you're not making sense. There is a prophecy that I am to fulfill?"

"Yes, my child. Your father and mother started the journey, and you are to finish it." Starlene sat up abruptly and grabbed Belladonna by the front of her corset and pulled her close.

"Listen to me, Belladonna. You are to go to the islands and find the Isla del Dragón, and there, you will find what your parents worked tirelessly to reclaim in their lives. I watched the power of their island consume them. Blackfoot will try to stop you as he did your father and mother before you. You cannot allow him. You must destroy him. You must. It is in the prophecy that you will slay the Demonclaw!"

As Starlene told her this, she began to convulse. She spoke through gritted teeth, her blood spewing between them and running down her chin. She was frightening to look at. Belladonna herself began to shake, feeling a mix of fright and exhilaration. Belladonna grabbed her wrists and pushed herself away from her face.

"Starlene, what is this? Where is this coming from? You must tell me more about them. Please, for my sake, why does Blackfoot want you? Why has he chased *you* year after year if my parents have been dead?"

"I have tried to take over their quest. I have tried to solve the puzzle of their lives, and I have doomed myself to die by Blackfoot's hand because I am not part of the prophecy. I am not the one who is to destroy him and find the Isla del Dragón, and it has consumed me. I felt I must avenge them. All this time, I tried to be the remnant, but you are the remnant."

An explosion rocked the ship, and the *Zodiac* keeled to the left. Snaggletooth jumped up to keep Starlene from rolling off of her bed as she wailed with the movement.

"How am I to do this? I know nothing of the islands, much less how to get there. What is to happen to me? Please, Starlene, I have been under your care and protection my whole life, and I don't feel prepared to do what you're saying I must do. All of this frightens me!"

"You will not be so afraid. You will grow. You will fight more battles than I ever have at sea. Your ancestors will guide you. And keep a weather eye for *the Mark*."

"The Mark?" None of this made sense to Belladonna. She tried to take a moment to think about all the pirate tales Starlene had told her over the years, remembering the hushed stories shared among her crew. They whispered tales of the Isla del Dragón, the Mark, and the Dragon Majestics.

Starlene's eyes began to roll back in her head.

"Captain!" Snaggletooth yelled. "Stay with us! Ye must finish telling Belladonna what she needs to do!"

"Look for the Mark," Starlene gasped, "and fight."

"Starlene, no, please! You cannot leave me yet! What do I need to do?"

"Fight." With that word, Starlene let her body fall back into the pillows. She arched her back, using her whole body to take in the air around her. Suddenly, her body ceased. Blood continued to seep out around the wood stuck through her stomach, but her body stopped fighting.

Captain Starlene breathed her last.

Belladonna screamed, allowing her body to give in to the grief. She shook, and her hands began to sweat. Then she let her gaping mouth release sobs that started deep in the pit of her stomach. Starlene was the only person that Belladonna had in her life. She had no family; she had no formal education, she had only stepped foot off the *Zodiac* a handful of times throughout her short life. The grief and fear twisted her gut as she started to think of a world without her beloved captain in it. She got to the floor and curled into herself, letting her tears fall to the floor. Snaggletooth lowered his head and sighed, crossing himself as he did so.

"May she rest in peace." He removed the rag from her side, giving up the idea that he could prevent her death. Romulus let out a series of low, sad snarls and paced the room. Belladonna was able to look up long enough to demand that Snaggletooth tell the crew that their captain was no more.

"You need to tell them. They need to know."

"Now is not the time, Belladonna. I am sorry for yer loss. I know how much she meant to ye. She was like a mum to ye. I watched 'er raise ye and all that. She was good to ye, and ye was good to 'er."

"If you will not tell them, then I will." She stood up, steadying herself as the ship rolled to the side. Snaggletooth grabbed her arm.

"No, ye don't. Now is not the time. Ye need to think about what Starlene done told ye. Ye suddenly have a lot to do. Ye need to think about that before ye be gettin' the crew stirred up. They got much on their hands right now, miss, defendin' the ship and all."

"I don't need to think. They need to know." She yanked out of Snaggletooth's grip. Before she could take two steps, she fell back. Romulus had the hem of her dress in his jaws and brought her to the ground with a thump.

"Don't test yer quartermaster, miss." Snaggletooth towered over her. The room felt grim.

"Romulus, I want ye to let those stinking dogs out there know that they must fight to the death." Romulus obeyed him and left through Starlene's doors. He ascended the stairs to the helm and once he could see the whole of the crew, he let out a deep, mournful roar. Not even Romulus could contain the mourning deep within him enough to keep the news until the fighting ceased. The crew, one by one, stopped their fighting with Blackfoot's crew and looked up at Romulus as his announcement of Starlene's death broke through the air. All of them knew what Romulus's cry meant for the *Zodiac.* The ones who had hats and could remove them did so and placed them over their hearts.

Cornelius Blackfoot looked up from his place in his quarters, tucked safely away from the war outside, when he heard a wild animal's cry pierce through the noise of battle. The silence that followed after the animal ceased told Cornelius everything he needed to know.

Captain Starlene was dead. And the *Zodiac* was likely on its way to the depths of the sea.

He smiled. *Finally.*

"Captain! That devil woman of a captain, Starlene, is dead!" Maximus, Blackfoot's first mate, cheered as he entered Blackfoot's quarters, uninvited and unannounced.

"Yes. I know." It satisfied him more than it should have to be so content with someone's death. He had been fighting Starlene for years, ever since he missed his chance to take her down with the Skylarks. He picked up his pen and dipped it in ink, his hand shaking with joy as he pulled out his log to record the date and time of Starlene's dark end.

"What are we to do with the ship, Captain? Are we to capture the remaining crew and run her alongside us?"

Blackfoot thought about this for a moment. He had not given much thought to what he would do once Starlene finally passed on. Starlene was merely a thorn in his side, a minor obstacle in his pursuit of the imminent destruction of the Isla del Dragón and the Dragon Majestics.

"She sails without a captain. I doubt any of her half-witted crew would try to command a vessel the size of the *Zodiac*. The ship means nothing to me. Let her be swallowed and eaten by the dreaded Kraken—along with her captain's corpse. A just end to a noble cause." He grinned and looked back up at Maximus, his ever-loyal but irritating first mate. He dipped his pen in the ink jar, finding a blank page.

Starlene has fallen – 10 September 1718

Blackfoot almost closed his logbook before he decided the words he had just written satisfied him. He left it open and stood up. He looked out his window, watching the *Zodiac* take every blow that was given to her.

"But you chased her for so long, sir. You want nothing? Not even for us to loot her cargo? Surely you want the body." Maximus felt a sting across his face. He placed his hand on his cheek and began to rub. Blackfoot had slapped him.

"I said let her sink. The whole lot. Did I say anything otherwise?"

"No, sir. Sorry, sir." Blackfoot turned back to his window to enjoy the view. A long moment of silence lapsed between them.

"Well then, where are we headed, Captain?" Maximus asked. Blackfoot turned and grinned his awful, black-toothed grin.

"I think you know very well our destination, my good man."

Belladonna felt herself being shaken. Slowly, she lifted her head and gazed around her. She wiped the drool from the corner of her mouth, willing herself to sit up. The blur faded from her vision, and she noticed she had not moved from where she had begun to mourn Starlene's death. Her face was caked with dry tears. Snaggletooth stood over her, looking down on her small, crumpled frame. When she looked toward the bed, she saw that Starlene's lifeless body had not been moved from its resting place. A moan escaped Belladonna's mouth.

"Enough of that," Snaggletooth commanded. "Allowing yerself to die along with 'er ain't gonna do ye no good. Ye need to get up."

Romulus appeared at Belladonna's side and nudged her with his soft snout. His low snorts encouraged her to stand.

"I cannot, Snaggletooth. How have you not moved her yet? How do you expect me to do anything after all I have endured this day?"

"Quite actin' like a spoiled child. Ye know what this means, don't ye? The *Zodiac* cannot sail without a captain. That title now belongs to ye."

Belladonna's eyes widened in disbelief. "I am *what?*" She gasped.

"Ye are the captain. And if ye are the captain, ye need to start actin' like one. Starting with gettin' off yer arse. A slew of men awaits ye out there." With his words, Belladonna felt Snaggletooth's hands in hers, lifting her to her feet. She wobbled, finding her footing to be seemingly impossible. Anger began to course through her veins.

"I don't think you understand the weight of what has happened. Starlene is *dead.* I cannot simply take command of her post and her ship. It isn't right. It isn't even *fair.* How am I to be the captain that Starlene was? How am I to do what she has told me I need to do?"

"The prophecy." Snaggletooth did not change his expression.

"I don't want to hear about—"

"The prophecy, m'lady. Ye heard her well and true. Ye are to fulfill the prophecy. Ye will be guided. *They* will show ye what to do."

Snaggletooth's words ignited a flame in Belladonna's heart. For her entire life, she knew nothing but the comfort of being cared for by Starlene. She suddenly felt stronger. She felt wiser. She felt a *call.* She knew not from where, and though it was faint, she felt it.

The tale of the Skylark parents now felt like something tangible, something able to be uncovered. The mystery of Belladonna's family had shrouded her for as long as she could remember, even though she had tried hard to think of it merely as a tall tale rather than true events. It could be an invitation to at least unearth what happened to them and how she ended up in Starlene's care. Not only could the journey be an opportunity to discover her family, but it could also be an invitation to discover herself. She knew already that what lay ahead of her would not be easy. It would not be comfortable, and she could not hide in anyone's shadow any longer. Quickly, she glanced at Starlene's body on the bed and looked down at her feet. Examining herself, she flattened the front of her skirts and looked up at Snaggletooth.

"You are right." As much as she hated to admit it, he *was* right. He had heard Starlene's words just as clearly as she had. He reached down to grab her hand and kissed it.

"I am at yer command, Cap'n Skylark."

This made her smile. She still felt the grief of Starlene's passing tugging in her heart, but she was too thrilled by this newfound courage to discover and live out.

"I must see to the crew then. And we must get rid of the body. Shall you join me?"

"As I said, at yer command, Cap'n Skylark."

Romulus nuzzled her thigh, pledging his allegiance as well. Belladonna took her first steps forward, Snaggletooth and Romulus flanking her on either side. As she emerged from the quarters, the crew gazed at her in wonder. She walked down the middle of the deck, dividing the onlookers as she made her way.

"I am sure you are all aware of what has happened this day," she yelled, loud enough for every crewmember to hear. "Captain Starlene has left this world and because of that, it is a little darker."

"May she rest in peace." The crew murmured solemnly in unison.

"But this does not mean that we stop fighting. This means that we continue the fight. We repair the damages. We do not let the *Zodiac* sink. We keep Starlene's legacy alive! And we must grant Starlene her final wish. She told me from as early as I could understand that her body belonged to the sea—and in her death, even still. I need two men to retrieve her body and heave it overboard."

"Are you sure that's such a good idea, miss?" Jedidiah, one of Starlene's skilled gunners, asked. "Pardon me for asking, but bein' as we are all a little superstitious, don't that sound like it will bring us ill favor with the sea?"

"Jedidiah, ye will do as yer new cap'n commands," Snaggletooth shouted, "so p'rhaps you would like to do the honors?"

"*Captain*?" Jedidiah gasped. The crew let out gasps behind him.

"What you've heard is true. With Starlene's passing, I am now in charge of the *Zodiac* . . . and all of you." She held her hands behind her back and laced her fingers, beginning to pace again. A stunned silence fell over the crew. "So Jedidiah, fetch her body and see that it is brought before me."

"Do we not get a say in these matters?" Jedidiah protested. "Who said she was to become captain when Starlene passed? We don't stand a chance with 'er as our captain. She ain't even old enough to know about piratin' and such."

Belladonna would remember Jedidiah's opposition.

"I suggest ye commence yer blabberin' and do as Cap'n Skylark has asked ye. That's an order." Snaggletooth was just an inch from Jedidiah's face. No one else dared to speak.

"Aye, sir." Jedidiah shared a resentful glance with Belladonna and walked toward Starlene's quarters. He grabbed another man, Daniel Cross, by the arm and dragged him behind.

The silence that filled the time while Belladonna waited for them to emerge with Starlene's body felt cold. The sails and colors, or what remained of both, whipped in the wind. She sensed that Jedidiah was not the only one present who held any objections. Surely they did not object to a female captain. But they would object to a *new* female captain, especially one as young as herself. She would have to handle these objections as she saw fit.

Jedidiah and Daniel trudged to the deck with Starlene's heavy body in their arms. Belladonna held her gaze away, willing herself to keep her eyes from the corpse in the men's arms so as not to lose her hold on her emotions.

"Now, throw her overboard," She commanded sharply.

"But captain, are we not allowed any remarks?" Daniel cried.

"No. Let us be done with it."

The two men who held Starlene's body looked up at her questioningly but listened. They hauled her to the side and began to swing. Quiet sniffs were heard among the crew as they were denied a formal parting with their beloved captain. Belladonna knew that Starlene's death would weigh heavy on not just herself when the time came, but also her crew. She was beloved among them, and even though she was stern, they were beloved to her as well. Soft, muffled prayers were heard all around. Some of the men closed their eyes and rocked back and forth as they prayed for mercy over her soul.

"God bless her, and God help us," Snaggletooth said quietly at Belladonna's side. There was a collective inhale as Starlene's body was heaved overboard. Belladonna closed her eyes in time to avoid the looks around her when her body hit the water with a dull splash. Many of the men crossed themselves.

Something stirred in Belladonna's heart at the sound of that splash. She felt full of life-giving fire, full of unquenchable fury. She put her hand to her breast, surprised by this bitter feeling. Her heart was *burning.* The pain was unimaginable.

"Cap'n, are ye alright?" Snaggletooth grabbed her shoulder.

Suddenly, she was more than fine. She was no longer burning. Hatred had just replaced the burning. Nothing had ever made her feel this much hatred toward the world around her. The grief she felt for Starlene had vanished entirely and been replaced by something new. Her heart was not the same human heart that she had possessed a moment before. Her heart had shriveled.

Belladonna's heart had turned black.

This new condition made her feel indestructible. Her heart was seemingly impenetrable. The confidence she felt moments earlier had caught fire, the embers igniting her heart, spreading pure rage in its place like wildfire.

"I've never felt better," she grinned at Snaggletooth. His face twisted with his lack of understanding. What had come over her?

As the men continued to mourn quietly among themselves, Belladonna ascended to the helm. All eyes turned to watch as she made her way slowly. This new version of her heart—this black heart—sharpened her newfound purpose. She now had what she needed to do as the prophecy stated she must do. Her newborn cruelty was aimed at a life she had never known, the life she did not get to have with her family. That rage was now aimed at destroying that cursed Cornelius Blackfoot, the man who had taken everything away from her, starting with her family and now today, her beloved captain. Her black heart would ensure that Blackfoot was cast to the bottom of the ocean for what he stole from her.

Somewhere along the way, she grabbed a sword she found on the ground, disregarding the dead surrounding her. The crew had been reduced, yes, but was easily replaceable. She would need to make a stop along the way, but no matter. Her quest was now laid before her—to seek the Isla del Dragón to find what the Skylark name held for her there.

As she stood at the wheel, she raised her sword in the air.

"Hail, Belladonna! Queen of *Zodiac!* Hail, Belladonna! Queen of *Zodiac!*"

The crew chanted this as fury beat in Belladonna's breast. At Starlene's bedside, she was a timid, insecure young girl who feared life itself. With Starlene's passing, she had transformed into a monster. She knew not why, but surely this transformation was all be part of the prophecy in which she was now so heavily steeped. Snaggletooth appeared at her side.

"Where are we headed, Cap'n Skylark?"

"To the Isla del Dragón . . ." She paused and couldn't help but grin before saying, "But first, prepare the pistol and bring me anyone who has any objections to my new station."

CHAPTER TWO

A GRUELING CAPTAIN

Almost two years had drifted by since Starlene had passed into the next life, and Belladonna had taken over as captain of the *Zodiac*. Belladonna was just shy of turning eighteen; she could feel in the weather that it was almost time for the day that Starlene had celebrated as her birth date. She was not sure if she was the youngest pirate captain who ever lived, nor did she really care for that matter. Already, she was making her name as one of the most notoriously ruthless captains of her day.

When she first took her place as captain, she set out to do what her black, bitter heart told her to do. Her first order of business was ridding the ship of anyone who had incorrect opinions about her new station. Her cruelty started there and only magnified itself with each passing month. The confidence she felt in herself was strong enough to care for little else but herself and what lay ahead on the Isla del Dragón.

Belladonna often thought back to the day she became captain all those years ago. Jedidiah had been the first to go after his outspoken dissension. Snaggletooth prepared the pistol for Belladonna as she had asked. When he delivered it to her, in her new quarters, she asked him to retrieve Jedidiah and bring him immediately before her. The rest of the crew started making the necessary repairs to the ship. Miraculously, though she had taken quite a bit of damage, the *Zodiac* did not suffer enough to sink. Blackfoot had been wrong when he believed the sturdy ship would meet her end. The only part of the *Zodiac* that now rested on the ocean floor was Starlene's set of bones. Snaggletooth had found Jedidiah leaning over a bucket of water with a brush in his hand, ready to scrub the deck of the blood and filth from the battle.

"Captain's askin' for ye." Snaggletooth knew what Belladonna intended to do. He felt a snag in his breath, the smallest bit of remorse beginning to take root in his heart. Other than his rebellious opinion of Belladonna, Jedidiah had been an outstanding gunner and a reliable member of the crew.

"Oh, yeah? Well, let me go see my *captain* then," Jedidiah said mockingly, throwing his bucket on the ground.

"I suggest ye mind yer tone with 'er. Yer liable to pay if ye don't," Snaggletooth tried to warn Jedidiah with his words and glaring blue eyes. Jedidiah chuckled, brushing off his quartermaster's warning, and headed for Belladonna's quarters.

Romulus was lying at Belladonna's feet when Jedidiah entered. Romulus was an obedient animal, partial to the feelings of whoever his master was. Starlene had been his master for most of his life, but he had known Belladonna for all of hers as well. Though just a jungle cat who could not reason in the ways of men, he *knew* that Belladonna would now be the one he served. He laid his ears back against his skull and let out a harsh growl. Belladonna reached out to stroke the deep fur on his head. She smirked at Jedidiah. The man showed no fear or unease. This surprised her. He clearly did not know what kind of captain he now faced.

"So you have something to say to me, don't you?"

"I don't know what you could possibly mean, miss."

"Miss?" She laughed out loud at this. "Don't you mean *captain*? I can't believe you've already made that mistake."

"Ain't no mistake been made. You ain't the captain. No one says you was except for yerself. That's not how this works. We all get to have a say in such matters."

"Do you? Well, what if Starlene had willed it so? What if I was always meant to captain the *Zodiac?* Would you go around questioning fate like that? Seems an awful big risk for someone who seems so worried about superstitions all of a sudden." It gave her far too much pleasure to squeeze Jedidiah like a bug between her fingers. "What if it was just *meant* to be this way?"

"I ain't ever heard Starlene's wishes for you, and I certainly can't predict fate. It would be wrong of me to just go along assuming."

"Aye, I guess it would." She stood up from her place. The hair on Romulus's back stiffened. He stood in a defensive crouch, his eyes piercing Jedidiah. "But would you be messing with fate, then, if you objected to me? Would you try to change the course of it?" She started to approach him. Her boots made a rhythmic *tap, tap* as she moved closer.

"No, ma'am." Belladonna was in his face. She looked up at him, and she could smell the fear that was beginning to grab hold of him. Romulus could smell it too. Jedidiah tried to turn away from her.

"Alright, then. So simply call this fate and accept. There is more to this than you know." Her words came out like a growl. She turned to walk back to her seat, certain that Jedidiah's fear would melt into compliance.

"I don't know that there's more to this. What I see is Starlene's whiny young maid-girl trying to take over our ship. And it ain't right!" She paused after Jedidiah said this and then turned to face him again.

"Just say it!" she demanded, tired of the back and forth. "Accept me as your captain."

"That, I will never do, ma'am. Starlene will be my captain until we decide otherwise." In a flash, Belladonna raised her pistol and cocked it.

"Say it, you bastard." Her finger slowly made its way to the trigger, ready to fire the minute she heard another peep from Jedidiah's cracked lips. Her anger burned red. It felt like a fire was dancing in her ribcage, and she was sure she'd start to see smoke slip through her tight lips.

"Never in my life will I—" Jedidiah's words stopped dead in their tracks. He had heard the ring in his ears before he knew what had happened to him. The bullet pierced through his filthy linen shirt and nestled in his stomach. He looked down at the wound, the crimson already blooming on his shirt like a rose in season. Belladonna held the pistol, still aimed directly at his chest, the smoke rising in thin wisps from the barrel. Her expression had not changed. Jedidiah expected her to falter on what she intended to do, remembering him as a soul who added value to the ship's crew. By golly, something was *wrong* with the girl, but what? Never had he seen her act this horrendously. Jedidiah moved one foot toward her, needing to be closer to her. He felt drawn to her cruelty.

Something about it was powerful. Whatever possessed her heart seemed strong and desirable.

"I hope you know now, in your final moments, that I hold true to my word. I will not suffer intolerance at the hands of any man. Not any loathsome soul." Belladonna snarled.

"Belladonna, what possesses you? 'Tis not the girl I remember that lived under Starlene's care." Jedidiah gasped, doing his best to stay alive long enough to solve this sudden mystery. Dying had become an afterthought. He started to paw desperately at his wound to stop the bleeding.

"I'm afraid I have not the slightest clue what you're talking about. Now, go show the crew what has happened to you here. Go, now." She shooed him toward the door. He stood in disbelief, fully aware of the evil that lurked in Belladonna's bosom.

"What has happened to you?"

Before he could receive an answer, he felt himself wheeled around by Belladonna's tight grasp. He was being dragged out through the doors on deck for the crew to see. As she pulled him forward, he stumbled.

"Get up, you wretch!" Belladonna yelled at him. Jedidiah only moaned and coughed up blood in response. "Romulus, come fetch this man." Romulus came behind him and grabbed him by the scruff of his neck like he would a small cub. As Romulus dragged him across the teakwood of the main deck, the wood splintered Jedidiah's skin. He screamed in pain, blood choking him. The pain that pierced his belly was insufferable. Now the skin of his legs was being shredded by the ship he had spent many of the years of his life in love and labor with. When Starlene took him on, he had lusted after the sea. He fell in love with the *Zodiac* and earned his keep as a prized gunner. Surely, he never imagined that Starlene would pass on before he would, and he surely never thought that he would die at the hands of Starlene's girl. His loyalty lay with the woman who gave him the life he had, and he would never renounce it, not even on his deathbed.

Jedidiah felt the eyes of the crew turn toward him. Humiliation rattled him. So many of the men he had grown up with were presently watching his final moments. He heard Belladonna's steps near his ear as Romulus plopped him down before the crew.

"Gentlemen, witness this man today! This is a man who has decided that he does not agree with my place as captain. His allegiances lay with Captain Starlene, but she is no longer. So here he is as a warning to you all. He will die today, whether that be seconds or hours from now, I know not. But heed this warning nonetheless! If I find that any one of you has any blasted thing to say about myself as your captain, I will not hesitate to put a bullet between your eyes. Or much worse. It all depends on how I feel at the time, perhaps. Today, I don't feel so kind. So if I so much as hear one thing like what this man—" Belladonna was interrupted by a tug on her skirts. She pulled away and looked down. Jedidiah clung to her skirts like a hungry child.

Tears flowed down his cheeks.

"Belladonna, I have known you for your entire life. Will ye not call me by name? Say my name; you know it well. Please, if I am to die by your hand, at least give me the honor of being called by my name." Belladonna considered this but decided to remain unmoved by his words. Even worse, she was unmoved by his humanity. Her heart only knew the passionate anger she felt against him. She stepped away, pulling her skirts from his grasp in disgust.

"As I was saying, before I was so rudely interrupted, if I so much as hear one thing like what this man has had to say, your time on this ship will come to an end. Do I make myself clear?"

Weighted silence hung in the air, the men too afraid to speak. "I asked, do I make myself clear?"

"Aye, Captain!"

"Aye, then," Belladonna smirked. She heard Jedidiah crying at her feet, whimpering to himself.

"She won't even say my name!" He yelled. "She is not human, ye dogs! Heed my warning as well before I pass on. Your captain is no more human than that wretched cat!"

Belladonna kicked him in the ribs. It took all his might to muster another breath from his lungs. He began to cry even harder, disbelieving how quickly the course of his life had been altered. He had been the first true witness of Belladonna's transformation. Just the day before, he had remembered her to be a shy soul, hiding in Starlene's shadow. The next day, she had exhibited a warrior spirit with an unforgiving heart.

"Ah, I am so delighted to finally hear you call me captain. But I hate to tell you that it's too late for me to save you. Romulus, I've had enough of this man. Do what must be done." Like the loyal animal he was, he listened to his new master. Jedidiah's pulse had slowed as Romulus dragged him away into the darkest corner of the ship.

None of the crew ever found out exactly how Jedidiah's life ended. Some said that after Romulus dragged him away, Snaggletooth threw him overboard as a final thanks for his services onboard, saving him from any further torture. Some said Belladonna kept him locked up in a cell that only she had access to until he breathed his last. Whether or not those two tales were true, the story most commonly shared among the crew was that Romulus had eaten Jedidiah. Even though the crew knew Romulus to be a loyal pet to the *Zodiac's* captain, trained in magic by a witch woman, he was still a wild cat. Surely his natural instincts took over every once in a while. No one had dared to ask Belladonna, or even Snaggletooth, what really happened to Jedidiah's body. They collectively decided to steer clear of Romulus from that day forward.

Many of the men who claimed Starlene as their one, true captain met their end under Belladonna's hand. But after the rumors of Jedidiah's death, they feared what she would do to them if they shared their thoughts aloud. The ones that did find fault in her position became loyal to one another, unintentionally dividing the crew. This, in fact, made it much easier to know who was loyal to Belladonna and who was not. In their attempts to stay quiet, they were speaking volumes.

Belladonna quickly put a stop to it by first doing as she said she would—firing a bullet between the eyes and then finishing them off in a medley of cruel ways. The crew that was left knew when another disloyal mate bit the dust when they heard the pistol's single fire. It took her close to two years to rid the *Zodiac* of its plague of rebellion, but she had done it nonetheless. Starlene's crew of fifty men had now been reduced to twenty under Belladonna's command.

Sea life under their new captain was equally as cruel. If Starlene ran a tight ship, then Belladonna squeezed it to a bloody pulp in her grasp. The men who were left after the killings were given more duties, some they were unaccustomed to handling. Every day, one of the crew was responsible for swabbing the deck. If the entirety of the ship was not completed by supper, the man responsible was given lashings from Snaggletooth and made to start anew the next day. When this happened, the men were not allowed to wear their shirts; they were forced to remain on their hands and knees, scrubbing with their fresh, raw wounds blistering in the sun. Belladonna did not allow these men any treatment from the surgeon. The men with the stripes on their backs endured the fever brought on by the sun shining into their wounds. This was only one of the ways in which Belladonna revealed that her heart had hardened toward the men she had been raised alongside.

They were given small rations, mostly because Belladonna's need to reach the Isla del Dragón took precedence over stopping to replenish food and drink. She could hardly think of eating. Her heart beat only for the Isla del Dragón and for her purpose there. With so many of their mates gone, the men did what they could to make it through the day on what little food and drink they were offered. She had not yet lost any men due to starvation. Because of her position, Snaggletooth daily reminded them to be grateful that she allowed them any food and drink at all.

There was little to no merriment onboard. The lively dinners that Starlene hosted every so often no longer existed. No dancing, no laughing, no mulling about on deck when they worked to lull themselves through the doldrums they sometimes found themselves in.

Generally, Belladonna remained content when she wasn't aroused by any happenings on the ship or looking on as one of the crew received his punishment. She had Snaggletooth and Romulus keep a watchful eye and interfere when necessary. For the past two years, the few men she was gracious enough to let live knew what irked her and did what they could to stay quiet moving forward. Every man avoided her berating them at any cost.

Surely she would be driven to madness, she thought. Though many suns had set since she took command, she felt as though no progress had been made toward the Isla del Dragón. In that time, she focused on attacking any ship that happened to interfere with the *Zodiac's* path. What she needed from these ships, which so unfortunately crossed her, was any plunder, food, or spirits her men could find. All three of those things were needed to keep her from having to stop in port, which meant more time could be spent finding her way to the island. She was still somewhat new to her station and still driven by blinding rage—so much so that she had spent the last two years concentrating her efforts on learning to control herself.

Now that she had some experience under her belt and all that she needed had been taken from other ships, she felt more prepared, especially as the *Zodiac* crossed the Atlantic, nearing the Caribbean day by day.

It had taken her many months to admit to herself that she also did not stop in port because Blackfoot had been very quiet since Starlene's death. She would not rouse him if she didn't have to. Perhaps she could keep this mission secret if she kept quiet at sea.

There was much she still did not know. Starlene's mention of a divine prophecy rang in her ears almost every hour of the day. The Isla del Dragón was not located on any map. In fact, she had only heard mention of it in tales told among the men during the night watch. The Isla del Dragón was plaguing her—was it even real? Or had she been sold into a hoax created by Cornelius Blackfoot himself to lure her into his trap? Everything about the world since Starlene died Belladonna saw as negative. Fulfilling what her parents started and living up to the Skylark name was the only thing that gave her enough hope to keep going. She would simply have to see what lay ahead.

Soon, she would need to stop off and recruit new men, as much as it pained her. She thought about how refreshing it would be to bring aboard new recruits who did not hold negative predispositions toward her, but she also worried about the risk of Blackfoot gaining knowledge about her and the *Zodiac.*

Where *was* Blackfoot? Why had they not crossed paths?

Snaggletooth remained true to his character, brightly optimistic and devoted to his post. It did not take a fool to know that some force had a hold of Belladonna; he had been an eyewitness on the day that changed her, had seen the hardening overtake her. The time passed, and he hadn't dared to ask her why she changed. From the time she was a young girl, Belladonna was a good lass, gentle and reserved. Her reserved nature had not changed. It was probably at its strongest at the present, yet she had lost that youthful gentility. Snaggletooth was proud of her courage in taking on the challenge of being captain. However, he worried about her still.

Many of the men aboard the *Zodiac* had sailed with Starlene for years. Snaggletooth considered them the closest things to a family that he would ever be able to possess, despite the rough conditions pirating brought about. Brotherhood was crucial if the crew was to work together in such closeness. It had taken her nearly two years to do, but Belladonna had single-handedly wiped out the men that he had grown with on the seas. Mentally, Snaggletooth endured more than he would let anyone know. Many nights he spent in his own private quarters—gifted to him by Starlene and which Belladonna had respected him enough to let him keep—mourning the deaths of his closest companions. Somehow, despite Belladonna's brutality, he still found himself able to respect her as his leader. He boiled his ability to do so down to the fact that she had to do what she must to establish her place among the crew. It was dirty work, certainly. But he had to give her credit for being strong enough to do it.

But if he was going to continue to be her quartermaster, he needed to know what plagued her.

As Belladonna sat in her quarters, legs propped on her desk, a map laid out in front of her, Snaggletooth knocked on the door. The door creaked open slowly when he stepped in.

Romulus stirred from his resting place next to Belladonna.

"Captain, may I have a word?"

"Of course you may." Belladonna may have been short on love in recent days, but she held a special place in her heart for Snaggletooth. He remained a constant to her (other than Romulus, of course). He shuffled forward, crossing his arms.

"I think it's time we address what's happened to ye. I know something's up with ye, and I haven't pried ye fer any information since the day I saw that *something* take over ye."

"I have not the slightest idea what this *something* is that you could be referring to." She slid the map aside on her desk and folded her hands.

"Oh, I think ye do, Captain." He raised his eyebrows at her. Belladonna was tough to crack, but Snaggletooth didn't find any fault in trying.

"I am absolutely fine. Nothing has taken over me. I am the same Belladonna I was from back when."

"I won't pry too much more, but I will say this. Ye lost yer captain and yer leader. Ye lived a quiet life, and ye were cared for under Starlene. She gets hurt and starts squirmin' and ye even showed some fear then, ma'am, need I remind ye. Then ye happen to grow stone-cold almost the second after Starlene dies. Don't mind me sayin' this, but I hope as yer quartermaster that ye feel enough trust in thee to tell me what in heaven and high seas has led ye to kill more than half of the crew, the men ye spent yer life around. Not to mention the fact that I am yer humble and faithful right hand, and I feel it's necessary fer me to know as much as I can to help ye. So, Captain, what'll it be? What is this madness?"

Belladonna knew that her heart had turned *black*. She was not sure how she knew that, but she was certain that if her heart was removed from her chest, whoever held it would find the beating thing to be the color of coal. Since the moment it happened, she told not one soul. Even worse, she had never been made to state her condition out loud. If she confessed to Snaggletooth, he would be the first man to know. It was not only hard for her to say it aloud, but it was hard for her to admit it to herself. Just because it happened and it had helped her in her post, it did not mean that she enjoyed it. She did not enjoy the passionate, yearning burn that brewed in her breast. All she desired was revenge—revenge against Blackfoot for the deaths of her family and Starlene. Nights passed by with little to no sleep because her mind would not cease its dangerous thoughts. She wanted to *feel* again. To recall with fondness the way the men made her laugh as a child when they sang. Starlene braiding her hair, humming old hymns to which she had never learned the words. The excitement of a successful quest. Now, all she felt was this anger. Any other feeling only existed as a memory, drifting away like embers from a glowing fire.

"Snaggletooth, I have not told one soul of that which possesses me now. But when Starlene died, I was made new. Maybe whole, if you want to look at it that way. It has taken me much time since that day to grasp what has happened to me. I have grown dark and cold-hearted, with rage burning me from the inside out. It has possessed me so that I cannot suppress it. Anger is my motive in all of my actions. Quite literally, my heart has shriveled and turned to stone. It has rotted—I am most certain of that. However, I can't help but think that these burning feelings contribute to my purpose. I could not carry on to complete the task my parents started being the silly girl I was before that day. No, I would not have made it one day beyond that. Every day, I wish these feelings would leave me, but a part of me has also been trying to accept them and grow in them and with them. Do you understand my meaning?"

"Aye, I think I do." Snaggletooth grinned.

"Why do you look at me so? Do you not understand the seriousness of this matter?"

"Oh, aye, I do, Captain, but I smirk because ye have not taken that bold leap into yer quest. Yet ye seem so sure of it. Why have ye not started to track down this Isla del Dragón if ye feel so sure yer whole being has changed for it?"

"Well, to put it simply, I have decided to use this time to get whatever is needed on the ship. I know not where this Isla del Dragón lies. My heart feels equipped for the quest, but my mind still doubts. I need a guide, someone who knows of this blasted place. I feel strong enough to start the quest, but I do not possess the knowledge of it. What I know of the island exists from the tall tales of mortal men. Do you know any more about it?"

"Quite the opposite, ma'am. Much like ye, I have only heard of it. I have perhaps heard more tales of it than ye, about men who had no business being there trying to reach it but meeting their end. But ye, ye have a purpose there."

"Aye." Belladonna sighed. "I need to avenge the Skylark name, Snaggletooth. I am the only one who can. Starlene foolishly thought she could take my place. She was bound to fail from the start because she was no Skylark. And I need Blackfoot dead. Those are the two desires behind my burning."

"He's been mighty silent since Starlene's fateful end that day. Perhaps he is no longer."

"No, he is around. I can feel him. My heart tells me that he is on his own quest toward there, believing there is no remaining heir to the Skylark name to thwart him." Belladonna raised her eyebrows at Snaggletooth. "If he had known of me, he may not have been so quick to sail away from the *Zodiac* when Starlene died. He thinks he has rid the earth of any possible obstacle in his wake."

"Ye could be onto him, that ye could." Snaggletooth seated himself in one of the velvet armchairs seated across the room from Belladonna. "Much like ye said, ye need a guide."

"That I do."

"I suggest we stop off shortly to find more crew. And potentially, yer guide. I know we have not stopped in a couple of years, but it must be done if ye wish to truly carry on to this island. Ye will need the manpower. And another thing, Captain, ye may need to hold a lighter hand over any new crew ye bring aboard. Ye have been terribly harsh toward the men." Belladonna looked at him when he ended his sentence and glared at him. Her expression was often soft toward Snaggletooth—the only one she could depend on now—but he needed to understand that her harsh treatment of the crew held its purpose.

"As quartermaster of this ship, I suggest you let me decide how the men are to be handled, and you do as I command," she growled. He threw up his arms in surrender.

"Alls I'm sayin' is that ye won't keep much of a crew if ye go on taking yer anger out on 'em. Do ye not think the way ye handled some of those men who are long dead and gone now harder than ye should have? I stand behind ye, but feel like ye are taking these raw feelings out on 'em."

"Leave it be, Snaggletooth!" she shouted then stood and put her hand to the butt of her pistol. He first looked at her eyes then down to where her hand rested. He chuckled aloud. He knew that she was full of fresh anger, but he would not allow himself to be afraid of her. Fear would shatter his allegiance to her.

"Aye, then. What's done is done anyway, I suppose."

"I intend to do as you recommend and make port in the next few days to gather a new crew. And potentially, someone who knows of Isla del Dragón. But we must be covert about it. I only intend to kill any crew from now on who I sense may harbor feelings of resentment against me. Anyone who betrays me dies in front of this pistol . . . or worse. I am to be eighteen soon, and I cannot think of a better time to make way to the island. No matter your feelings about this journey and my treatment of the crew, you must rid yourself of them. I admire you most of all among men, but I will not hesitate to send you to your Maker. Do you understand me, Snaggletooth?" Belladonna still stood, towering over her desk as if she had grown in the time it took her to say these things. The room felt cavernous, the waves lapping against the sides of the ship, producing an eerie hum. Candles flickered with each lap of the waves.

"As clearly as any uneducated man can, Captain." Snaggletooth stood from his seat. Romulus stood as well, twitching his tail, indicating that he agreed with every word his master had spoken. "Shall I have the men prepare to make port, then?"

"Aye. Port Royal, if you will. I'm sure that filthy place is buzzing with men ready to give their lives to this blasted ocean. When we get there, have some of the men load the hold with as many rations as they can find. We will need them. I want you to help me find a new crew. Gather and bring me whoever you can find that you see fit to join us. But please, for heaven's sake, don't bring me anyone that I will have to kill as soon as we set sail. Make them well aware of who their captain will be."

"Aye, Captain. And thank ye. For trusting me well enough to tell yer heart. I won't fail ye. I will remain ever true and noble to the quest, whatever it may be."

"Right then." Belladonna went back to looking at the map laid out before her. Based upon the coordinates, they were about a day's journey from Port Royal. It would only make sense for Isla del Dragón to lie somewhere close in the Caribbean, being an island itself.

Snaggletooth thumped toward the door but paused and turned back to Belladonna.

"One more thing. I remember Starlene's mention of the Mark. Have you gained any knowledge of it? Have you seen it?"

"I am just as much in the dark on that matter as you are, Master Snaggletooth. All in due time, I suppose."

Uneasiness settled deep in Snaggletooth's gut. His captain had certainly seemed to grapple internally with who she had become over the last two years. She had not, however, seemed to give much thought to the warnings heeded by Starlene. Snaggletooth decided that, much like Belladonna had said, time would surely reveal these things.

CHAPTER 3
BLACKFOOT'S DISCOVERY

Tea sloshed over the side of the delicate teacup, courtesy of the steady pounding of the waves underneath *The Temptress.*

"Blasted thing," Cornelius Blackfoot muttered, reaching for a nearby white cloth to wipe up the mess. He could not risk dampening any of the documents he had collected over the years of the Skylark family. In a way, he had created his own map of their family history. Following the Skylarks for centuries meant keeping abreast of every damned thing that happened to them. As he soaked up the tea with the cloth, he became particularly interested in one of the more recent documents he obtained on the Skylark name. It made mention of an Obadiah Skylark, just seven years old when he disappeared. Interestingly, it also named Abraham and Jade Skylark as the parents of the young boy. Blackfoot did not know until he found the document that a Skylark heir had ever even existed.

Since the destruction of the *Zodiac* and Captain Starlene, Blackfoot had ventured out to find the Isla del Dragón. Along the way, whenever *The Temptress* made port, he asked the locals if anything was known of the last living Skylark. Everyone he spoke to claimed that he was killed shortly after the death of the Skylark parents, too young to care for himself. There was also a rumor that he had found himself in Paris and, completely overwhelmed by his new surroundings, threw himself into the Seine. Either way, Blackfoot was satisfied in believing that the Skylark heir was dead, thus making his path clear to the Isla del Dragón. After all, if a Skylark was still alive, he would know.

Truthfully, Blackfoot had spent a great deal of time since Starlene's defeat puzzled by how exactly he would find the Isla del Dragón. The Demonclaw Court was hard-pressed for him to expose the secrets of that hidden place. He had not failed them—not yet—but he was left with very little to go on. All he knew were the pirate tales of the island, which the men whispered about.

Much like his probing questions about Obadiah Skylark, most could never say exactly if the island existed. Or perhaps it did, but no one who visited lived to report on it. If this was the Demonclaw Court's way of forcing him to earn his stripes, then it was a cruel, sick joke.

Cornelius Blackfoot had lurked in the shadows of history for many centuries. Vaguely did he remember being present when Pontius Pilate washed his hands of the crucifixion of Jesus Christ. He had seen many empires rise and fall. The world had turned to rot around him, yet here he was. Operating as a Scatterclaw, an accomplice to the mission of the Demonclaw Court to reap destruction on the Earth, for so very long was daunting.

After all the passing years, the Demonclaw presented him with an opportunity to take a High Seat at the Court. Though few got this chance, it was the most desirable position for any Scatterclaw. Besides, living as an ordinary accomplice for thousands upon thousands of years had grown boring after the first century or so. To obtain his seat at the Demonclaw Court meant he needed to become one of the chief agents of destruction. The only information given to him was that he needed to pursue the Isla del Dragón and kill the Dragon Majestics. It seemed far too easy. Conveniently, the Court came to him at what would later in history become known as the Golden Age of Piracy. He would mold himself into a tyrannical, bloodthirsty pirate captain, in search of a hoard of treasure hidden somewhere in the Caribbean islands. This treasure reserve, he decided, would be his latest discovery, and he would make himself the only known pursuer of it. He had grown proud of this cover over the years. No one would be suspicious of a humble pirate captain when the sea was crawling with them.

However genius he was with his plans, the Skylarks had thwarted him early on. Quickly, he resolved with himself that the Demonclaw wouldn't make it *that* easy to obtain a highly acclaimed Seat in the Court. And in crossing paths with the Skylarks, he had learned much about the entities that inhabited the Isla del Dragón.

Oh, he had learned far *too* much. What inhabited the Isla del Dragón was power itself, and he was leading a clear path to the destruction of that power.

After almost two years of slow progress, he had begun to assume that the Isla del Dragón was a delusion. No matter the fact the Court insisted he must find it, he felt used. In fact, he still felt like a simply accomplice, which he had been already—since the beginning of time. Maybe he was not wise enough to decipher the vague clues on the map he was given. Perhaps he needed someone wiser than himself in the ways of pirating to decode them.

It was hard to work toward a High Seat when all he knew was resentment toward his journey to reach it.

A southerly wind blew mightily, pushing *The Temptress* away from the direction of the Caribbean Islands. Blackfoot had no doubt that if the Isla del Dragón existed, it was quite possible it existed somewhere in the region, perhaps as an unnamed island to the locals. There were still so many islands to be discovered. Circling the islands and asking around in port might guide them. None of the ports on the other side of the Atlantic seemed to know.

Standing next to Maximus at the helm, Blackfoot fought with the map he held. The wind threatened to snatch it at any moment. He jumped when Jonas yelled from the crow's nest, his voice shrill.

"Oy! Captain! There's a ship over yon!" Jonas leaned his front half over the basket of the crow's nest and peered at Blackfoot. Blackfoot sighed.

"Of course there are ships in the bloody ocean, you fool," he muttered under his breath. Maximus was the only one close enough to hear it and chuckled. Blackfoot scowled at him, and he stopped snickering immediately. He shaded his eyes and looked up at Jonas. "Whereabouts is this ship you speak of, Master Jonas?"

"Just over to the starboard side, Captain!" He pointed in the direction. "Looks to be they is heading toward Port Royal to make port."

"Fine then. Do you suspect anything of it, lad?"

"Perhaps you'd better take a look, Captain Blackfoot. Something about it feels *strange.*" Blackfoot let out another sigh and tapped Maximus for the telescope. How could another ship at sea feel strange? Blackfoot was growing weary of the act of pirating—the plundering, the looting, the division of treasure that had been agreed to in each man's contract—and needed to focus on his hopeful Seat in the Court. Enough pirating had been done to establish himself as a tried-and-true pirate. The cover was entirely put on; now he needed to act.

He extended the telescope and strode to the starboard side of the quarterdeck. Doubtful that anything could be made of the ship ahead, he held it up to his eye and peered through. It took a moment for him to steady his hand and the telescope. When it focused, Blackfoot gasped.

It cannot be. His heart began to flutter, then feeling as though it had dropped all the way to the deck beneath him. *Mary, Mother of God and all the saints . . . it cannot be.*

Quickly, he dropped the telescope from his eye and took a deep, labored breath. Surely, it was not so. When he looked through again, he found that it was indeed so.

The *Zodiac* was making its way across the sea, heading straight for Port Royal.

But the Zodiac was beyond repair the last I saw her. She should be resting on the ocean floor!

Rage boiled in Blackfoot's blood. He clenched his fist around the telescope and felt his body begin to quake. For far too long, Blackfoot had wasted his precious time pursuing the *Zodiac* and its members. Complete annihilation of the Skylark bloodline and their cursed ally Starlene had been necessary. Silently, he looked out over the water and felt a scream attempting to escape his throat. But he knew he must look again before he gave himself over completely to his rage. Maximus appeared at his side.

"Who goes out there, Cap'n?"

"This is none of your concern, Maximus." Peering through again, he wanted to see if he could identify anyone on board. If Starlene still lived . . . oh, how he would murder her again.

The ship looked sparse, seemingly fewer men working on deck than his last encounter with the *Zodiac.* Many of Starlene's men had been lost during that battle, but even fewer men were there now. He saw two more enticing, more familiar sights. Snaggletooth, that idiot with his pointy tooth poking out from his bottom lip, lit a pipe while leaning over the side, looking into the sea. Blackfoot remembered having a strong desire to cut that tooth out of his mouth if he ever got the chance. An orange and brown *thing* slunk slowly across the quarterdeck, focusing its attention on the man at the wheel. *Ah, so the Hoodoo jungle cat had lived.* He had also previously imagined what he would do to that cat if he were able to trap it. It would make a beautiful rug in his cabin, he had thought.

It would be impossible for Starlene to be alive.

As he thought this, he moved his telescope to the left. Through the lens, he saw a young woman—a welcome sight when one has only been around filthy men for months on end—standing next to the helmsman that the cat watched. The young woman bore an expression of perpetual malice. Blackfoot felt a kinship in his heart for that expression as he felt stuck with its potency. The man Snaggletooth ascended the steps to the helm and seemed to consult the young lady as if she were in charge.

Perhaps Starlene has a charge these days. A young woman to rear in her glamorous profession—if she is still alive, after all.

He quickly navigated the telescope to scan the entire ship, front to end, for any sign of Starlene. Nothing gave any indication that Starlene was on board. A chilling notion crept into his mind.

Perhaps the young woman is *the captain.*

When he looked at her again, he spent a few moments examining her movements. She appeared to be a wild thing, much like the cat on board. Her nature seemed hot-headed and maddening. Her skirts were of luxurious silk, costly no doubt, and probably from

China. Her scarlet hair was twisted down her left shoulder. She was bodacious yet commanding, two contradictory qualities for a woman, Blackfoot thought. Though his intentions in watching her for as long as he did were rooted in manly desires, he found himself becoming deeply allured by the commanding aspect of her person. An aura of power—and of mystery, perhaps—shrouded her. The lady was hard to look away from, not simply because she was young and beautiful. The lady seemed the embodiment of strength.

"I have never in my life seen a woman such as she," Blackfoot whispered to himself, holding the telescope to his breast.

"A woman? Let me have a peep—" Maximus reached greedily for the telescope. But Blackfoot pulled it away in a flashing moment and reached for the cutlass he kept. The edge of the cutlass floated over Maximus's neck.

"Don't you go trying to interfere with a captain's business, or I'll slice your throat and paint the sails with your blood." Maximus raised his hands in surrender and Blackfoot dropped the knife. What he saw on the *Zodiac* enticed him in a maniacal way. Whoever this woman was, her power was unlike any mistress he had ever known. The *Zodiac* called to him, and he must follow yet again.

"I'm sorry, Captain. Didn't mean to overstep." Maximus anxiously wiped the front of his shirt. "What do you say we do about that ship? Do we pursue her or what?"

"Aye, we pursue her." Blackfoot grinned. Looting is not what Blackfoot was after. He had to find out who the woman was and why he was drawn to her.

"But, sir, what of the course we charted in discovering the island you seek?"

Following the *Zodiac* again would be a setback, but it needed to be done.

"Forget that cursed island for now and follow her. She be the *Zodiac* that I thought we sunk a few years ago."

"Heavens!" Maximus gasped. "You're certain of it?" Blackfoot held the telescope up for Maximus to look. His captain was right. The name of the ship read *Zodiac.* "Impossible."

"Evidently not, my good man. Which is why we must follow it. If she ports, we port. Tell the crew."

"Right away." Maximus trudged off to spread word of *The Temptress's* newest endeavor. Blackfoot peeped through the telescope again to take one last look at the woman before he went back to his map. Just because he was following the *Zodiac* again did not mean he had to slack on riddling with the Isla del Dragón.

On the Zodiac, the scarlet-haired woman stroked the tiger's fur and walked away, disappearing from his sight.

Who are you, O strange and powerful one?

CHAPTER 4
NEW RECRUITS

I should have changed the name of the Zodiac. *Blast, why did I not, after all this time has passed?*

Belladonna felt vulnerable as the *Zodiac* sailed into the bustling city of Port Royal. A port that relied heavily on the plunder of pirates, she wondered if any tales of the new captain of Starlene's beloved *Zodiac* had been told. Starlene's was a well-known name among respectable pirates. They must know that she was no longer sailing the seas. Belladonna, fierce as she was, fought hard to remain a mystery to those who sailed around her. When her crew attacked another ship for their cargo and whatever fortunes they had hidden, she made sure that every man (or woman and animal, for that matter) onboard ended up dead. After each attack and Snaggletooth's report, she crossed over to the defeated ship and did her own survey. Oftentimes, she would find a man hidden away, thinking himself safe. Usually, the man begged for mercy in whatever tongue he spoke. Belladonna would have him captured and tortured, or she would end him without a thought. Word traveled fast among pirates about who to avoid and the fewer who knew of her meant fewer who would stand in her way. The risk of entering Port Royal was great, but she needed men. And she needed to find someone who would help her locate the Isla del Dragón. In a place such as Port Royal, who knew: she might possibly find someone who had seen it with their own eyes.

The *Zodiac* dropped anchor, and the crew tied her off. She would permit the men this single night in port to give themselves over to whatever pleasures they desired. Little did they know, if they showed up the next day still drunk or wreaking of sex, she would cut out their tongue. Then, they would never be able to enjoy the taste of a strong drink or a woman again.

That would learn them.

Snaggletooth approached Belladonna as she looked out over the port.

"As ye have asked, I will gather a gaggle of men and present them to ye if I see 'em fit fer work. Ye need not worry yerself with the finding, captain. Ol' Snaggletooth has much experience weedin' the good 'n the bad. The men I found served Starlene well, mind ye."

"I trust you . . . as much as I can." Belladonna grabbed his hand, squeezed it, and smirked. The only feeling of something close to love she felt in her heart was for her quartermaster. Perhaps it was more endearment than love. She didn't know anymore, for love had become so very distant from her.

"A'right then, miss. Do ye really feel safe with just Romulus here to protect ye?" The man looked down at Romulus, who gazed at him with assurance. Snaggletooth had been around Romulus for many years yet still stood in awe of the emotion the cat could show in its eyes. He let out a snort and rubbed his head affectionately against Belladonna's hip.

Romulus ain't nothin' but a house cat, Snaggletooth thought.

"You seem to forget that old Romulus is a predator of the forest. You could send a whole hoard of men my way, and he would rip every one of them in half," Belladonna said flatly. Snaggletooth shuddered, still finding himself appalled by the violent nature of his captain. He nodded to her and turned to leave the ship. The crew left the ship in groups, paying their respects to their captain before they embarked on a night of debauchery and drunkenness. If Snaggletooth had not convinced her what little crew she had would not jump ship in Port Royal to find a new one, she would not have allowed her men to leave the ship. Snaggletooth knew the desires of a man held a strong hold over him and advised Belladonna to let them give themselves over to those desires for a night. They would probably resume their work in a better frame of mind when they returned.

Being the young woman she was, Belladonna would have given into these same types of desires had she known anything about passion other than the passionate rage that consumed her. Had she been normal, she assumed she would have already given herself to a man, potentially more than one. Giving herself to a man never crossed her mind until Snaggletooth mentioned those male desires. No time existed for such things when one was so preoccupied with bringing justice upon her family name.

Too much time on deck meant too much time to be seen. It struck her that tonight, stories may be told of her among her men and the other pirates who sought relief and pleasure on the island. Who knows what tales would be spread? Most would undoubtedly tell of her cruelty. For the past few months, the men began to secretly call her the Dragon Lady. Though they whispered the nickname among themselves, nothing slipped past their captain. It couldn't be said that she entirely disliked the nickname. It meant the men feared her. That was a thing to be prized among her achievements.

The morning sun began to peek into the windows of Belladonna's cabin when Snaggletooth jerked her awake.

"You scoundrel!" She grumbled as she jerked awake.

"Pardon me for botherin' ye, Captain, but it's well-nigh time fer ye to start sortin' through the recruits. I found a great many men, surprisin'ly sober, and I can only assume they was lookin' for work and wanted to give their best faces. Did ye leave the ship at all? Find any pleasures for the night?"

"I did not a damn thing, Snaggletooth. I need not go around spreading my legs and making myself the talk of the town. I am quite sure the men did enough of that in my place. You know that I haven't stepped foot on land in years, and I do not intend to again until we arrive at the Isla del Dragón." It infuriated her that Snaggletooth would think her so stupid.

"I didn't mean to pry, Captain." Snaggletooth gulped. "I just thought maybe it would be good fer ye." Being in the advising position Snaggletooth often found himself in, he knew it would do her good to act like a young lady occasionally. Clearly, age was not a consideration of hers.

Belladonna rose from her bed and shuffled toward her washbasin. Romulus leaped off the bed.

"Give me just a few moments to prepare myself. Then we will begin. Have all of my men reported back?"

"Well, all but about two of 'em. Roger Fleetwood and Nicholas Scrimmer seem to be gone and not a one of the men claims they know where the fools ran off to."

"Romulus needs to fetch them. They were supposed to report back," Belladonna stated through gritted teeth. "Romulus, go and find those no-goods!" Romulus began to slink toward the door when Snaggletooth stepped in front of him.

"Ye need not do that, miss. I know ye have grown up around this cat, but 'tis not a common thing among men to cross paths with a beast such as he. Ye risk him gettin' captured or killed. Ye must let them go."

Silence permeated the room as Belladonna considered this. He served as her voice of reason amidst her greatest fury. Besides, it was true: she could not risk her greatest and constant protector.

"Aye. Disregard my command, Romulus. To me, now." It pained her that Roger and Nicholas would escape her command without consequence. Had Snaggletooth not spoken, she would have set out to find them herself. Her anger must not get in the way of her ultimate prize, and stepping on land would draw too many eyes.

Snaggletooth had an eye for men who would work hard and work well. He had lined them up on deck, one next to the other, about forty men in all. Some looked to be drunkards, who Belladonna quickly turned away. Most of the lot looked anxious and ready to work. Presumably, these were men who had left the British Royal Navy, seeking a great deal more independence. This they would receive—anything was better than the Royal Navy—but little did they know they would be subjected to the brutality of their new captain if they failed her.

Belladonna wanted desperately to send them running from her now, cowering in fear, but she decided she needed to be favorable to win their hearts and join her crew. The *Zodiac* was a fully-functional ship and needed a solid crew to operate her. Surely, the men who remained from Starlene would feel relieved. After all the articles were signed, Belladonna began to pace up and down the line.

"This is a great day for you, lads. Welcome to the *Zodiac*," Belladonna began. "This life is fraught with perils unimaginable, yet it can also heap its rewards. Do as I command, and do not question me unless you want to spend the rest of your days in a living hell. If you do as I say, I shall leave you alone. There are no traitors permitted on this ship. I will not allow it. Prepare your sea legs because where we are going is a long, long journey and you will hardly remember the sight of land on the horizon by the time we see it again. I am in quest of the Isla del Dragón."

The new men gasped. All of them were young, likely around Belladonna's age or slightly older. They began to murmur among themselves. Belladonna smirked.

"Captain, I don't know a living soul who has seen that island. It's dangerous!" Thomas Quint, one of the new men, shouted. He took his hat in his hands and held it to his breast.

Belladonna whipped her hair behind her and turned to face him.

"Aye, it is. What of it, then? Are you too afraid? Shall you go back to your bondage with the country of England? I am sure they would be simply delighted to have you back after you serve your time in a cell for jumping ship. Or much worse." Belladonna's answer made Thomas gulp.

"No, ma'am." He muttered, looking down.

"Lovely. Now that we know Master Thomas is not afraid, we can move forward, can't we gentlemen?"

"Aye, Captain!" The men agreed.

"Get to work, you dogs. We sail until we reach the Isla del Dragón unless I tell you otherwise."

"Hoist the anchor, lads! Let down the sails! Get her movin'!" Snaggletooth commanded. Fortunately, the new men knew how to operate a ship. This knowledge and experience were essential in Snaggletooth's search. Just when he started to make way to his post to continue overseeing the crew, he remembered the prisoner. He turned toward Belladonna, who was watching Romulus pick up the scents of the new bodies he would be surrounded by. The men were cautious not to turn their backs on him and cower, as men are taught to do when encountering a ferocious cat.

"If ye don't mind steppin' away right quickly, I have something to show ye in the cell down below. It could be very beneficial to ye in yer quest."

"In the cell? Why would you try to conceal such a thing from me in the cell? Could you not have presented this to me at the time you presented me with these new sea rats?" Frustration rose in her voice, unwillingly. Everything came out of her with irritation, whether she meant it or not.

Truthfully, Snaggletooth did not trust the prisoner. The accent was thick on that one, and they didn't speak directly. He often did not trust a person who did not speak directly. The prisoner insisted they already knew the name and the mission of Belladonna Skylark and could serve as a guide. Uneasiness stirred in him. Finding a guide was one of the things that he expected to accomplish, but he did not expect one to come to him—and so quickly after stopping in port. One could not trust another who already knew too much outright. The prisoner's promises of the Isla del Dragón were enough to at least let Belladonna decide for herself. Even still, he worried. Belladonna was not the most clear-headed at the present. He shackled the prisoner, locked them away in the cell belowdecks. After the lock-up, a shudder rushed through Snaggletooth. The prisoner's very presence on the ship felt ominous.

"I didn't mean to conceal a thing, Captain. Should we have Romulus keep an eye on the crew?"

"No, I am quite sure that if you felt the need to lock whatever this is away in a cell, it must present some sort of threat." Belladonna stuck her hand deep into the pocket of her gown and pulled out her pistol. "Perhaps I will need this?"

"Best if you keep it with ye, I suppose. They know yer name and what ye are setting out to do." Snaggletooth felt the same unease from their meeting creep back up his spine. Would the prisoner try to hurt Belladonna? Was the prisoner seeking the path to the Isla del Dragón for themself?

"Romulus, darling, come. We have something that needs tended to." She pet Romulus behind the ears and looked at Snaggletooth. "The men will be fine for a moment alone. They are new; they won't try to run yet."

Romulus lifted his nose in the air, sniffing the prisoner that was huddled in the cell of the ship. A deep, rumbling growl escaped him. Belladonna did not fear any warnings from Romulus, but she would listen. She cocked the hammer of her pistol and held it to her side. Snaggletooth fingered the cutlass in his trouser pocket.

The dampness of the salty-aired sleeping quarters stuck to Belladonna's skin. It was not often that she found herself belowdecks. Her domain was far removed from that of her crew, and she preferred to remain only an occasional visitor. As she listened closely and stepped heavy-footed toward the cell, she heard rhythmic mumblings coming from the prisoner. They were bent in the corner, laughing ever so often to themselves and muttering unintelligible nothings. Belladonna felt goosebumps break out on her flesh. An evil lurked within the prisoner, that much she knew. Whatever evil that lurked within the prisoner must not have been strong enough if Snaggletooth had allowed them to step even one foot on the *Zodiac*.

"Speak to me, prisoner. Who are you?" Belladonna demanded.

The thing in the corner of the cell turned their body halfway to reveal their face. In that face, they saw a woman, not much older than Belladonna. She looked youthful, yet her skin was stained by dirt and heaven knows what else. Her dreadlocked hair hung in heavy strands around her dirt-pocked cheeks and neck. Wandering eyes, blue and murky, shone through the hair that veiled her. She toyed with the shells hanging from her neck, her nails black with grime and hands caked in filth. What in the devil's name had Snaggletooth thought by bringing this woman here? The prisoner went back to her corner, continuing her mutterings.

"Speak to me, you wench. You will be missing that tongue if you don't." Still nothing from the prisoner.

"Ye knew the conditions when I told ye I would bring ye in front of my captain. Now speak." Snaggletooth stepped forward, thrusting his hand through the cell bars, brandishing the cutlass not far from her face. She looked at it quizzically and tried to push it away. Snaggletooth lunged it back near her face. She looked at it again, not so quizzically this time, and stuck out her tongue. She ran her tongue along the edge of the blade, giggling deep within her gut, eyes never leaving Snaggletooth's. Slowly, he pulled the cutlass away, expecting the blade to drip with blood. When there was none, he gazed at her with fright. Her tongue, still protruding from her mouth, was slit down the middle. Her tongue had been bifurcated many years before.

This caused the prisoner to cackle loudly.

Belladonna was done with this woman's games. Either she would talk, or she would die.

"Open the door and let Romulus have his way with her. She is useless to me."

Romulus crouched low to the ground, ready to pounce when the gate flung open. At the sound of Romulus's name, the prisoner quickly turned her head. Her attention was won.

"Romulus? Cannot be deh Romulus dat I wav'd me hand over one dey and made it magic! Where be dat mean ol' kitty?" She moved on her knees toward the door, sticking her hand out through the bars toward Romulus. He did not move toward her in recognition. He was ready to shred the prisoner, fangs exposed in a cruel snarl. Snaggletooth placed the key in the cell lock and twisted it. The door swung open on the rusted hinges. Romulus leaped toward the cell. As Belladonna prepared for the bloodbath to ensue, she was surprised when Romulus stopped, his body seemingly suspended in the air. The prisoner had her palm toward him. Whoever the prisoner was, she knew Romulus, and she knew of the magic that had domesticated him. Belladonna only knew a little of his magic; after all, the magic only made sense when one considered a tiger living among mortal men as a faithful guardian.

Already, the female prisoner had proven she possessed two valuable assets that could assist Belladonna: a knowledge of the Isla del Dragón and a knowledge of Romulus. She needed help understanding both in their own way.

"It cannot be," Belladonna muttered quietly.

"Aye, so 'tis, Belladonna Skylark." The woman winked at her. She brought her hand back down to her lap and Romulus bowed in submission. He leaned his velvety muzzle toward her, and she stroked it with her fingertips.

"You are strong in something. I demand to know who you are. How do you know me? How do you know of Romulus? I have not heard of one living soul who has been able to command Romulus the way any of his masters have."

"Yuh be Starlene's girl, yes? Deh heir o' ole 'Braham n' Jade Skylark, yes?" Belladonna nodded, wary of the woman still. The woman's words oozed with her native accent, and Belladonna realized she was blind. "I be Arimetta, Hoodoo woman of deh island yuh leave now. Dis island my home for many, many a moon. I knew yuh fadda and motha, 'n yuh old cap'n, may she rest. I e'en train'd dis cat. A mighty beast he think he were, madame, but aye, Arimetta laid a 'and on 'im and spoke deh spell on 'im to make 'im a humble servant tuh Captain Starlene." Arimetta laid her forehead against Romulus's, her hand stroking under his chin. Romulus purred.

"You knew Starlene and my parents? How?"

"Oh, dey come to Arimetta seekin' deh Isla del Dragón, dey did. Come to my islan' just as yuh done. But I known Starlene wey afore den. Afore e'en she sought deh Island o' deh Dragons. Dey was close to't. Dat ol' Blackfoot run dem off again afore they could get dere. So 'twas always wid dem. Always chasin' an' chasin'. Until he brung deh end tuh all a' dem. But yuh, aye, yuh Belladonna, yuh deh one tuh find it. Arimetta come tuh offer to advise yuh in deh wey of deh spirits. Arimetta did not offer in time afore wit your fadda and motha when she should 'ave. Arimetta not gonna make deh same mistake again."

"So you know of the Isla del Dragón then?" Belladonna crouched down to look into Arimetta's sightless eyes. She reeked of island filth. Belladonna did not care; she was beginning to see the importance of this meeting with Arimetta. She felt that Arimetta held a deep connection to her purpose on the Isla del Dragón. "Tell me of this island. And why do you offer your help to me? What is in this quest for you?"

"What will happ'n if yuh don't make it dere will lead to an Eart' filled wit destruction like not a one has e'er seen. Tis ver' important for yuh tuh make it. As for Arimetta, she will suffer much at deh hands of dis destruction if yuh don' settle matters on deh island. Arimetta offers 'er service todey tuh stop deh destruction. Yuh know yuh need a guide tuh find de island. Dat much yuh know, Belladonna a smart lass. Yuh need Arimetta, love; yuh need her tuh look into deh future and offer counsel. I can help." Arimetta smiled, revealing shale-black teeth.

"How should I know to trust you?"

"Did yuh not see deh wey deh cat Romulus stopp'd in 'is tracks at de utterance o' one word from Arimetta? I has deh power yuh need, bot' in deh magic and deh future. If yuh find Arimetta not tuh yuh standards, we strike a bargain dis dey dat yuh let Romulus tear her limb tuh limb."

"And what of when we reach the island? What will you want in return for your service?"

"Nothin', good Captain. Arimetta wan' nothin' but freedom from the pain she will suffer if yuh do not stop deh destruction."

"I need to consult with my quartermaster, Arimetta. I'm sure you understand every precaution of mine."

"Arimetta know dat yuh blood boils unda'neath dat alabaster skin, she does. Yuh 'ave a hold on yuh, jus' deh wey deh cat do, just deh way Arimetta do too. In time, it will simmer back down." Belladonna stopped dead in her tracks. She turned back to Arimetta, feeling her face redden.

"You know nothing of me, scum. I know your work as a Hoodoo prophetess means something to me, and I know you have learned much of me from that, but you do not know what lies in my heart. I will have Romulus tear you apart right here if you speak of it any further."

"Yuh jus' said much 'bout yuh heart, Belladonna." Belladonna felt the jab of Arimetta's truthful words prick her. She hated that Arimetta spoke so accurately. Not a soul had questioned or spoken that way of her heart since it first blackened. Arimetta knew more than she thought.

"I think this needs no further consultation." She looked at Snaggletooth, who shrugged.

Snaggletooth would not share the mutual feeling of Arimetta's connection to her mission. In fact, even with time, he would never fully trust her. Perhaps no one would fully trust Arimetta, what with her way of speaking and her dull, depthless eyes. "If you know the way to the Isla del Dragón, you must be direct with me. If you get me there safely and without interference, I will owe you much. What I will owe you remains to be seen. Do you understand me, Arimetta?" The Hoodoo prophetess considered these terms in her head. "And for as long as you are on my ship and under my command, you will release any holding power you have over Romulus. He is my guardian and mine alone. If he turns on me, it obviously means that without me you suffer the pain you spoke of before. You will pay for any enchantment you attempt to cast over the *Zodiac*."

"Yes, Miss Skylark, yes. Arimetta will do what she can to keep herself from deh sufferin', yes. She be at yuh command."

"Good." Belladonna motioned for Snaggletooth to remove Arimetta's feet from the shackles that bound her. Romulus had been pulled out of the spell that she held over him and strode to

Belladonna. "And for the love of all sea life, you must call me Captain Skylark. Few are permitted to call me Belladonna, and you are not one of them."

As she stepped back on deck, her eyes burned against the sun that beat down on her. The dark corner of the cell below had shrouded her. The crew seemed to be functioning as they should. Occasionally, one of the new men would glance at her and then look away quickly. She sensed wariness in their looks. Had the crew had enough time to warn the new men of their captain's nature?

Let them think what they will, she thought to herself. Fearful respect was not often a bad thing.

Slowly, she made her way to the port side of the ship. Port Royal faded away in the distance as the *Zodiac* began its course to sail around the Caribbean islands in search of the Isla del Dragón. A feeling arose in Belladonna that she had not felt in quite some time: hope. Arimetta's words indicated that the Isla del Dragón was, in fact, a *real* place. Perhaps it did not mean quite as much to Arimetta as it did to Belladonna, but it meant something. For Arimetta, the Isla del Dragón meant freedom. It meant freedom for Belladonna as well, but it meant so many things beyond freedom. Fate had spoken. Belladonna was in need of a guide, and one had been given.

Thank the stars.

The Skylark name was one step closer to justice and redemption . . . and, presumably, future notoriety. Deep in thought, Belladonna cursed when she felt Arimetta's hand on hers.

"Arimetta can see deh tings of deh future, as she 'as a'ready said." She turned her blind eyes toward Belladonna's face. Gently, she placed her hand on Belladonna's cheek. Belladonna reached up to hold the wrist of the hand on her face. She felt the seriousness that Arimetta felt in that instance. "She sees yuh must pass through many storms tuh reach deh Isla del Dragón. A storm leads deh wey." Arimetta pulled her hand back quickly and began to wander away, muttering to herself as she did in the cell.

She is so very strange. Belladonna brushed the cheek that Arimetta had touched. Her eyes followed Arimetta as she passed in front of the ballast, the men turning their heads to watch her. Undoubtedly, Snaggletooth would need to warn the men that they could not lay a finger on Arimetta unless they wished to forfeit their life for a few minutes of pleasure. She was sure there existed one or two men who would risk that.

Storms were an unavoidable part of being at sea. In her life, and as captain, Belladonna had endured storms of all kinds. The *Zodiac* always made it through.

Certainly, Belladonna and the *Zodiac* could weather the storms ahead.

CHAPTER 5
THE STOWAWAY AND THE DRAGON

Ephraim Howell awoke in a haze, his vision fuzzy from alcohol. The world around him rocked wildly. He propped himself up, back pressed against the barrel he had helped himself to the night before. So far, he seemed to have found a freedom he had never experienced. Before he could focus his gaze on one thing or locate where exactly he was, he lunged forward, vomiting on the ground next to him. He did not want to know how much of whatever spirit he drank remained in the barrel behind him. Just the thought made him dry heave. Clean drinking water was bound to be not too far from where he was now.

The young man, recently nineteen years old, had escaped the life he'd known since he was old enough to remember such things. His father, a drunken fool, was not shy with the belt. His mother, Christine, remained passive, aware of the heavy hand of Jacob Howell, yet she cowered in fear of him herself. She did not want to become the object of scorn in the family. Ephraim was left to assume this was the only reason she was glad a son existed in the family, to take the beatings that would have otherwise landed elsewhere. Thus, Ephraim spent his young life growing in fear.

At seventeen, Ephraim had enough of his home life. He would fight under the British Royal Navy, leaving his home behind to start a new life of military success. What he ended up in resembled that of the Howell household far more closely than he liked, only with more bloodshed. The discipline Ephraim received at home on the shores of England was mere child's play to the discipline he would endure in the Navy. The punishment was far more severe than he could have imagined. Not to mention the number of Spaniards he slaughtered, as Britain far too often found itself at odds with Spain, was staggering. He killed these men with a sense of injustice. But he wondered: Why was he killing for a regime that would not hesitate to kill him if he deserted it? The last skirmish he was involved in prevented Spain from reclaiming Sicily and Sardinia. He was a witness to death upon death of the men he thought to be innocent, the Navy masking their murderous ways as a duty to their country.

It was after the Royal Navy prevented Spain from reclaiming Sicily and Sardinia that he decided he would escape. He could not stay in England; they would have his head if they found him. Ephraim sought freedom. He longed for freedom from the duty and discipline he had fallen victim to since his childhood, as well as freedom from his duty to one nation. For this reason, pirating, though extremely dangerous, appealed to him. Sailing the seas to unleash havoc over the men he once answered to satisfied him tremendously. Ephraim spent several months as a stowaway on quite a few ships to get himself to Jamaica, the home of pirate pleasure. Now, he found himself aboard the *Zodiac,* certain that the freedom he craved was now within reach.

Why did I not simply confront the quartermaster who was recruiting men for this ship? Why did I insist upon being a stowaway once again? Ephraim thought to himself as he regrouped, trying to focus on one object in the hold around him long enough to orient himself. Already, he appeared to be in a tight spot. This was not how he should have commenced his new life as a pirate. One of two scenarios would happen: either he would start working with the crew and blend in, unnoticed, or he would be ratted out by one of the crew, resulting in punishment, or worse, death. Nothing about the captain of this ship was known to him.

It was morning; he knew that much. When the sun sunk below the horizon and the men went to their quarters, he would need to listen in. For now, he would try to sneak out of the hold and hide in the shadows on deck. It was a risk he had to take if he wanted to learn anything.

Ephraim stayed quiet as he worked. He took to cleaning guns—his specialty in the Navy—and minded his business. From what he had heard so far, the ship he was on was called the *Zodiac.*

He gathered that the quartermaster was named Snaggletooth. He appreciated the nickname so he knew to hide his face when the man came near. There was also talk of *The Cat*, but Ephraim did not yet know what that meant.

As much as he did not want to, Ephraim stood out among the other men. He was tall and lanky. His hair, deep brown and wavy, flopped in front of his eyes more than it should. He was lean, his thin muscles taught and refined on his thin frame, unlike most of the men he'd been around who were more muscular. He'd heard it said before in the Navy that he looked to be from a painting, too pretty for the jobs he did. His brown, sunken eyes looked down more than up. The confidence that he should have possessed had been brutally damaged by the life he had led. Feeling less-than had taken a toll on him, and it showed now more than ever, a time when he should have felt proud of himself for escaping his own personal captivity.

Nearby, a group of the men huddled around two others who were playing cards. They acted as if this was not a usual activity. The quartermaster stood at the helm, occasionally catching glimpses of the game being played below. He now saw why his name was Snaggletooth. One of his bottom teeth, unusually sharp and pointed, protruded from his closed mouth. Ephraim found his appearance to be comical yet knew the man garnered much respect from the crew, considering the way he was spoken of. When the quartermaster seemed distracted, Ephraim slid over to the card game. He needed to hear what he could and possibly ask questions of his own.

"You think we will be reachin' this dragon place any day soon?" One of the men asked quietly to another as they watched the game.

"I reckon the cap'n will keep us going until she finds it. She is persistent, that I have noticed so far." This man took out a match and lit the pipe in his hand. *She?* Ephraim leaned closer to them, pretending to be very interested in the card game happening in front of them. He must have heard incorrectly.

"Aye, she will never stop. So's the men say who's been on here for many years. She ain't found it yet. Mayhaps this time will be her lucky break." Ephraim had *not* heard incorrectly. He tapped one of the men on the shoulder.

"Excuse me, sirs. I wanted to make sure I heard you right. This captain is a woman?"

"Aye, she is. And who are you?" The one with the pipe asked. "Did you not see her the day she stood before you and selected you to be part of her crew?"

Ephraim bit his lip, realizing the bind he had placed himself in by asking this question. "Um, well, yes, I did see her, but I don't think I realized she was the *real* captain." *Blasted stupid thing to say,*

Ephraim thought to himself. "My name is Ephraim, by the way." He stuck a hand out to the two men. The one with the pipe took it first.

"Name's Mace. This here is Swann. But aye, she be the real captain, as you call it. A real nasty one at that. What you see going on here ain't normally allowed. 'Parently she's been preoccupied with her health these last few days. Others say if she saw us out here doin' this she would line us up and slit each of our throats."

Ephraim pondered this. Of course, he'd heard of pirates, but he had never heard of a female pirate. Especially a captain. He heard the strumming of an instrument, noticing it came from above him in the crow's nest. Next, a voice started to sing:

"Oh, my Captain!
Her breast a-blazes with red,
One puff of her breathe,
And you're better off dead—"

The ship erupted in laughter. The men scattered around the card table pounded their fists, laughing in drunken hysterics.

"Quiet up there, Mr. Lancer!" The quartermaster yelled from the wheel. "If ye don't stop yer singing, ye'll be feelin' the cat-o-nine-tails across yer back!"

"Alright, Snag, that'll do!" The man, Lancer, shouted from the crow's nest. He continued to strum to a different tune.

"Ye dogs need to find thanks in this time of solitude. This be the first time in many moons that Captain Skylark has allowed any merry happenings on this ship. Ye need to be grateful, lads. Keep that in the back of yer minds, all of ye." When he said this, the men grumbled among themselves.

"What ails the captain?" Ephraim asked Mace and Swann when the grumbling died down.

"We know not," Mace said after a puff from his pipe. He eyed Ephraim suspiciously. His heart began to pound. Mace had caught on to him. He grabbed him by the shoulder and led him away from the group. "I suspect you of something, Ephraim."

"I'm not sure what you could mean by that. I just wanted to ensure I had all of my facts straight before—"

"You're a stowaway is what you is. I know it. I would remember a face such as yours if I seen it that first day the quartermaster brought us here. Your face is as polished as a child's. You don't necessarily look the part of a pirate. You from the Navy, boy? You jump ship with them?"

Ephraim sighed. "Yes, I did. I needed to find a ship fast, and I had no time to spend being questioned by anyone. Not much time has passed, but I know without a doubt that the Royal Navy is looking for me. I cannot go back to that life."

"How old are you?"

"Nineteen, sir." At this, Mace chuckled.

"You will be quite lucky if you can keep hidden one more day. I assume you've been hiding in the hold? I haven't seen your face around the sleeping quarters. That cat will sniff you out before long—if one of the men doesn't find you first sprawled out drunk and fat from what you've been stealing down there."

"The cat?" Before Ephraim could get an answer, the two men playing cards started shouting at one another. Fists flew at one another. The men watching began to shout as well, egging them on to a full-blown fight. Snaggletooth started to run down the stairs but stopped when an orange flash streaked through the scuffle. Ephraim could not believe what he saw.

A tiger, fierce and striking, stood on his hind legs and clawed at the man who started the brawl. Ear-piercing growls came from the open mouth of the tiger, each tooth showing and his paws scratching the man wildly. Snaggletooth, teeth bared as well, stepped between the man and the beast with a knife.

"Enough, Romulus! To yer master at once!" Snaggletooth yelled. The tiger, who Ephraim knew now to be called Romulus, eased back down on four paws, looking defeated. A chill made its way down Ephraim's spine, his skin breaking out in goose flesh. On what he thought to be a humble pirate ship, he had just witnessed a wild animal attack. Not just that, but he saw the *anger* in the cat's eyes. Already he had seen more today than any other day of his life. Panic shot through him. Did these men allow themselves to share the same quarters with a tiger who could pluck them off one by one during the night? Ephraim had no doubt that every man on board the *Zodiac* was mad.

"Mr. Gibbons, I'll have ye know that while I have allowed ye to have yer fun, ye have fallen out of line." Snaggletooth roared at the card player. "I'll have yer opponent lash ye until ye can no longer see straight." He turned to glare at the crowd that gathered around the fight. "No more of this—back to work, all of ye!" The men broke off to their individual tasks, grumbling to themselves. Their taste of life without Captain Skylark's interference ended in violence. Gibbons stood with Snaggletooth holding his arm, preparing himself to be dragged away to receive his punishment. The tiger had mauled him badly. Between the open wounds and the lashings, Ephraim wondered if he would see Gibbons after that night.

Ephraim made off to go back to the guns, which, God bless them, no one had taken up before he could. Mace followed him to where he sat cleaning.

"Looky here, Ephraim." He jumped when he heard Mace's voice near his ear. He turned to look at him. "I will not speak of you if you keep a quiet countenance. I can sympathize with ya, for I once sailed the seas in another occupation, one viewed with much more esteem than this. Mind the quartermaster, mind the cat, and mind the captain. If you get caught by one of 'em, do not go tellin' them I kept your little secret."

"This ship is madness. What have I stepped into?"

"You've come under the command of the Dragon Lady, so we call her. Best not wake a sleeping dragon." Mace smiled, showing all of his rotten teeth, and clapped him on the shoulder.

The freedom and confidence that Ephraim felt that morning, after vomiting the alcohol from his system, seemed to vanish. He sensed he now lived under the tyranny of a kind he had not yet witnessed.

Meanwhile, Belladonna lay on her bed, her linen shirt clinging to her figure. She had developed a fever—or likely, driven herself to fever—the morning after the *Zodiac* left Port Royal. *So much for sailing directly to the Isla del Dragón,* she thought. Her fever fell upon her as the result of her fear of a thing that lurked quietly in the back of her mind and was now manifesting. She had not forgotten it since Starlene's warning. It haunted her; however, she had preoccupied her mind with thoughts of the Isla del Dragón to suppress the haunting. Now, she could not escape that which haunted her.

The Mark. *Keep a weather eye for the Mark,* Starlene warned her. *Look for the Mark and fight.*

The Mark held her in its grasp. She awoke the morning after leaving Port Royal to bathe herself as best she could. She lifted her thigh to run water from the basin over it and nearly screamed. She pulled her skirts down to cover it but could not escape the knowledge that it was *there.* Slowly, she lifted her skirts back up and peered at the thing she saw there.

On the side of her right thigh, the figure of a green dragon flowered beneath her skin. She could see the fine detail in it. As if to peel it away, she went to touch it. When she pressed her hand to the dragon, she felt nothing. She had heard of tattoos as a thing among different cultures but had never seen one in person. Now, she had what appeared to be a green dragon tattoo, existing between the layers of her skin. The dragon was no longer than her forefinger and no wider than a rope. It both fascinated her and repulsed her.

Look for the Mark.

Belladonna thought about Starlene's words and felt light-headed. Whatever the Mark was, she knew without a doubt this dragon was it. The dragon marked the beginning of a new chapter she would have to face.

Romulus came to her side, sensing her distress, and sniffed the Mark. Puzzled, he looked at Belladonna and tilted his head to the side. She reached down to steady herself, using Romulus to keep her from falling. Resentment for her family name suddenly welled up deep within her.

The Mark did not yet mean anything to her, but she knew it was connected to the Skylark name. Why had this weight been placed on her?

Before she could move to her bed, her body warmed. The resentment that was rooted deep in her gut spread to the outside of her body. Heat began to radiate from her body, feeling like falling embers popping on her skin. Sweat poured from her instantly, drenching the clothes she wore.

"Romulus, fetch Snaggletooth and have him come to me." She pushed Romulus, who grumbled at her when she did so, and he then pushed his way through the doors to find the quartermaster.

Arimetta. Belladonna practically screamed this name to herself in her head. Arimetta, the woman with the magic power, the woman Belladonna could not find a reason to fully trust no matter what she said of helping her. She had not been on the *Zodiac* for more than a day and already strange things were happening. The resentment she felt for the Skylarks shifted to the Hoodoo woman. The surging pain from the burning in her unleashed itself throughout her entire body, causing more sweat to pour from her skin.

"What ails ye, Captain?" Snaggletooth cried, putting his arm around her and moving her to the bed. To her, the air around her was frigid. When Snaggletooth touched her skin, he jumped back. "Yer skin simmers to the touch, my lady! Do ye feel unwell otherwise?"

"Snaggletooth, it's the Mark." Belladonna could not keep her voice from shaking. She shook with rage at herself and Arimetta. Why had she let such a woman as Arimetta come near her? A knowing fear spread over Snaggletooth's face.

"Ye have seen the Mark that Starlene warned ye of?" He gulped. "Let me 'ave a look, if ye will." Belladonna pulled up her skirts to reveal her thigh. Snaggletooth, leaning close, now jumped back again. "Holy high seas, when did this happen?"

"This very morning is the first I have seen of it. Ever since I first laid my eyes on it, I've felt ill. And *hot.* So wretchedly hot that my body feels as if it has been submerged in the deepest circles of hell. Yet the air feels so cold."

"Do I need to send the surgeon to ye, Captain?"

"No, but you can send that witch woman or whatever she is here directly. I am afraid she has already used her magic to try to ruin me. I knew that I had no reason to trust her."

"Do ye really believe it's that Hoodoo prophetess down there that causes this? Starlene did warn ye—"

"I am aware, quartermaster, of the warning, but it seems oddly timed for Arimetta to come aboard and this Mark to suddenly reveal itself. It seems all too connected."

"Ye will not kill her, will ye? Ye must remember that she is powerful. She be the one tamed old Romulus, for goodness sake, and not just with a beating. Romulus only tends to ye now because of what she done."

"How reassuring to see that you have fallen prey to her glamour." Belladonna sighed, piercing Snaggletooth with her stare. "I will not kill her if she can prove to me this was not her doing. Now, bring her here and chain her hands. I do not need her using her hands to cast anything else upon us."

Her rage did not falter. In fact, it still surged but, it was dulling, becoming bearable. Almost as if she had developed an immunity to it already.

Belladonna heard the dragging of feet, of chains clanging against the wood of the ship in a clamorous rhythm.

"Yuh ask fuh Arimetta, muh Captin?" Arimetta croaked.

"Oh, I certainly do because Arimetta seems to be owing her captain an explanation," Belladonna smoldered, lifting her leg to reveal the small dragon that bloomed there. Arimetta crept toward her, dragging her feet one at a time. Belladonna's reaction was to back away. Arimetta's cold, clammy hand flattened over the dragon. She muttered to herself in words Belladonna did not know. Gently, the prophetess's fingers traced the dragon beneath Belladonna's skin, wishing she could feel the lines with the fingertips. Her dull eyes looked up into Belladonna's, unseeing. Then, Arimetta jumped back quickly.

"*Baxide,* chile!" Arimetta started. "Yuh has deh Mark. Aye, Arimetta know much about deh Mark, yes."

"Don't act like you did not inflict this upon me with your own hand, you devil!" Belladonna grabbed the hand that Arimetta used to trace the tattoo and slapped her with the other. "It seems mighty convenient that you happen to mix yourself in my business, and then this shows up. I'll have your hands bound so you cannot submit Romulus as he rips your heart out." Arimetta eased back on her knees and lifted her arms in surrender.

"Yuh tink Arimetta dwi'it to Captain Skylark? It be deh Mark, deh symbol o' deh Dragon Majestics. Arimetta cannot dwi'it wit 'er own hand." She looked away, off to the window, as if she could glimpse the sea that rolled beneath the *Zodiac.* "Aye thought deh Skylark reign o' deh Dragon Majestics cyame to deh end with Abraham n' Jade."

"You did not do this?"

"No mum, dis always meant tuh happen, if ya's deh next in line o' deh Skylark reign. I thought it impossible. Arimetta been cut-off from deh Dragon Majestics since deh passin' of ol' Abraham n' Jade. Dat be deh last aye heard." Belladonna was intrigued, beginning to believe Arimetta had no hand in this. Starlene had warned her of the Mark, after all, and though it was suspicious that it waited until Arimetta showed up, perhaps that was just how fate worked with these things. Suddenly, feeling stupid that she had not made the connection, a revelation occurred deep in Belladonna's mind.

"The prophecy!" Belladonna gasped, grabbing Arimetta's wrists. "Arimetta, you are a prophetess. You know the prophecy that I am to fulfill? Something about my parents. You just said their names. You *knew* them. What is this prophecy that attaches itself to my name? What could they not finish that I must?"

Without hesitation, Arimetta smirked. "Alauda dragon will crush the head of the demon with the heel of her foot. Upon Alaudidae all will look."

Belladonna rolled the words around in her head. The stanza did not mean much to her; she had never heard it before. However, *dragon* was becoming a common word that appeared in ways that struck Belladonna with a sense of duty. She could not think where a demon had come into play.

Perhaps a demon is what possessed her spirit after Starlene's death? And what did Alauda mean? "This prophecy means more to me than I know, doesn't it?" Belladonna asked knowingly.

"It mean much, yes."

"I want you to show me what I need to see. I know you have some knowledge of where this prophecy started, and I think it is meant for you to show it to me. Can you do that, Arimetta?" Belladonna filled her voice with trust.

"'Tis power yuh will feel. 'Tis strong, but yuh must see. Come down to Arimetta, chile."

Reluctantly, Belladonna sank to her knees. Arimetta placed her right hand on the side of Belladonna's face; her left grasped the shells dangling from her neck. She whispered to herself, rubbing the shells with her fingertips. Belladonna's eyes glanced back and forth to the shells and then to her useless eyes. Then, she saw white.

Belladonna stood at an apex of time, unfamiliar with the world she saw around her. A battle was raging before her. Seven dragons—dragons as large as the *Zodiac,* maybe even larger—clawed and ripped at the bodies of a horde of black creatures. Belladonna cowered away, dumbfounded by the enormity of the magical beasts that beat their wings before her. Smoke filled the air as fire sprayed from their mouths. Belladonna had never seen a dragon, let alone believed one existed. She thought them simply to be part of old tall tales. As far as she knew, they existed only in the minds and mouths of storytellers. To behold a dragon in all its splendor, and so close, gave her chills. The black creatures that fought against the dragons she had never known before but likened them to the tales she heard of goblins. Not knowing where they came from, the hate that she felt for Arimetta moments before welled up in her again. Belladonna *wanted* the magnificent dragons to destroy the goblin-like creatures. Watching their heads ripped from their bodies and their shrieks of pain escaping them gave Belladonna far more pleasure than she wanted.

After settling in to witness the end of the battle she now watched, she blinked and found herself in a different time, in a new place. She looked down and wiggled her toes in the grass that sprouted between them. When she looked up, she saw the seven dragons yet again. This time, they looked back at her. All seven of them crowded their massive bodies around her, peering at her like a babe in a cradle. Two dragons that moved to the forefront made her feel a twinge of recognition and longing. This place—this island, she noticed as she looked around—seemed familiar to her as well.

This is the Isla del Dragón, she thought to herself. *This is the place that I will find soon enough. But now I have seen it. I know it exists.*

The peace that filled her soul as she looked into the eyes of the seven dragons overwhelmed her. Tears rolled down her cheeks. Something about this place filled her with belonging. The tears would not stop, no matter how hard she tried to stop them.

Belladonna blinked again and when she opened her eyes, she found herself in a room of black. Rather than seven dragons, seven of the goblin-like creatures glared at her, elevated in their seats above her. Their stares were filled with disapproval. After a moment, they turned back to whatever business they had started before she arrived.

"They bring peace," one of the goblin creatures said. "Peace must not be so. We *must* demolish the root. With the root destroyed, the tree cannot stand! We all know who the roots of that tree on Isla del Dragón are. Alaudidae will reign no more, and the rest of the dragons will fall with them!"

"This is good and true!" The remaining six goblins shouted in unison. A foreboding aura hung in the balance. Wherever this place was, it filled Belladonna with the opposite of what she had just felt on the Isla del Dragón. Much like her earlier visit to the battle, Belladonna thought about how satisfying it would be to rip out the heart of each of the seven goblins, one by one.

The next time Belladonna opened her eyes, she stood on a ship. The ship resembled her own in some ways. Rain poured down on her, and she blinked the water away as she turned to survey the ship. When she had turned a full circle, taking in the world around her in this vision, an enormous man with long, stringy hair stood directly in front of her, unmoving. Belladonna gasped with recognition. The man that stood before her meant far too much to the Skylark name for her to be unfamiliar with him.

"Cornelius Blackfoot?" she whispered to the man, thinking him an apparition.

Blackfoot did not say anything. Instead, he offered her a smile that chilled her to her bones. He began to laugh like a man who has told himself a joke. That laugh turned into a shrill cackle. Belladonna stared expressionless at the crooked, laughing face of Blackfoot. Before another moment passed, Blackfoot fell silent and expressionless himself.

"I am right behind you, Belladonna Skylark." He smirked this time, showing only a corner of his teeth. He blew at her, knocking her out of the ship she stood upon into the darkness.

Great wars.

Innocent men pleading for mercy.

Corrupt leaders.

Children taken from their mothers.

Natural disasters.

Belladonna flashed through time, seeing these things as they happened as if she was living through them. All of them—every vision of destruction, every death, every battle, every injustice—fell under one word that she released from her lips in the trance Arimetta held her under: "Demonclaw."

Rain pattered softly on the ship around Belladonna as she slowly came down from the magic Arimetta used to show her what she needed to see. Her eyes fluttered open, glimpsing the rain that she heard above her. The memories of the visions she saw flooded her as she awoke, and she jumped up. Her eyes widened, looking back and forth between Arimetta and Snaggletooth, who had witnessed the exchange between the two women.

"I know what I need to do now. I have seen what I needed to see. Starlene mentioned the destructive Demonclaw before and that Blackfoot was an 'Emissary of Destruction.'" She remembered the vision of Blackfoot standing in front of her. His words haunted her: *I am right behind you.*

"Now yuh know, Captin Skylark. Yuh is deh inheritor o' deh work yuh parents begun."

"Arimetta, who were my parents? When you showed me the Isla del Dragón, I felt like I knew two of them, though really I felt like I knew all of them. But two of them struck me as most familiar."

"Yuh parents were deh empr'r and deh emp'ress of deh Dragon Majestics." The prophetess smiled. "Yuh deh next in line. 'Tis why deh Mark appear now."

"And who are the Dragon Majestics? I have only ever heard tales of them."

"Dey be deh emissaries o' Peace. Deh opposite o' deh Demonclaw yuh seen. Dey deh ones keep deh world from ruin."

"They are the balance. The Dragon Majestics keep destruction from overtaking the world. They offer peace in place of a world of hate."

"Jah know't," Arimetta agreed.

"If I understand it right, it goes like this: my parents were the emperor and empress of the Dragon Majestics, and the Dragon Majestics maintain peace throughout the land. The Demonclaw is the cause behind every tragedy that has fallen upon the land. Because my parents are dead, that leaves me as the heir to the title of empress of the Dragon Majestics." Belladonna paused here, taking a moment to absorb the enormity of what she was saying. This was not simply a matter of riddling distant family history; this involved the weight of the world. The world would depend upon *her*. "The prophecy states that a dragon will crush the demon under its foot. If I am to finish what my parents started and defeat the Demonclaw, where do I start?" Her words lodged themselves in her throat.

I am right behind you.

"Snaggletooth, go have a look behind us. See if you can find any ships on the horizon and report back to me at once. I must know what you see. I have been a fool to think that simply because I have not run across Blackfoot that he does not pursue me."

"Aye, Captain." Snaggletooth exited the room, leaving Arimetta and Belladonna alone.

"I bear the Mark of the Dragon Majestics, do I not? Does this mean that I *myself* am a dragon?"

"Let yuhself grow, young Skylark. Yuh will know soon 'nuff. Deh wey yuh skin burn, Arimetta would say yuh know ver' soon."

Belladonna had just heard a great deal of information that had flipped her world upside down in a matter of minutes. From the dragon tattoo to Arimetta's casting of the past onto her revealed much about the Skylark family. Why did Starlene keep all of this from her? Belladonna tried to assume that Starlene wanted to finish business with Blackfoot and the Demonclaw personally; to spare Belladonna the danger of it, perhaps ushering her into her place as Dragon empress without having to suffer through the fight. The way Starlene died was the way she was always meant to die: she stuck her nose in the Skylark quest and messed with fate. Fate and prophecy were quick to push her out of the way. Since Starlene died, Belladonna had not felt sorrowful toward her old captain. Today, she pitied her, felt sorry that Starlene had to die because of business that involved the Skylark family. However, it was Starlene's fault. Starlene knew the prophecy but tried to step in anyway. Snaggletooth entered again, disrupting Belladonna's thoughts.

"What do you see out there, quartermaster? Does a ship follow?"

"Aye, it does." Snaggletooth seemed to understand that this was not good news. "She follows quite a few leagues behind, not close enough for me to identify, but she follows nonetheless."

"I am right behind you," Belladonna said to herself.

"Speak, chile, say't again."

"I am right behind you. Blackfoot. That is what he said to me in one of the visions you cast on me. Did you know he was trailing us?" Belladonna was becoming angry with Arimetta again, ignoring the searing burn inside of her that came with the anger.

"Arimetta hed not known dis until yuh seen it. But aye, he follow. He do deh werk of deh Demonclaw. He been offer'd deh High Seat in deh Demonclaw Court. Dey deh masta-minds behind deh destruction yuh see. Dey offa him deh seat, he mus' destroy deh Isla del Dragón. Part o' deh deal. He been at it many a-year, he been 'round since deh beginning o' time. He didn't start 'til yuh parents came into dey rightful place. Den dey offas him deh seat, he become a captin to many-a man to destroy deh Skylarks. Now, he know yuh. He not know yuh 'afore today. But aye, he seen yuh. Now, he set out tuh destroy *Belladonna Skylark.* Dey not want anotha Dragon empress sittin' on dat island."

"You mean to tell me that after eighteen years," Belladonna had to think on this, realizing she had just entered her eighteenth year, "Cornelius Blackfoot has not known of me?"

"Allow me to explain a little, Captain," Snaggletooth interjected. Snaggletooth felt the guilt as he spoke, guilt for all of the years he had allowed Belladonna to live without the knowledge of Blackfoot. He stepped forward. "Starlene worked hard to destroy Blackfoot so ye would not have to. Blackfoot knew that a Skylark heir existed—yer brother—but the heir that was known to the world died. He thought that the Dragon Majestics would be easy pickin's once all the Skylarks died. Ye, however, were kept secret. Blackfoot knew not that ye even existed. Starlene hid ye. She did not want ye to die the way yer mum and dad did. She wanted to create a safe passage for ye to take yer rightful place as the next Dragon empress without a soul knowin' ye. I know not how Blackfoot has found ye. I assumed he was out of the picture as no one has heard of him or from him since Starlene's death."

"And you? Snaggletooth, you knew what I was to become?" She scoffed. "How many other souls on this ship knew this and thought it would be fine for their captain to be hid from this knowledge?"

"No one but me." Snaggletooth sighed. "I have always known. I have known since Abraham and Jade allied with Starlene. I saw their power; I saw their strength. I am one of the only who saw them in their truest forms, their dragon forms. And, Belladonna, what magnificence they were!"

Belladonna thought about what Snaggletooth told her. It struck her like an arrow to the heart that so much of who she was remained hidden from her. It was no wonder now why she never truly felt like she knew who she was. This new knowledge, much like the knowledge she acquired when Starlene died, ignited a flame in her, incomparable to the flame that grew from her anger. Belladonna was beginning to feel whole. However, she knew that her heart remained black and bitter. What would she need to do to remove that curse from her?

"Well, seeing as I would very much like to be angry with both of you for knowing such things about me and choosing not to tell me, I find that I cannot be so angry. I find that I am, in fact, beginning to make sense of this life I have been given. Even though I do still feel full of hate, now I think I know why. It is probable that I will not learn to rid myself of that hate until I have avenged my name or until I have crushed that Blackfoot serpent under my heel once and for all. I have lost much in this short life of mine. But with each passing day, things are made just a little clearer to me. I will bear my family name. I will find the Isla del Dragón. I will cast that Blackfoot demon back to hell, without his promotion. I will become the Dragon empress, distributing peace throughout the land. This is my purpose, and I will fight."

Arimetta took Belladonna's hand from her place on the floor and kissed it, twiddling with Belladonna's rings as she did so, smiling up at her. Snaggletooth grinned. Belladonna herself was filled with pride.

"We will fight with ye, Captain Skylark," Snaggletooth promised.

"I know you will. I know all of you will." Coming down from her moment of pride left her feeling ill yet again. There was now so much to think about, so much to consider. She needed to decide how she would meet Blackfoot and deal him his death. Blackfoot was not part of the picture until Arimetta's vision. She felt faint, lowering to her bed. "Now, if you will leave me be, I have much to think about. Snaggletooth, I would ask that you take command until I have sorted through all of this. And Arimetta, you have earned my trust. You have free range of the ship as you like. But be careful of my men. Do not lay a hand on them, do not even do so much as look in their direction. Though you cannot see them, they will fill their head with ideas. I need your mind to remain *pure,* in the event that I may need you to cast your vision on me again or look into my future."

"Arimetta remain clean, Captin. She want her freedom jus' as much as her captin do."

"You can rely on my leadership," Snaggletooth promised.

As the two left the room, Romulus came back to her. Belladonna still burned with fever, ignoring it long enough to listen to her quartermaster and prophetess. She glanced at the dragon on her leg and felt a fresh surge of heat wash over her body. The small dragon meant so much to who she was. Not too long ago, she feared Arimetta, or anyone for that matter, had placed a curse on her. Though she still feared its ultimate meaning, she accepted the Mark as a part of herself, the Mark of a young lady becoming who she was created to be.

Over the following days, Belladonna would fight the fever ravaging her, going back and forth between the seething anger of knowing Blackfoot would now become an obstacle and overwhelming, philosophical ponderings about her identity. Many questions came to her regarding these things, but one seemingly meaningless question kept recurring: If Abraham and Jade had been Dragon emperor and empress, and she herself was to become empress, who was the Dragon emperor to be?

CHAPTER 6
ACQUIRED KNOWLEDGE

The *Zodiac* led the way, but *The Temptress* followed not too far behind. Keeping his distance, Blackfoot chose to make his ship's speed slow but steady. In a quick, flashing moment, he knew why the lady captain on the *Zodiac* had drawn him.

The captain heard a voice, tucked away inside his brain, speak to him. Startled by its presence, he jumped back. Where had it come from? None around him had spoken. No, he *felt* the voice inside his head. The voice promised things that he did not think possible. Briefly, for only just a few seconds, he saw her. There could be no doubt that she was the same girl that he glimpsed distantly on her ship.

"I am right behind you," he said to the wind, though in his mind, she stood before him.

I have been a fool to believe the Skylarks were gone. Blackfoot had previously resolved that the Demonclaw Court would not make his voyage easy. He was presently being forced to face the fact that the Skylarks would lie in his wake until he destroyed every last one of them. But he could not help but wonder, how had he missed a *second* Skylark offspring?

Blackfoot plodded heavy-footed to his quarters where he kept every scrap of information on the Skylarks that he could find. Rifling through the information, he scanned for anything he could find on another Skylark. The only name in relation to Jade and Abraham was Obadiah, who was known to be dead. No mention of a girl was listed anywhere.

She was their secret. Blackfoot dropped the papers to the ground in a daze. *Her name is Belladonna Skylark, and she sails for the Isla del Dragón.* The knowledge of her life was breathed into him. This newly acquired knowledge was useful. Besides that, Blackfoot praised the voice that spoke quietly to him. This new voice would be helpful, and it would feed him along the way. Never had the Demonclaw Court been so gracious to provide a gift such as this! He quickly pushed aside any thoughts that the Court might have sent the voice because they were disappointed in his slow progress.

Giddiness crept into Blackfoot's spirit. The lady captain allured him, and he knew now that her allure was neither her beauty nor her station. Blackfoot was drawn to her because he was *meant* to follow her.

"Is she one of them?" He asked aloud to whoever or whatever it was that fed his mind. There was no answer except the whipping of the sails. The prospect of Belladonna Skylark being one of *them* was all too much for Blackfoot. "Whether or not she is one of *them,* I will follow her to the Isla del Dragón, and I will kill her before she can even step one foot off her ship."

It was too good of a plan. He was being led to where he needed to go, to become who he was meant to be. He would kill her. After that, he would be exalted among the Demonclaw.

However perfect it all seemed, Blackfoot could not help but acknowledge the suspicion that crept up his spine. *I know who she is now, but does* she *know who I am?*

He could not help but think that she did, in fact, know that he lurked in the shadows of her sails.

CHAPTER 7
RUNNING THE GAUNTLET

Belladonna felt a fool for not thinking about Blackfoot. She always assumed that she would have encountered him by now during her two years of active pirating. If she had come across him then, he would have been dead by now.

Killing him was not optional. She knew not where or when she would kill him, but she knew she must if she was to be the chief emissary of peace in a world that unknowingly relied upon her.

Snaggletooth came to her often in the few days she remained in her quarters, wrestling with the hot fever that gripped her flesh. In fact, he had cried to her, begging her for mercy for not telling her about her destiny as a Dragon Majestic sooner. Snaggletooth found himself in a fever of his own, sick with guilt. She did her best to console him: "You knew not what would befall me, good man."

"But I did! I did, and I kept it from ye. I thought that maybe it was not *ye* that were meant to bear the peace of the world. I thought it befell yer brother, and with him long dead, I should've known better."

"I would not expect you, Snaggletooth, a mere man, to know all the secrets of the Dragon Majestics. For I am one, and I still do not even know all the secrets. You have been forgiven."

Nodding in acceptance, Belladonna knew that Snaggletooth had not, and would maybe never, truly receive her forgiveness. His thinking made sense to her. With the eldest heir dead, perhaps the title of Dragon emperor passed on to another generation from a different time. Would the title have befallen her, with or without her brother dead? She knew not.

The fever raged on within her, never ceasing. Rather than defeat it with rest or medicine, she found herself growing immune to the burning. She assumed it was a side effect of her brittle, charred heart. She wondered how her heart could endure any more hardening.

The heaviest weight upon her now was her ever-increasing need to understand the Dragon Majestics and the Demonclaw. Their feud had been waged since the beginning of time, the two realms constantly at war to bring either peace or destruction to the masses. Selfishly, Belladonna thought about how all of this would affect her. Once she took her place on the Isla del Dragón, she would not live a normal life. She would reign as a dragon forevermore, rid of the earthly vessel her soul inhabited. This she assumed, at least.

All of what she came to know was weighty, so weighty that she accepted she would not be able to comprehend all of it. Contrary to her current desire to control her course, she would simply have to let each day come, and with each day, she hoped she would learn more about herself.

Alistair Kent had served faithfully as the *Zodiac's* cook since Captain Starlene first set sail as captain. Fortunately, he survived his new captain's fits of rage and managed to stay out of her way almost entirely. She did not like to deal directly with him. Occasionally, when she had complaints, she would let Snaggletooth handle them. Alistair had been struck when he came to learn the young girl who grew up on the *Zodiac*—the girl who was very curious about his craft, the girl who taste-tested every meal before she rushed it to Starlene for him—had fledged into a beastly tyrant. Starlene had been so gentle toward her, so motherly. What happened to the girl he once knew? He longed for the days of her innocence and mourned for the men, including himself, who would die by her hand if her favor was not earned.

Much like some of the men who remained from Starlene's rule, Alistair held his own opinions of her. He, unlike the ones who had been killed, was wise enough to keep them to himself. His loftiest opinion was that of the democratic vote among the crew as to who the next captain would be. On a ship, if a captain died or was mutinied, the crew elected who they saw fit to be the next captain. Traditionally, this should have happened after Starlene's passing. He found it best to keep his mouth shut, considering a female captain was not a convention of the day. And certainly, nothing was traditional about keeping a tiger as a beloved companion.

Remaining constant in his duty and away from his captain, Alistair whiled away the days, making sure she and her men stayed fed. On this particular day, he realized he needed to go below to the hold to update his stock. *One must make do with what he has,* Alistair thought to himself, which is what he knew he must do so since Belladonna did not intend on stopping off again any time soon, and he needed to prepare for that.

Before he saw the man, Ephraim heard his clunky footfalls and his whistling. Whoever was descending into the hold was humming a tune he knew but could not place. Just as it had for almost a week now, the rum he drank the night before carried him to a place of mental fog.

Too busy thinking about the name of the tune the man whistled, Ephraim's eyes widened. He was a *stowaway* for heaven's sake, on a ship abounding with dangerous curiosities, yet he lay in the open for anyone to see. Ephraim had grown too comfortable in his resting place, thinking of the hold as his own personal quarters and not the belly of a pirate ship. The prospect of someone finding him hidden had not crossed his mind. He got on all fours, trying to scramble to a place that would cover him. The alcohol impaired his movement, his spider-like attempt at crawling away looking more like a pig escaping slaughter. The noises he made while trying to hide did not help him.

The man that Ephraim would later learn to call Alistair stood on the last step of the hold. He paused, looking around with his lantern held close to his face.

"Is someone down here?" Alistair called. "If there be someone down here, make yourself known to me. And I hope ya don't intend to kill me. Without a cook, there be no meals for the crew."

Ephraim hid behind barrels of rum, crouching low to the planks underneath him. His crouch made him unsteady. The rolling of the ship along the sea attempted to take his footing out from under him. All at once, Ephraim felt the rolling of the ship in his gut. His quick movement to hide had roused his stomach and sent the alcohol up to his throat. He swallowed hard, doing his best to keep from vomiting and giving himself away. The feeling would not leave him no matter how hard he fought it. Quickly, he peered around the barrel and saw that the man still stood on the bottom step, scanning the hold. Trying to shift his position noiselessly, his stomach erupted, sending the alcohol out of his body in a violent hurry.

Alistair heard the gagging, rushed to the source of the sound. He peered over the barrels and found a boy, probably not much older than the captain, bent on all fours like Romulus, coughing up his dinner. He saw the puddle of liquid under the boy.

"Not too good at holding that liquor, are ya, boy?" Alistair chuckled. Ephraim lifted himself and sat on his haunches, wiping his mouth with the back of his hand.

"Have never had a high tolerance for it, sir. But have always liked it nonetheless."

"I hope ya haven't been drinking that from these barrels," Alistair said, kicking the barrel Ephraim sat behind. The hollow sound the barrel made against his shoe indicated otherwise.

"And I hope ya haven't been eating from what I got down here, lad. This will last us until Belladonna thinks we will get to land again. Have I seen ya before? Ya don't look too familiar to me. And why are ya down here and not in the sleeping quarters like e'ryone else?"

"You have probably seen me, just can't place me is all. Just came down here to fetch something." Ephraim rubbed his eyes with his palms and hiccupped. He knew the cook's discovery would give him away, as would his excessive drinking. Alistair did not believe him.

"What's your title, and what's your name?"

"Seeing as you're just a humble cook, I don't know that you are entitled to any of that information. You have no power over me. I answer to my captain, Belladonna." Ephraim mustered enough gusto to state this information confidently, though he really did not know much at all about his captain.

"Oh, yeah? Shall I go get her and ya can answer those questions when she asks ya, if ya only be answerin' to her?" Ephraim remained silent, his head pounding from dehydration. There was not much he could say now that would convince the cook that he was not a stowaway. "Or perhaps maybe I will go fetch the kitty and have him sniff you out. I'm sure his rations have left him licking his chops for an extra meal these days."

"No, please!" Ephraim jumped up. The cat scared him more than the captain. Little did he know at the time that a quick end with Romulus would be better than what Belladonna would bestow upon him. "Please, sir, my name is Ephraim Howell. I stowed away when the ship left Port Royal, and I've been doing my best to work without notice. Please, don't give me away. I can't go back where I came from, but I don't want to die either. Have mercy on me, sir."

"And where do ya come from, Ephraim Howell, that's so bad ya'd rather work under the Dragon Lady? Have you not come to find that what ya had might have been better?" Fear shot up Ephraim's spine. Even the cook called her that wretched name. What reputation had their captain won to be called the Dragon Lady?

"That's not important. What is important is that—"

"What's important is that if Captain Skylark finds out about ya, I don't find ya worth dying over. So I will do my duty to my captain and report ya to her immediately. She would certainly kill me if she knew I kept ya a secret down here. Besides, can't have ya eatin' and drinkin' off what is rightfully ours if ya don't pull ya weight around here." Alistair went for Ephraim's wrist. Ephraim ducked away, pulling out the knife he kept at his side.

"You will not lay a hand on me," Ephraim warned. "And if you so much as open your mouth to shout for anyone, I will slit your throat." Alistair glared at him. Then he started to chuckle.

"Romulus!" Alistair shouted. Romulus could hear his call from anywhere on the ship. He lay peacefully on deck, entirely in the way of the men that worked. Occasionally, he lifted an eyelid, letting the men know if they even so much as attempted to raise a fuss about his massive body being in the way, he would attack. Romulus was always listening.

Ephraim went to dash the knife into the cook's neck before he thought about what Alistair shouted. Over the past week, he had become very familiar with the names of the men on board and knew the name the men used for the cat. His hand paused mid-swing, frozen in time. Gooseflesh crawled on his skin from his neck down to his ankles. He heard the four paws of the tiger thump across the ship above in a hurry. Alistair grinned at Ephraim.

"Ya should not have done that, Mr. Howell. Ya should not have forced me to get him involved in this business."

Romulus appeared, his lumbering, striped body descending the steps with the agility only a wild animal could possess. When he turned the front half of his body in their direction, he snarled.

Ephraim could see the cat crouch, his shoulder muscles extending to attack. Ephraim raised his hands and dropped to his knees in surrender. This, however, was a cat, not a man. He was not sure if the cat would accept his surrender or if he would see Ephraim as an easier target. Romulus growled, licking his teeth the closer he got to Ephraim. His nose continued to twitch, smelling the stranger before him. Romulus did not recognize the boy nor his scent. Now just inches away, Romulus's eyes bore intently into

Ephraim's. Ephraim felt the urge to urinate, doing his best to hold his composure. The cat would surely eat him.

I should never have left the Navy, he thought to himself. The Royal Navy did not have predators of this kind living onboard.

Just as Romulus widened his jaws to clamp down on the boy's face in front of him, Alistair whistled. Romulus snapped to attention. His growling ceased.

"As quick as it would be for Romulus to destroy ya, I suddenly find no satisfaction in that." Alistair looked down at the frightened boy in front of him. "I find your offense worthy of a longer, slower death. Ya will follow me to Captain Skylark, and ya will face her. Come with me, boy."

Ephraim wanted to fight. He wanted to dash the cook to pieces and find a way to throw them overboard at night. His hiding among the cargo had grown so comfortable, so secure. The prospect of facing the captain that held such a nasty reputation made him quiver. Ephraim had to face the reality that he could hide from the woman whose very ship he leeched off. Best to get the meeting over with, he reluctantly accepted.

He also knew his hiding and his violent plans against the cook would not hold now that the tiger had taken a good whiff of him. The tiger would be tracking his every move.

Ephraim stood up slowly, offering his wrists to the cook. The cook uncoiled a thin rope from his belt loop and bound Ephraim's hands.

"Name's Alistair," he muttered to Ephraim. "If she lets ya live, you'll be knowin' me anyway as yar cook, as ya have already guessed. I hate to do this to ya, but ya must understand. She be a fierce lady, and I fear her. I have lived too long to give her a reason to kill me."

The only thing Ephraim could do was glower back at him. He made no attempt to be cordial. When Alistair finished tying his hands, he motioned for him to start walking. When he did not move, Romulus growled and nudged him. The cat could not be ignored when all Ephraim could think about was the pain that would rock his body if its teeth ever bore into his skin. Slowly and silently, Ephraim shuffled forward, taking his time to accept his oncoming death.

As Alistair followed behind Ephraim, he replayed the last few minutes in his head. He thought about the brutality of the threats he laid upon the boy. Those threats were not like him. They sounded more like the threats that Captain Skylark would speak. Alistair thought about his captain's cruelty imprinting upon him and shuddered. He could only wonder how much more his captain would influence him and feared for the life of the boy that he now delivered to his doom.

Every man on deck turned his head toward Ephraim, Alistair, and Romulus as they approached Belladonna. Ephraim kept his eyes cast down to the ground, embarrassed for himself. To his right, he heard a man scoff under his breath. Probably Mace, the man who had kept his secret. Ephraim assumed that scoff was one of agony, as he was sure Mace knew the price for concealing information from their captain.

Alistair stopped walking, told Ephraim to stay where he was, and moved on. Romulus remained by Ephraim. The cat kept his glistening eyes on the boy. He heard voices somewhere not too far off, perhaps up at the wheel, and took a moment to consider his fate. Now that he had a few moments to think about it, he probably would have died soon in the Navy at the hands of a Spaniard or the like. Life at sea was often short, no matter how you spent it. And if this captain truly held to her reputation of being the

Dragon Lady, he would consider it God's grace if he lived beyond the next hour.

Boots stomped one at a time from somewhere above. The stomps got closer, closer, closer with each footfall. Someone now stood before him. He still had not looked up.

"So you have been helping yourself to a share of the rum down below, aye?" The voice that spoke before him was feminine, yet he couldn't ignore the attention that voice commanded. When he looked up, he nearly gasped. Standing in front of him was one of the most dazzling women he had ever seen. Her hair, scarlet and shining, framed her pale complexion well. She wore a linen shirt with, bless it, men's trousers that were fitted to her exact proportions. Had she looked like this in London, she would have been considered a walking crime. Her clothing was scandalous, but then again, so was a lady captain.

As beautiful as she was, Ephraim could not overlook her Amazonian qualities. Her breasts, her hips, and her thighs were shapely. Something about her body made Ephraim think of a Greek goddess prepared for battle. He was entranced with her strong yet womanly features. Oddly, heat radiated from her body. The pale, delicate skin appeared dewy. Lastly, he noticed her cheeks, rosy and bright underneath high cheekbones.

Though it would never happen, not by his estimations, he wanted her. The urge of man began to take hold of him.

She, standing before him, gave no indication of these same feelings. Green eyes framed by long, thick eyelashes bore into his, demanding an answer. The urge he felt quickly melted into submission to her.

"Um, aye, I have." He gulped. The men that had gathered around them laughed quietly.

"I did not even need you to say a dang thing before I knew what would come out of your mouth. Can you smell it, boys?" She looked around to the men, all of them nodding in agreement. "Well, I am certainly glad you have found merriment aboard my *Zodiac*. I am also glad to hear you've been working for free for me."

"Miss, I—"

"That'll be Captain Skylark to you. Nothing else. But go on."

"Captain Skylark, I really meant no harm."

"What is your purpose here, boy?" She twisted her arms behind her back, starting to walk in a circle around Ephraim.

"Work, Captain Skylark. I come seeking work."

"Work? Then why did you not present yourself to me when all these other fine gentlemen did? Would that not be a fair way to gain employment in this lovely occupation you've chased after?"

"Aye, yes, I should have."

"You would think I would be glad to hear that I have one less man to pay who will work. You would think that I should praise you for all of your free labor." At this, she stopped in front of him, grabbed him by the neck, and pulled him down to her face. To his surprise, her grip seared his skin. Her fingers, clenched tightly around his throat, burned like the fire from hell. It took all of his strength to keep from screaming. "But in fact, it makes me sick when a man thinks he can sneak past me. A man often thinks he can fool a woman and that he can keep fooling her for she must be too stupid to notice. But I always find out. I look for honest men, men who don't find their means sneaking around me and taking what is rightfully mine." Belladonna let go of his neck, shoving him back. He wished he could move his hands to his neck to feel the damage she likely caused, but they remained bound. "What is your name?"

"Ephraim Howell, Captain."

"Ephraim Howell, then. What am I to do with you? Am I to trust you and think you an honest man now? Certainly not. What have you done to earn my trust? You have used me, plain and simple. I am quite certain you have run from somewhere you do not want to go back to. I am sure you thought something about this life sounded romantic to you. Quite charming to hide with the rats and suck from the teat of a woman's hard work, isn't it? Have I got you pegged, Ephraim Howell?" Ephraim said nothing, only blinked in acknowledgment of her accusations.

Honestly, she *did* have him pegged. "This is what I will do with you, Mr. Howell. I will not have you working on my ship. Not when you have done nothing to prove that I should trust you. I am on a very important voyage, and I cannot have anyone betraying me. It'll be the gauntlet for you."

The men gasped. Running the gauntlet was barbarous. Normally, Belladonna preferred torturing her victims with her own hand. In the case of Ephraim Howell, she was so furious that she wanted to simply sit back and watch the brutality rather than deal it out herself.

"No, please!" Ephraim howled. Two sets of hands grabbed him. One set belonged to Snaggletooth, the other belonged to Mace, who looked at him wildly. His eyes told Ephraim he knew one day he would get caught and that he would not confess to knowing him. Ephraim was foolish enough to trust the man. "Captain, please, I will get off at the next port. You can maroon me, if you like, but please, why this torture? I have done nothing!"

"Oh, how dull you must be, Mr. Howell. You come on my ship without my knowledge and drink from the rum that I have purchased with my own hard work. I know your type. All you want is freedom, but you live in a fantasy. You think everything about this life is beautiful—that you get to play the hero, robbing the rich and feeding the poor, or some hogwash like that. And I know your type well enough to tell you that you would not last long on this ship if you worked under my command. You're too fragile for this life. When you think about it, I am doing you a service. I am showing you what this life is really, truly like."

As Ephraim begged, Alistair fetched the whips the crew would use to lash Belladonna's newest victim. He began to tremble, doing his best to fight his fear. He thought he had come to terms with the reality of his death, but he found he was not ready for it. Urine splashed down the legs of his trousers, dowsing the deck beneath him. Belladonna let out a terrifying laugh when she noticed the fear escaping his body.

"Captain Skylark, please have mercy on me!"

"Oh, please, Mr. Howell. I have known nothing of mercy for nearly two years now. I have only known hate for those who betray me and the lust for watching those very ones die. Nothing you could do or say will sway me."

Snaggletooth dragged Ephraim to the end of the line, the crew standing in lines on both sides of him. Some of them looked ready to offer a fresh beating; others looked regretful and sorrowful. Some of the men probably sided with Belladonna's thinking. The others simply didn't want to get killed if they did not participate.

Ephraim knew he would not die from the lashings. He would die from the agony after they had been dealt.

Belladonna stood opposite him at the front of the line. She sneered at him, prepared to enjoy the torture of the boy who tried to take advantage of her. From her face she told the story; she had been taken advantage of before and would kill anyone who tried to do it again.

Romulus peered up at Belladonna, a nasty snarl on his whiskered mug. She nodded to him. Deep within the recesses of the cat, he mustered everything to unleash a mighty roar, beginning Belladonna's game.

Limbs heavy from hard labor and excessive drinking, Ephraim began to trudge through the wall of men on each side of him. He did something he never thought he would need to; Ephraim began to pray for his soul.

"God in heaven, hallow'd be Thy name—" Lashings rained down on the skin of his bare back on both sides. He winced, keeping his composure for the time being.

"Faster, you wretched dogs, the man needs to scream!" Belladonna commanded from her post. Romulus watched on with her. Both woman and beast seemed to be driven to a frenzy by the bloodshed.

When he reached the end of the line, he turned to go back where he had started. The second round of lashings ripped his already open wounds. His breath fluttered in his chest by the time he reached the end of the line again. Deep, wheezing gasps escaped him. He turned again, bracing himself for a third round of fresh whippings.

Twelve times Ephraim ran the gauntlet. The stripes on his back were searing and raw. There was not one bit of his flesh that did not escape the blood oozing from the cuts. Ephraim himself had lost count of how many times he thought he had been flogged.

Belladonna raised her hand for a pause in the commotion when Ephraim fell to his knees midway through the line. She walked to him slowly. The boy bent to all fours, his open back arched and heaving. Belladonna dropped to her knees, feeling far too much satisfaction from the way in which the boy in front of her suffered. She grabbed his face with her hand and made him look into her eyes.

"This boy can bear much pain; I will give him that." The men who found satisfaction in their work along with Belladonna chuckled at this. "But perhaps this is too quick of a death for him. Some traitors deserve to die slowly, so I think."

Three versions of the captain blurred back and forth in front of Ephraim. His parched throat begged for water, his raw stomach ached for food. Yet all he wanted to do was close his eyes and drift away.

"Take him below. He will certainly be dead by the time the sun sets." He heard the captain say this but did not care any longer. Breathing had become his sole focus. A man heaved him up on his feet and nudged him with the handle of the whip he held. When Ephraim looked behind him, he saw the man with the pointed tooth jabbing out from his bottom lip.

"Ye have heard the voice of yer captain. Down with ye," Snaggletooth commanded. Ephraim tried to move but one step brought him mindlessly to his knees again. The skin of his back burned as if chemicals had been poured into them. "Alright, so it's like that now, innit?" Snaggletooth grabbed him by one of his elbows and began to drag him. Splintered wood jabbed through Ephraim's pants and ripped through his skin. *What is more pain?* Ephraim asked himself. He felt confident, as Captain Skylark said, that we would be dead by nightfall.

As much as Ephraim wanted to believe he would be dead by that night, all he did was lapse into what seemed like a dark, bottomless slumber. He dreamed deeply, seeing visions of a visitor. When the visitor came to him in his visions, the pain in his back intensified but then subsided after some time, like the coming and going of waves on sand. Ephraim could not get a good look at his visitor. When he tried to open his eyes to get a peek, he found it impossible to keep them open. On one occasion he was able to gather some knowledge of the visitor. A spindly, spidery shadow of a woman with a long mane of tangled hair knelt before him, brushing the curls that lay on his forehead to the side. Once—maybe more than once . . . he did not really know nor could he even try to count—she lifted a vessel to his lips that sent lukewarm water over his tongue and down his throat. Nothing more stood out about the woman other than the floating, milky orbs that could only have been her eyes. They glowed at him gently, offering him condolence that he could feel deep in his heart. Sometimes, she whispered unintelligible nothings to him, and sometimes, she said these things with the glowing orbs looking toward the heavens. The kind and mysterious visitor was the only thing that made what Ephraim thought to be his passage into death a little less frightening.

Several days passed since Belladonna's discovery of the stowaway. She cursed her youth, attributing her inattentiveness to all things that required her attention to her lack of aging wisdom. Much had been learned since she had become captain of the *Zodiac,* but she still had far more to learn.

Today, she would go down to the cell she kept below and see what remained of the boy named Ephraim. The boy's eyes spoke of innocence and fear, but she could not find a care to offer him. Innocence and fear had marked her once upon a time, as well, when her beloved captain died before her eyes. She did not think herself ready to take on a task such as she had. One must grow out of that innocence and fear of life, she thought, to become anyone of value in the world.

A small part of her hoped that the boy's death down below had been quick. The smallest twinge of pity nicked at her, but she was quick to brush it away.

"Snaggletooth," she called as she looked out into the sea, "have you gone to check on that stowaway below? Do you know if he has died?"

"No, Captain, I have not. I assumed him dead long ago, probably half or wholly eaten by the rats by now. I am surprised ye have not yet allowed Romulus to pick at the scraps." Snaggletooth chuckled at this, feeling just as much contempt for the boy as Belladonna. Being a pirate did require a degree of heartlessness toward dishonest men, which Snaggletooth had allowed to callous his heart over his many years at sea.

"I will go see today. I ask that you keep away, for if he is alive, I would like to be the one to finish him off."

"Aye, Captain." Snaggletooth tilted his hat to her and headed back to his duty. In the moments before she would decide to step away toward the stairs that led to the cell, Belladonna felt a presence behind her.

"Mey I hev a word wit deh cap'n, if it do yuh?" Belladonna felt Arimetta's warm, rank breath on the back of her neck. She resisted the urge to turn and slap her for getting too close.

"I suppose I have a moment. What concerns you, Arimetta?"

"Arimetta know dat yuh wan' ta finish deh boy yuh hold in deh cell, deh very same cell yuh held Arimetta in herself. Arimetta, she have a feelin' dat yuh mey wanna tink again afore yuh go down dere."

"Does he live? Does the boy live?" Belladonna turned abruptly to face Arimetta.

"Oh, he live. He fight hard but he live. He deh reason I wanna talk to captin. Yuh need tuh

let 'im live."

Arimetta's suggestion struck Belladonna as odd. She could think of no reason for him to live if he had started on such dishonest footing.

"Give me your reasons as you see fit."

"Yuh needa tink, yuh deh next Dragon emp'rss, yes. But tink a dis: ya fadda n motha ruled as deh empr'r n deh emp'rss. Dey was two 'n yuh only one. Dere is anodda dat will need replacin' even afta yuh take yuh place."

It was as if Arimetta lived in Belladonna's head. Though not one of her primary concerns at the moment, Belladonna *had* toyed with the idea that maybe she was not the only one meant to rule. Surely, if there had always been seven Dragon Majestics, she must be responsible for ushering in the seventh along with herself. But what about Ephraim Howell led the prophetess to believe that she thought his life worthy of sparing, let alone being worthy of such an honor?

"I cannot say I haven't considered that very thing. The time I spent grappling with my fever made me pause and ask many questions about these things. All of it is so new to me, and there seem to be so many pieces missing. But what of the boy? Why do you think he deserves to live?"

"'Cuz Arimetta gots a feelin' dat deh boy mean more den jus' anodda soul on deh ship. Arimetta suspect deh boy hold great purpose. Yuh must decide fuh yuhself, but Arimetta speak on what she feel in 'er heart. Mayhap she also seen some o' duh future fuh him, and in what she see, he is dere."

"But I am assuming you did not see what type of part he played, did you?" Belladonna asked.

"Ah, no, not always how a vision work. But yuh claim tuh trust Arimetta; continue tuh trust 'er on dis matter."

"Suppose I find him truly deserving of death? Do you think his death will break the web upon which I have built thus far?"

Arimetta's eyes met Belladonna's, and she pursed her lips. It had not been very often that Arimetta remained silent when asked about these kinds of things. Arimetta had a way of making all of her visions cryptic, as Belladonna was sure most prophetesses did. The rage she had felt toward Arimetta upon their first meeting had subsided completely once she decided to trust her. She now ranked her with Snaggletooth and Romulus as someone who truly sided with her.

"I will accept your silence as the utmost urgency to keep him alive." Arimetta made to leave Belladonna's side, but another question nagged Belladonna, which she felt she must ask her now. "Arimetta, you mentioned that your motive to help me find the Isla del Dragón was your freedom. I would like to know exactly what you meant."

"Arimetta sold her soul to deh Demonclaw many a year ago. When deh Dragonclaw no longer, she be free from deh bondage."

"Do you work for them?" Belladonna asked, feeling icy cold spread through her veins. Did she have a betrayer on board? Worst of all, had she trusted her too soon?

"No, Arimetta a free agent. If I cannot help yuh, den when I die, I go down wit' deh devil in hell, serving deh Demonclaw fer all eternity. If Arimetta help yuh and yuh defeat dem, and dey is no more, den I am free."

Belladonna understood this. In some ways, the two women were similar. Though Belladonna had not sold her very soul to the Demonclaw as Arimetta had, her freedom also depended on their total and complete annihilation. Wiping the Demonclaw from the face of the earth would free many, she supposed.

"Rest assured," Belladonna stated, "that I will make sure you get your freedom when I have taken my oath as Dragon empress." She squeezed Arimetta's hand, not feeling love toward the prophetess—that she was not capable of—but feeling a sense of oneness. She had not felt this oneness of prolonged purpose with another woman since Starlene's death. Arimetta smiled at Belladonna, then quickly pulled away to continue roaming the ship. Arimetta spent most of her days pacing the entirety of the ship, fingering the shells that hung from her neck and talking to herself in a dialect beyond anyone's understanding. Once upon a time, Belladonna had assumed she would become a distraction among the men, but much like herself and Romulus, she was avoided. The men did not understand her, and it was best that way.

A few moments later, Belladonna found herself stepping quietly toward the iron cell that held her victim. The closer she got to him, the more she could make of his physical state. The boy's back was blistered and scabbed, still red around the edges of each gash. His body curled into itself, hugging himself. Gray, lifeless skin clung loosely to his bones, and his lips looked purple and cracked. His tight, young muscles rippled with the labor of his breathing. When she found him, he appeared to be in a deep sleep, or something similar. She could hear raspy whispers coming from him.

She knocked the iron door with the heel of her boot. Ephraim jumped to attention, his eyes still half-closed. She could smell the illness from his infection permeating the stale air. How had this boy lived through such torture and sickness? This question started Belladonna's mind to think that maybe he *did* serve a purpose for her.

"Who is it?" he wheezed.

"It's your captain, Mr. Howell."

"Have you followed me to hell then, Captain Skylark? I think that is where I am."

"No, boy, you are alive. I cannot say how alive you are, but your earthly body still lives and breathes." She began tapping her foot. "I have someone who is very valuable onboard who has insisted that I extend you some grace. I personally do not think you deserve it, but I trust in what she says. Despite my own reservations, I am going to let you live."

With these words, Ephraim began to weep. He rested his elbows on his knees and hid his face in his hands. *What a waste of moisture for a man who has dried up,* Belladonna thought to herself. The longer she sat and watched him shed his tears, the more she realized she felt something unfamiliar. The little naggings of pity that had earlier tried to break her fledged into an agonizing sorrow. The boy before her was broken. His body was broken, and certainly, his soul had been broken with each crack of the whip on his back. Ephraim had not truly committed enough of an offense to deserve the slow torture he had endured. Certainly, he had been dishonest and had helped himself to what belonged to her, but had he harmed Belladonna in any way to deserve the punishment she bestowed upon him?

The feelings of pity had become so foreign to her that she was repulsed by them. No one deserved more pity than she, the one who was bearing the weight of the world for the sake of her last name. Finally, Ephraim's tears began to subside. His voice shaking, he said, "Thank you, Captain Skylark."

"But before I really decide that you are worthy of becoming another soul on the *Zodiac,* I must know about you. What can you bring me? I am on a quest to find the Isla del Dragón and must fulfill my purpose there."

"You search for that island?" Ephraim sniffed. "I have come to hear it does not even exist."

"A bunch of doubters you men are! It is as real as you and me. I have seen it; I have touched it with my mind, shown to me in a vision. Tell me how you can aid me in this and where you come from."

"Well, where does one even begin?" Ephraim asked out loud, drawing air into his weak, fragile body to tell his tale. "I come from England, a merchant in the Royal Navy. I felt less than satisfied by the work that I did. Killing men when I didn't even know if they had done wrong. All for king and country. But I—I wanted to have a say in my own life. No longer did I want to be ruled by a monarchy. Pirating seemed like honest work. Pirating seemed like a way to live in terms of freedom."

"I was correct about you, then." Belladonna leaned against the cell, which she still had not opened. "You have taken a marvelously romantic view of what we do. What we do is not pretty, nor is it safe. And what I do is even less safe. Let's just say there are far stronger forces than militias at odds against me. If you choose to follow me to the Isla del Dragón, you could potentially die. I cannot guarantee your life."

"I have taken that into consideration. I still find that I can be allotted more freedom in the ranks of a pirate ship than that of the Royal Navy."

"What did you do for the Navy?"

"Gunner, Captain. I made a fierce gunner."

Belladonna stopped to consider Ephraim's occupation. A highly-skilled gunner, especially one well-trained, was useful no matter the end goal. If Blackfoot ever caught up to her, which she knew he likely would, having another man to blow a hole through him and *The Temptress* would not hurt. Besides, she had killed Jedidiah two years ago, the one who had served as Starlene's gunner, and he had not yet been truly replaced. She could also feel a little of what Arimetta might have felt in him. How many times had Arimetta crept down here in the dark to look into this boy's mind?

"My offer to you is this: become my master gunner and help me defeat those I tell you to defeat. I am willing to bring on an expertly trained man for such a role. When I tell you to fire, you do not hesitate, no matter what your gut says about the ones you are shooting. Perhaps you have more skills beyond those you obtained in the Navy that you have not told me about, such as handiwork or navigation. Like I have said, someone I trust on my ship has told me that you may become very important to me and what I ultimately seek. However, if I find that you are not as valuable to me as I have been told you will be, then I will decide what I will do with you. Do you understand me?"

Ephraim cowered in the corner, and though she was softer today than she was previously, he still feared her. One thing was certain: despite his fear, he could not help but behold the beauty that masked itself behind her fierceness. Much like the day he saw her for the first time, her skin shone. Now that he could see her more clearly, he found that her dewy skin looked like a result of a steady fever, her crimson cheeks flushed with it. Instead of making her look ill, it made her radiant. Ephraim had not spent much time with women outside of the saloons and the whorehouses he visited, but no woman he had seen thus far compared to Captain Skylark.

Admiration locked his words in his throat.

"Mr. Howell, do you agree to my terms?" she asked impatiently.

"Oh, yes, Captain Skylark. I accept," Ephraim choked out. In the moments that he sat before her, he had forgotten about his thirst, his hunger, and his biting pain. Belladonna removed the cell key from the pocket of her trousers and unlocked the gate. It swung open wide. Ephraim did not know what he had done to deserve such favor from the one the men called the Dragon Lady. He could only think of one thing as he remembered his visitor.

"The lady in the shadows has protected me thus."

Belladonna raised her eyebrows at him. She started to ask him what he meant but decided it was no use. The boy, her new master gunner, was sick from his stripey wounds and needed to get clear of that before he stepped foot behind a gun.

"You will need to visit the surgeon, Cromley. I am sure you have been made aware of who my quartermaster is. Find him and tell him I have given you permission to visit Cromley. When you have mostly recovered, have Snaggletooth bring you to me to sign the articles."

"Yes, Captain." Ephraim stood slowly and began to stagger out of the cell. He took a few steps then fell into the cell gate, weak from lack of nourishment. "And thank you for your mercy."

As she watched him struggle to leave his holding place, feelings of sorrow toward him flooded her yet again. He was pitiful and ruined because of her. Quite honestly, she did not know how he could thank her. She was wicked. Belladonna began to resolve with herself that she was, indeed, sorry for the way she treated him.

I must focus. These feelings must be suppressed, she felt a voice deep within her command. *This journey is not a time for feeling.*

It had been a few days since she last glimpsed the green dragon on her thigh. Now, alone by the prison cell, she decided to take a look at it once more. Her feverish burn continued and at this point, she had seemed to have developed an immunity to it. Burning had become part of her physical body.

She rolled the leg of her trousers up to her thigh and felt herself swoon when she saw it.

The dragon was *bigger.*

The small dragon with blazon eyes had grown to the size of her hand. Every detail of it remained the same otherwise. Not every day could be spent locked away in her quarters sulking over the thing. The thought of cutting it out of her skin had crossed her mind more than once, and the thought arose again. Belladonna considered it a bad omen to cut it out and rolled the fabric back down over it.

The dragon was growing, and in some time, it would be far too large to keep in its cage.

CHAPTER 8
BOATSWAIN

Several months passed after Belladonna's decision to spare Ephraim Howell. He had been presented a small handful of occasions to prove himself, and so far, he had not disappointed his captain. The *Zodiac* sailed along the shipping lanes of the Caribbean islands, straying just close enough to land to avoid making herself known to the islanders. And just as before, when the *Zodiac* befell a ship and plundered her, Belladonna left no survivors.

In the beginning, the task that Ephraim took on as part of Captain Skylark's crew reminded him far too much of the reasons that caused him to flee the Royal Navy. He found himself behind the gun of a seemingly unknown pirate brig that took the lives of men who simply wanted to work and raided what they left behind. Before much time passed, he found his views on their plundering to be far different; he was becoming more of a pirate and less of a soldier. His humanity was still intact, but a pirate's love of liberty, independence, and anarchy overrode his prior feelings. Equality was shared among the men—no man greater than his brother—which was unheard of in the Navy. Yes, Ephraim was shaping up to become a version of himself he never supposed he would become, including his increasing love of rum, which was shared often among the men.

The Crown be defeated, he thought to himself more often with each passing day.

One attack left him particularly shaken in the first month after Belladonna had recruited him for his skills. Just west of Havana, the *Zodiac* overtook a merchant ship, *The Intercessor,* for supplies and any ammunition they possessed. The *Zodiac* herself was not necessarily running low on these things by any means, but the opportunity presented itself, and Belladonna needed to see her newest recruit in action. Ephraim took his place on deck behind the swivel gun, coordinating the other men behind their guns in the gun deck below, while Belladonna ordered *The Intercessor's* captain to come aboard to inquire about what the ship held and if any of it was of value to the needs of the *Zodiac.*

Before he heard any mention of a fight, he heard the pleas of mercy from the captain of *The Intercessor* as he was moved to the prison cell. Belladonna had ensnared him in her trap. The crew that remained on deck was summoned to loot *The Intercessor,* killing each and every member of her crew before they could fight back or jump ship themselves. Ephraim knew that if any tried to jump—which some would—these waters were filled with sharks. Those who jumped would not live long enough to find land or another ship to save them before their flesh was ripped apart by those monsters.

Wiping sweat obsessively from his body and waiting for the signal to open fire, Ephraim's nerves racked upon themselves. A successful attack meant approval from Captain Skylark. Something about that approval Ephraim desperately wanted. Captain Skylark's endorsement was not simply a matter of whether he remained in his position as the master gunner or faced certain death. Her approval would cause his heart to glow with pride. A certain giddiness about her had developed in that heart of his, and her good favor only amplified it.

Just as he found himself lost in his thoughts about his captain, Snaggletooth shouted from somewhere close, even though in Ephraim's head it felt far: *"Open fire!"*

What *The Intercessor* carried was taken and most of her men lay dead on her deck. Cannon fire would only kill any remaining men who still lived but were injured and would leave the ship unaccounted for when it came time for expected arrival, wherever she was flying to. Ephraim held the fire to the fuse, feeding the powder to unleash the bombs of destruction upon the merchant ship. The ring in his ears always satisfied him afterward. But as he lit fuse after fuse, he began to feel sick. He thought about the men who lay hidden, reciting their last rites to themselves on *The Intercessor.* Their faces came into his mind—some stricken blind from a whack by the hilt of a sword, some dumbstruck by the speed of the attack, others begging God to forgive them of their sins so they could be taken into His loving arms. Thinking about these men numbed him enough to continue to fire. After what felt like just a few moments, Snaggletooth came and grabbed him by the shoulder.

"You've done it, Master Howell. She is sinking!" he declared proudly. Ephraim mindlessly peered out over the rail in front of him. *The Intercessor,* sleek and majestic before Belladonna had arrived, now crumbled under the orange glow that engulfed her. Black smoke drifted to the west behind it.

Ephraim could guarantee that no living thing on her still breathed.

He thought he would be sick with regret, but he never once felt queasy after the fight. Whatever veil his captain had over her heart had come over his as well. Ephraim would never feel his heart turn into a black stone, but what he felt was *nothing*.

Just business, he allowed himself to think. Certainly, the other men must have fallen into this pit of unfeeling, as well, for none of them showed *any* feeling after the fight either. It was their duty, and they protected only themselves. Ephraim swelled with pride. Since that first fight (there had been four since his time joining the crew and the present), he was content with the life of independence and victory he now lived under Belladonna and the *Zodiac's* flag.

And just as he had longed for, Captain Skylark found favor in him.

Just as Ephraim was letting himself fall into the unfeeling nature of pirates, Belladonna was experiencing some unexpected changes in her own character. The dragon under her skin, that twisted, scaly serpent, grew to cover the entire side of her thigh. It no longer concerned her as it did when it first appeared. In fact, she became more fascinated with it. Did her fascination with it border on obsession? At times, perhaps. But she grew proud of it, wearing it like a badge of honor. At night she would trace the detail of it, seeing if she could feel any part of it with her fingertips. It was perfectly inlaid under her skin as a glowing reminder of her heritage. That heritage still terrified her when she thought too long and hard about it, but everything regarding the prophecy would fall into place in its time.

Blackfoot remained a good distance behind her still. Her heart told her to turn the *Zodiac* around, to kill him as quickly as she could. However, her mind told her to let him follow, and she would deal with him when the time was right. She relied heavily on the prophecy that Alauda (whatever that meant, she still did not know) would slay the demon; at times, perhaps too heavily. For now, she still could not find the Isla del Dragón. This troubled her.

She was also troubled by certain *feelings* she noticed trying to tap through the glass of her black heart. These feelings regarded the stowaway-turned-gunner. On the day she freed him from his cell, back torn open from running the gauntlet, pity for his broken body loosened her desire to be done with him. Killing had been her instinct, yet somehow, the appearance of the boy reached around that instinct and unlocked the part of her that would think of him as someone other than her next victim. So she had given him a chance, and thus far, she had not been disappointed. The gunner was agile and militant, presumably from his strict training in the Navy. Quite honestly, it was what she needed. Pirates oftentimes became lazy, and she needed a man she could kick back into attention. Though she was not entirely sure, she sensed Ephraim revered her, which made him want to do well for her. And, if she was being honest with herself, that delighted her. Most of the men only did their jobs because they *feared* her wrath. Ephraim feared her in some ways, but for the most part, he did as he was commanded because he beheld her as someone worthy of respect.

As a result of her observations of him, she felt herself growing attached to her gunner. Not in the way that she shared an attachment with Snaggletooth and Arimetta, no. This was something different, something new for her. Hating to admit it to herself but knowing she must, she felt stirrings akin to what she remembered to be *love.*

But it was ridiculous. It could never be. Belladonna had far bigger tasks to take on than love. It would be ridiculous if she allowed herself to tangle with love with so much else on the line. Besides that, she was the *captain,* and he was merely a part of a miscreant crew.

She wanted to act to see if she could put out the fire of these feelings she held for Ephraim, but how? Loving him was not an option, but showing him she acknowledged his reverence for her might help.

The *Zodiac* had not had a boatswain for many years, not since Belladonna lived and breathed as a child. Snaggletooth handled a great deal of the responsibilities among the crew, doling out punishment when needed, ordering the men around, and for the most part, sailing the *Zodiac* wherever Belladonna wished it to go. Was Ephraim worthy of the position of boatswain? She argued that he was. He was the only one on board who was professionally trained to deal with ranks of men and bloody battles. Unswayed by any notion that proved he would not do well as a boatswain was overridden by her absolute certainty that promoting him would alleviate Snaggletooth, who was positively overworked, and hopefully snuff out any attraction toward the boy, for he was terribly easy on the eyes.

Nodding out her mental pictures of Ephraim, she decided to approach Snaggletooth on the matter. Even if he approved it, Ephraim's new rank would cause yet another stir among her crew. She cared not for this, for the men should surely have learned by now that as long as she was captain, and as long as the state of the globe upon which they sailed depended on her, she would veto their democratic voice.

It was late when she snuck out of her quarters. All the men would either be sleeping or drinking below; only the night watch would be out at this hour. She had night watch keep constant surveillance of *The Temptress* as Blackfoot sailed behind her. If any new developments arose, they should report to her immediately, even if she was asleep. She nodded at them as they kept watch and padded to Snaggletooth's quarters. She knocked lightly. As she waited for his answer, she peeked around the deck. Romulus raised his head from his nightly watch, seeming to ask if Belladonna needed him. She shook her head, and he groaned, lowering his head on his paws.

"Ye may enter!" Snaggletooth shouted. Belladonna entered slowly. In his lap, Snaggletooth was whittling something she could not identify.

"Good to see you have taken something up in your own time," she said approvingly, for Snaggletooth truly *was* overworked.

"Aye, just something to keep me occupied. Ye know I don't know how to sit idle." His voice cracked with fatigue. Belladonna, with arms crossed, came to him and stood over him. She swayed slightly as the ship glided gently through the night.

"I know the hour is late, and I will not keep you long, but I have had a thought arise in my mind that I cannot seem to let go of. The gunner, Ephraim, how have you felt about him thus far?" Snaggletooth placed his work next to him and considered the question.

"He's right trig if I say so, Captain. Has a good head on his shoulders and becomes one with the gun when he is behind it. I appreciate that he keeps his head hung low. He don't get into fights or nothin' like that. Not sure if he's humble or just don't like talkin' much, but me thinks he is a good lad." Snaggletooth raised his brow inquisitively. "Thinkin' of gettin' rid of him, are ye?"

"My heavens, have I become such a heartless wench you think me ready to kill him?"

"Didn't mean to offend, ma'am—just used to the way ye usually handle things these days." Belladonna, feeling the slightest uptick in her ever-raging fever, chose to overlook the offense and headed straight to her point.

"No, I want to make him boatswain. And before you go saying we have not had one, not in a long while that is, I must defend my decision. Ephraim has *grown.* I have seen it. Even though he keeps his head down, I have sensed a maturation in him. I do not know all the details about what caused him to want to become a pirate, but whatever that reason was seems to be far removed from him now. I also get the feeling he wants to please me, which is unlike all the others. Not to mention his Navy training. In my thinking, he is an asset to us, and we best hold onto him for when we must fight for the Isla del Dragón."

"Ye say true, so ye do." Snaggletooth stroked his beard, his eyes wandering around the room. "The boy came aboard eager to do the job, with or without pay, and without ye knowing ye had a free hand. I sense the regard ye sense, as well. He seems good and noble." He stopped for a moment, the silence growing between them. "But I also sense ye be comin' to me about this for more reasons than ye have already mentioned."

"You are precisely right, quartermaster," Belladonna spoke quickly, doing her best to rid Snaggletooth of any suspicions he hold. "You have been the most dedicated man on this ship for more years than I have been alive. You have worked long and hard years, all while not getting any younger. So, simply put, I am proposing Ephraim Howell as boatswain for all the reasons I have already aforementioned *and* to help alleviate some of your duties so we may prolong your years and your service."

"All of it makes sense. I cannot say I find any reason to object. 'Twould be nice to have a man share in my duties, I suppose. Yer quartermaster does grow older by the minute, he does. 'Tis a pity ye cannot find a way to preserve me!" The two laughed together, both of them wishing it were true. Snaggletooth loved the sea so much he wished himself immortal. He could not help but think that maybe, if Belladonna took her place as Dragon empress after all, it could be granted to him.

The two continued to laugh together, only stopping when they heard the familiar mutterings of Arimetta outside the cabin. Arimetta had grown stagnant in her visions lately, becoming less useful. Belladonna only held onto her because she hoped she would one day be teeming with visions when they got closer to the island. Nevertheless, visions or not, she wandered the deck spewing her usual mutterings and whispers.

"Does that crazed woman ever sleep?" Snaggletooth asked. They erupted into laughter yet again.

"Oh, I cannot remember the last time I have shared a laugh with anyone, especially not like that," Belladonna said as she wiped tears from her cheeks.

"Something is different with ye, Captain." Just as Snaggletooth finished speaking, Belladonna's face slackened. Dabbling in romantic feelings had indeed taken some of the edge off, her but she had hoped it did not show. Evidently, it had. Snaggletooth removed a bottle of rum from the cabinet beside him and poured two small glasses. He handed one to Belladonna, staring at her intently, inquiring of the secret to her difference in character.

"I suppose I feel a little bit closer to where I need to be. We haven't found the bloody place yet, doggonit, but perhaps it lies just around the corner," she lied through her teeth.

"I suppose I could see how that would fill one with some ecstasy." Snaggletooth held up his glass to her. "Shall we toast our new boatswain, then, and our getting closer to our destination?"

"To the boatswain." She tipped the glass back, sending the rum down her throat. The fever in her breast swooped up like kindling had been heaped upon it, then it settled. She grimaced, feeling uneasy about the last part of their toast. "And to seeing the Isla del Dragón soon."

Belladonna could only hope that they would see the island soon. After a few more glasses and some conversation, Belladonna made to leave and rest for the night.

"I thank you for sharing in merriment with me, Snaggletooth. And thank you for all that you are to the *Zodiac.*"

"Oh, it really is nothing, ma'am. It is a gift to be able to work such as I do." He took his final sip, slamming the glass down on the table before him. "Now, moving ahead, how shall we let Master Howell know of his new title. Are ye allowing the others to have a say?"

"As before, no. This is something that must be done for the betterment of the quest. That is my notion."

"'Tis bound to cause an uprising like last time. Ye have considered this, I am sure?"

"Aye. And like last time, I will do what must be done to clear my path if need be."

"Right. We will cross that bridge if we comes to it, I suppose then. Good night, Captain Skylark."

Belladonna left Snaggletooth's cabin to find rest, ready to revel in her violence in the morning if the need arose.

I must not give anything away, for if I do, I have weakened myself and damaged my reputation.

Belladonna had to talk herself down before her appointment with Ephraim. As captain, and as a budding *empress* for heaven's sake, she must not appear vulnerable. Her developing feelings for him could not overtake her. Even so, she hoped this small act of appreciation would remove those feelings from her heart altogether.

In the early morning light of the rising sun, Snaggletooth marched out of his cabin to find Ephraim. He was not hard to find; Ephraim could always be found anywhere near his station on the gun deck.

"Mr. Howell, the captain seeks a word with ye."

"Right away, sir." Ephraim dropped his cleaning kit (he had cleaned the guns well-nigh a thousand times) and made to see Belladonna.

What have I done to deserve the gauntlet this time? he pondered. Ephraim, as best he could, shied away from Captain Skylark. Not simply because he had won her good graces and wanted to stay in them, but because he hoped staying away would help him settle with the fact that no matter how lovely he found her, she would never be his. Before he could take another step, Snaggletooth grabbed his arm to stop him.

"But before ye see her, for she is not expecting ye for a quarter of an hour, I wanted to mention a few things to ye." Snaggletooth raised his eyebrows. "For I know ye must have some questions about her. The crew talks, but there are some questions even they cannot answer."

"I suppose I have a few questions." Ephraim looked around, saw the men at their work listening indiscreetly. "But perhaps we should take this conversation elsewhere."

"I understand." The quartermaster nodded, acknowledging the listening ears around them. They left the gun deck and ascended to the helm, Snaggletooth dismissing the man at the wheel so he could take over. Once he had a firm grip on the spoked wheel, he nodded at Ephraim, indicating he was prepared for any question he might have.

"My first question is this: why are you allowing me to ask questions of the captain? I mean, is this a trick? I cannot do anything that's going to get me killed."

"Ye assume that I would tell ye if this were a trick?" Snaggletooth laughed, roaring and clapping Ephraim on the back. "Ye must decide for yourself what ye think. Yer own self-judgment will be needed in the days ahead."

Ephraim considered his words. "You seem an honest man, and I know you are beloved among the crew, so I am not so sure you would betray me as such."

"Alright then. Ye made yer decision; now ask away."

"Blimey, I don't even know where to begin." Ephraim began to think, resting his head in his palm. "I guess I will start with this . . . because I have felt this deep down and have not seemed to have figured it out. The men, they know we are looking for the Isla del Dragón, but something tells me this is not simply a treasure-seeking visit. The captain's urgency seems very foreboding. Do you understand what I am trying to get at?"

"Aye, I do."

"Is there something more to this than that?"

"Ye will know in time, Mr. Howell—the sum of all of this. But ye are correct in yer assumptions. Captain Skylark is, how should I say, very *important* to the balance of the world. And what she goes to Isla del Dragón to do will determine the balance of the world."

"I'm afraid I don't understand."

"That is all I can tell ye on that."

"But you said I could ask any question I wanted?"

"So I did. Didn't say I would provide an answer to all of 'em."

"That's fair enough." Ephraim sighed. He tried to think of another question. "Have any of the other men been visited by the lady in the shadows?"

"What fool nonsense do ye ask about?" Snaggletooth seemed offended. "Things of that nature are not important. Just sea tales, they are."

"No, this is not just a tale. She came to me when I was locked in that cell, thinking myself dead. I believe she is the reason I live today. I can't say for certain, but I think she cleaned my wounds and gave me water. All I could make out of her were her murky eyes, almost like she was blind."

"Say true?" Snaggletooth nodded, raising his eyebrows yet again. "That weren't no lady o' the shadows then. That be Arimetta, the captain's prophetess. She only be comin' out at night these days—an order from the captain—as her seein' the future ain't been too good lately. She's a Hoodoo woman. I don't like to dabble in that, personally, but the captain seems to think it means somethin'. Ye ain't seen her since then?"

"Not at all."

"Well, perhaps she been stayin' away from ye so as not to give herself away."

"I was not dying, then? She was coming to me for a reason. I wonder why?"

"One thing I can tell ye about that . . . that prophetess saved yer hide. Captain Skylark meant to dismiss ye or kill ye, one of the two, but she told her that ye would be important to her."

Now it was Ephraim's turn to raise his eyebrows. Could his admiration for the captain be true then?

"Thanks must be in order to the prophetess, then. When I can find her. But do she and the captain truly suppose that I am a pawn in her game?"

"Funny way of talking about it, but it seems they do. I can't say that I understand it all, but considerin' that Arimetta says she can see visions, you must mean something." Snaggletooth suddenly got serious. "I find it in my best interest to be truthful with ye. Captain Skylark is *unwell.* She be unwell because she ain't yet in her truest form. She will be, though, when she gets to the Isla del Dragón. As for the rest of us, I ain't too certain what will happen. Could be we stay in service; could be that we all die. But ye—aye, ye—ye mean much. I can't place my finger on it, but I know ye fit into the puzzle somewhere."

"I sensed something must be unwell about her. That day she wanted to kill me, she touched me. When she touched me, her touch was like a branding iron. Quite literally, her skin was *burning.* I felt it on her even as I stood before her, untouched."

"She still burns, that she does. When ye meet her in a moment, ye will still feel it. I'm sure ye wonder why she is called the Dragon Lady among the men?"

"I have wondered about this."

"Captain Skylark seeks the Isla del Dragón to take her place as Dragon empress. Have ye heard of them?"

"Now *that* I thought to be sea tales." Ephraim felt like someone had punched him in the gut. "But this is true? The peace-keeping dragons are *real*?"

"They are. As real as ye and me. I confess to it because I lived among two of the finest, may they rest in peace." Snaggletooth crossed himself. "The Skylark mother and father were on their way to becoming the emperor and empress of the Dragon Majestics when they allied with the *Zodiac's* first captain, Starlene. And when they died, I saw the destruction start to seep back through the cracks of the world that they had worked on mending together. We are being followed at this very moment by the man that Captain Skylark has been prophesied to crush with the heel of her foot, shutting the Demonclaw out for as long as she lives. Do ye know any of what I speak of?"

Ephraim knew some of this, and it sounded so grandiose that he assumed it had to be a sea tale. "I do. 'Alauda will crush the head of the demon with the heel of her foot. Upon Alaudidae all will look.' I have heard the tale passed around. But this all is true, you say? I live and breathe this day on a ship that carries the next Dragon empress to her exotic realm?"

"Ye should feel honored." Snaggletooth smiled. All of this felt like the pages of a book. Yet in a way, it made sense to him. The men did not call her Dragon Lady because she was a brutal tyrant. They called her that, knowingly or unknowingly, because she truly *was* the Dragon Lady.

"Do the crew know this about her?"

"No. And I don't want ye to go tellin' it, either. I've seen ye keep yer head down when it comes to talk about the ship, and I demand that it stay that way."

"Aye, sir." Ephraim could feel the weight of Snaggletooth's command. It was so much to take in at one time.

"I know ye must be doubtin' some, or maybe all, of what I have just told ye, but ye will know by the Mark."

"The Mark? I don't follow?"

"Ye may one day see the Mark on her, and just as Jesus with his disciples, when you touch the Mark, you will believe."

Ephraim knew the story of which Snaggletooth spoke. Growing up in a Christian family in England meant he had spent much time in the Bible. The story that Snaggletooth referred to was after Jesus had been crucified and resurrected. When his disciples saw him and did not believe him risen, he told them to touch the wounds in his palms and on his side. Then, as the story says, they believed it was he when they touched and beheld the wounds.

"How can I see this Mark?" Ephraim asked in return, wanting desperately to believe what he had been told were simple tall tales.

"Ye will see it when ye are meant to, or should I say *if* ye are even meant to. Now come, it is time for ye to appear before Captain Skylark." Snaggletooth told the man who steered the boat before him to come back and led Ephraim away to where Belladonna sat in her quarters. If Ephraim was to be her boatswain, he had to be made aware of the facts that he *needed* to know, the ones that would be crucial to his understanding of the post. Thus truth had resulted in Snaggletooth's back and forth with him. Belladonna used the time to strategize her words, thinking carefully about what to say so as not to lay her emotions on the table.

Emotions? Belladonna asked herself. It felt odd to think about that word. She thought her emotions had shut down for good when Starlene passed.

Snaggletooth entered her quarters with Ephraim trailing behind him. Romulus arose from his watch at Belladonna's feet. Ephraim tensed, still not used to turning a corner and finding a tiger, especially on a ship. Then he looked to his captain.

Captain Skylark was a goddess incarnate. Today, she wore a gown (he noticed she liked to switch up her looks every now and then). Her lips were pink and plump; her cheeks pinched with that feverish red. Their eyes locked—both pairs green—and for just a moment, both swore something in the air snapped. They held their stare for the briefest moment before Belladonna broke it. After their introductory encounter, a loud commotion outside the doors interrupted the moment. Someone pounded on the doors.

"Let me in, chile. Arimetta here now." Snaggletooth opened the door and Arimetta spilled in clumsily. "Kinnit see, makes it hard tuh find deh door." She laughed at her own words.

Ephraim started.

This is my lady in the shadows, my savior.

Before he could open his mouth to thank her for her care and kindness, she passed a knowing glance at him.

She has read my mind, he thought.

Arimetta had a loose grip on his mind with her power, warning him: *Not yet.*

He nodded, even though she could not see him. The mental acknowledgment is what she understood, and she bowed to him.

"Dis deh one dat yuh decided tuh keep 'round, huh?" she asked Belladonna.

"Yes. Ephraim, I want you to meet Arimetta, my trusted guide and prophetess." Arimetta bowed again in Ephraim's direction. Her eyes looked somewhere beyond him.

"'Tis muh pleasure, darlin'." She smiled, revealing all of her broken, blackened teeth. At his lowest moment, Ephraim thought her an angel. Seeing her this close made him think more of the devil in a woman's body.

"Now, right to business then," Belladonna interjected, hands steepled in front of her on her desk. A map, brown and dusty, spread out underneath her. "I must say I have been very impressed with your skill and your order. You've come from a very militant background, and I respect that. What I like most of all about you is that you seem to care about keeping my favor. Would you agree with that?"

"Yes, Captain. I hold a very high regard for you and all you—"

"Lovely, how splendid. But as I was saying, you have impressed me. Your dexterity in bringing down the five ships we attacked since you joined us has shown that you are highly capable in combat. I do not want to say too much in trying to get my point across, but you understand what I mean. I would like to offer you the opportunity of becoming my boatswain. There has not been one on the *Zodiac* since well before my time. Snaggletooth has handled much of it on his own under one title. But seeing as I have someone who is now, in my opinion, qualified to do the job, I want to extend the offer to you."

Ephraim's face must have shown quite a bit of shock. Captain Skylark did not *sound* as if she was that impressed with him, but if she wasn't, why would she offer him this position?

"Would I still be your gunner?" he asked.

"Yes, you would be both. If that suits you, of course. You will have much to learn in the way of leading, but I think you will do fine."

"Well, I am assuming this will remain up for a vote. Or perhaps the men have already voted on it?"

"Captain Skylark runs things a bit differently," Snaggletooth interjected. "Seein' as this quest is a tad different than the ones most crews find themselves in. The democratic vote has become null and void. Ye need only accept."

Did this feel slightly suspicious? Absolutely. However, would it be wise for Ephraim to turn it down? What would become of him if he did not throw himself at his captain's every whim? If she possessed a notion that he needed to become boatswain, then perhaps he should.

For just a moment, he thought about what would happen to him if he decided to say no. The thought vanished when the scars on his back began to sing in remembrance. He could not endure the gauntlet again.

“Then I assume I have no choice but to accept,” Ephraim stated with pride.

“You assume? Are you already not confident in yourself?” Belladonna raised her brow.

“Because if you cannot perform to my standards I can demote you . . . and worse, of course.”

“No, I gladly accept. I am grateful for the chance to further prove myself to you, Captain Skylark.”

Belladonna smiled stiffly. “Welcome then, Master Howell. Your duty will be to maintain the ship overall. Starting immediately. The crew will be made aware of your new command.”

Hope welled in Ephraim’s breast. He may not be able to love her the way he wanted to, but at least, he could work closely beside her. Maybe this would be enough for him to live a contented life.

Across the desk, Belladonna felt similarly. She thought she had done well enough to conceal her interest in him, sticking to the subject while also showing him she acknowledged his dedication. In the tiniest corner of her heart, she hoped that he knew she cared for him.

Romulus picked up his four heavy paws and sauntered to Ephraim. He lowered his head, bowing to the man who would now be one of his masters along with the ones he already served. Hand trembling, Ephraim reached out to touch him. Romulus lifted his large head against his palm, closing his eyes with acceptance. Ephraim grinned.

“So this is what a tiger feels like. I never imagined I would ever see one up close, let alone touch one.”

“He, like many wild beasts, has a rough exterior, but inside, he longs to be loved just as anyone does.” Belladonna kicked her feet up on her desk as she said this, blushing at the double meaning behind her words. She could relate to Romulus in this way. "Now, go—off with you. You have work that needs tended to."

With that, she flicked her fingers, telling everyone to leave her presence. When Ephraim stepped out, he stood by and waited for the blind woman to exit. When she did, he grabbed her by the wrist and pulled her close to him, speaking in whispers.

"I know it was you that cared for my wounds and brought me water down below, Prophetess. You hung in the shadows. Why?" Ephraim felt that there was certainly a reason for her care beyond simple human kindness. Arimetta seemed to recoil at his words, eyes moving all around.

"Arimetta take care o' yuh fuh deh captin. Arimetta know she need yuh."

"What have you seen?" he asked firmly. "What do you know that I don't know? You have seen something about me. I know you have."

"I seen yuh wit' 'er on deh Island. Deh one she seek. Yuh stood beneat' her ultimate form. 'N yuh shared deh bonds o' love, Masta Howell. Dey run so ver' deep in yuh both."

"I stood beneath Alauda on the Isla del Dragón," Ephraim stated, almost as if he knew it already.

"Aye, Alauda, yes, Masta. But, oft'times what Arimetta see not always deh way 'tis. Arimetta tell her yuh would be important tuh 'er if she kept yuh, and she listen tuh deh Hoodoo woman."

"You have not told Captain Skylark of this vision, have you?"

"Not a word. She do what she need tuh get dere first. In time, she see what Arimetta see. She don' e'en know Alauda yet."

"So Alauda is still the piece of the prophecy she does not understand. She must not know what it means. And she must not know *she* is Alauda."

"She know nuthin'. She must learn. Arimetta n' deh quartermasta knows she Alauda, and we both a-knowin' what it mean, but she don't."

It was true then. Love between Captain Skylark and Ephraim could be possible. Arimetta had seen it as something that could be written in the stars. Ephraim wondered how she could love him. She certainly had not shown any of the first fruits of love, and for a while, she had wanted him dead. Belladonna was violence wrapped in human flesh. Was she so violent because she did not understand her very nature, the very identity that would befall her when the time came?

Things were starting to make sense. Belladonna did not know who she was. Marked by a life filled with loss, wandering, and searching, she did not possess the foreknowledge of her family history to know where she belonged and what she would become. Ephraim related her violence to a way of coping with the identity she felt had been stolen from her grasp. Belladonna Skylark lived in the shadow of her own insecurity.

Yet whatever Ephraim's purpose in her life was, he began to feel certain it was to draw her out of those shadows, pushing her to discover herself. To break the dark captivity that she fell prisoner to. To love her in a way that made up for all the love she lost.

He needed to help her become Alauda. That was his fate.

Ephraim smiled, overwhelmed by the prospect of both loving her and guiding her. But how much of this *did* she know? He would need to think about that.

"I should warn you that concealing what you see from the captain is not wise. She will find out one day, of that I am sure, and she will have your head." Ephraim, knowing that Arimetta could not *see* him the way he could see her, scowled at her in warning.

"Arimetta will consida' what 'er new boatswain has sed." With this, she curtsied and waltzed off, surely back to whatever hole she burrowed in during the day.

Much like Belladonna as she came to learn the tales of her family's dragon history, so Ephraim was learning as well. And it was all so very overwhelming.

Later that night, Snaggletooth gathered the men and placed Ephraim before them.

Belladonna had not necessarily told Snaggletooth to do this, but he felt like it was important, considering the way the last change of command had gone over. Just over two years had passed since Starlene's death. Belladonna could not afford to lose more men. Besides that, the men were getting restless. To them, it felt as if they were aimlessly sailing, and many missed land. The time to find the Isla del Dragón needed to come quickly.

"Listen up, ye of *Zodiac!* I have gathered ye all tonight to bring yer attention to a change in command." He raised Ephraim's arm. "This here man is to be our boatswain. He be in charge just as much as thyself, so ye listen to him, or it'll be me ye deal with."

Thus ensued the grumbling and the objections.

"But, sir, he ain't been on here for more than half a year!"

"How does this lad go from almost being killed to bein' top dog?"

"That captain of ours is insane!"

"He ain't deservin' of it!"

"Where's our say in all this?" The man Swann, one of Ephraim's earliest acquaintances, shouted. Ephraim noticed that Mace stayed quiet, he being one of the last men who lived through Belladonna's first massacre. Mace felt it in his heart to stay loyal to the boy, while the others who stayed quiet did not want to get killed. It was the fresher faces that had something to say.

"I know ye have been used to the crew voting on such matters, but I assure ye, it must be done this way!" Snaggletooth shouted over the commotion. "Ye men are neck-deep in something that is far larger than ye will ever understand."

"Then tell us then . . . what be this fantastic voyage we have set upon?" asked Geoffrey Taylor, one of the quickest men in the crew.

"And why him of all of these others?" The cook, Alistair, questioned. "I remember finding him below decks drunker than I seen any of these other men. I agree with these men. He don't deserve it."

Snaggletooth stepped lightly toward Alistair.

"Do ye not remember her tirade when ye all opened your sea-forsaken traps the first time?" He growled. "Did ye not live through it to tell the tale? And ye, a cook of all things, having such an opinion as this. Ye know deep in yer heart that it is dangerous to go messin' with her again."

"Perhaps we mutiny, then?" This from Cromley, the surgeon. Snaggletooth turned toward the surgeon and approached very slowly. Ephraim's eyes widened. Objection was very likely. He had no intention of his post causing such strife.

"If ye mutiny, may God curse you and throw all of ye into hell without so much as a second glance. Ye would be heaping His great judgment upon ye if ye did that. No, can't go doin' that."

"And why not?" Lancer questioned from his place in the crow's nest. He looked down upon the men.

"Because you can't, and that's an order," Ephraim interrupted. "What Snaggletooth means to say is you either accept me as your boatswain and keep your head down or be punished. Captain Skylark is embarking on a quest of utter importance. Come on, I know all of you can feel it. You don't call her the Dragon Lady without reason."

All the seamen looked around at one another. It was true; every one of them *felt* that their place on the *Zodiac* was more than humble pirating. Snaggletooth gritted his teeth.

He should not be telling them this.

"What is it that you say of her? What is the song you sing about her?

> *"Oh, my Captain!*
> *Her breast a-blazes with red,*
> *One puff of her breath*
> *And you're better off dead—"*

"I've heard all of you sing it, but you sing it because you know more than you think you do. All of you will be repaid handsomely if you allow this to happen the way it should. I promise you that."

"What yer boatswain means to say," Snaggletooth added quickly, "is that yer captain commands ye to do so; therefore, ye should listen. Captain Skylark holds yer life in her hands, and she ain't afraid to snuff a one of ye out. And much like Master Howell stated, ye know ye play a part in somethin' much larger than ye realize. And in fact, me thinks some celebration is to be in order. Ye will be allowed yer rum rations threefold tonight in celebration of Master Howell!"

"Well, if Master Howell promises a handsome reward for our participation, and if we get more drink tonight, I suppose we have but one choice." Mace stepped in, doing his best to encourage the masses. "For Captain Skylark has allowed us to live another day, has she not? That alone is cause for celebration."

"Right ye are, good man," Snaggletooth agreed. "Now below, all of ye, and if there be any talk of mutiny again, I will finish ye before Captain Skylark can even think of it. And Mace, fetch the rum. Tonight calls for celebration."

Still reluctant, the seamen made their way to their sleeping quarters to have their fill of rum and festivity. Snaggletooth could not guarantee that the men felt any better about Ephraim as boatswain, but for tonight, they had calmed. But before Ephraim joined them for their festivity, Snaggletooth needed to speak with him. He grabbed him firmly by the shoulder and spun him around to face him.

"What kind of fancy reward are ye promising these lowly men that ye have no business promising anything to? Ye are not the captain. Do not let this title make yer head big, Master Howell."

"They needed calming. I needed to take the focus off myself, and I put it back on their task. That is all. I did not mean anything by it."

"Which is exactly the problem! I told ye just this mornin' that I was most certain most of these men would not make it by the time we found the island, did I not? Now ye go promisin' them riches and eternal life and the like? Ye have filled these men with false hope already."

"Let them think what they will as long as it prevents a mutiny. They need something to live for if they are to stay in this for as long as she needs them."

Snaggletooth started to speak but stopped. In a way, Ephraim was right. The approach was merciless. Even Ephraim himself was surprised at his willingness to lie, even if it meant certain death for each man later.

"What ye say is fair. I will accept it. However, I prohibit ye from touching on the subject again. Discipline is where I come in, not ye. Do not overstep yer boundaries. And seein' as ye have just begun yer duties, I am willing to overlook this offense and keep it from Captain Skylark. She does not need to know that ye have said too much. Nor does she need to know the men have such objections. I am sure you know, last time she murdered over half the crew to spite the others. She gained their loyalty through fear, ye understand?"

"I apologize for the oversight, sir. And I understand," Ephraim apologized. He admired Snaggletooth and the respect the men had for him. Emulating his leadership would become one of Ephraim's most desirable goals.

Meanwhile, locked away in her quarters, Belladonna was aware of the shouting outside. She kept herself away for fear of the desire to slit their throats down the line. Belladonna already endured pushback once; she did not need to involve herself again when she had more pressing matters.

One of them she watched presently out her porthole through the lens of her telescope.

The Temptress drifted smoothly, passing effortlessly over the night waves. Since her view of the ship was from the front, she could not see the meeting being held in Cornelius Blackfoot's chambers that would interest her. His ship was not any closer than it was before. She maintained her distance, that was for sure.

Belladonna often wondered, as she did now, how she managed to sail almost two years without crossing Blackfoot's path. Divine protection was the only assumption she alluded to. Much like the end times she'd heard about in the Book of Revelation, Blackfoot's pursuit could only mean things were falling into place for the final battle.

Alauda.

The word popped into her head as if spoken to her. Was Arimetta trying to get back into her head? In fact, she had been hearing the word more and more. It disrupted her thoughts, woke her up at night, was breathed into her somehow. A kinship with that name grew within her. Sometimes, when alone, she said it to herself out loud, letting the syllables roll off of her tongue. The name *Alauda* satisfied her, but she was searching for the reason.

CHAPTER 9
THE DEMONCLAW ASSEMBLY

While exciting things happened on the *Zodiac,* Blackfoot was growing restless. His craving for a fight increased daily.

It seemed a good idea to overtake the Skylark girl—beat her to her own destination, swords ready to swing as soon as she got near. It had been quite some time since Blackfoot found himself in combat, and he longed for it.

The only fight that would satisfy him now would be with Belladonna Skylark.

Oh, how he could conjure up the scene in his brain. He would be waiting on deck for the presence of his victim. She would traipse her way before him, thinking it a simple meeting to negotiate. However, before she could open her mouth, he himself would strike her through her stone-cold heart, shattering it into thousands of little pieces as she screamed. The heart would first break free of the hardened shell around it. Then the organ itself would burst. But would it be better to strike her elsewhere so he could rip her heart out, intact, to present it at his appointment for his Seat in the High Court?

Imagining Belladonna's death was a good pastime, but no good could be done if no real progress was made toward acting on those imaginings. He assumed it must be written in the stars for him to remain behind her, but his patience was growing thin.

And the voice that spoke to him, the one that fed his ever-increasing knowledge of Belladonna's end of the quest, told him that he would soon be visited. But visited by whom?

As he labored over his map, searching for any clue about the location of the Isla del Dragón—just as Belladonna did—he felt eyes watching him. At first, he simply brushed it off. Since the voice that spoke to him had first come, he always felt watched. It was part of the task at hand, he thought, considering he *was,* in fact, being watched by many pairs of eyes (for some of the Demonclaw had more than just one set of eyes). Picking up his pen to cross off the coast of Cuba, the watching suddenly felt stronger. It could not be ignored this time.

Blackfoot looked up and jumped up from his seat. In all his time spent at sea, a demon hidden under human flesh, he had never been visited. Before Blackfoot's desk stood seven ghost-like figures: five men and two women. Their feet melted away into wisps of gray mist that upheld them, suspending them in the air. Many years had passed since Blackfoot left his true home with the Demonclaw, but he would never forget the faces of the ones that stood before him.

The apparitions that floated in front of him with their hands folded at their chests were the seven reigning members of the Demonclaw Court: Dart Rockwall, Perpetua Primrose, Aurelias Morgana, Bartholomew Hadley, Anders Wardon, Gladiolus Evergreen, and lastly, Blackfoot's dreaded sister, Aranxta Blackfoot.

Blackfoot's mouth hung open, dumbstruck by their phantom presence. He lowered himself to the ground, bowing low before them.

"My Most Highly Regarded," he nearly sang.

"Good to see you, brother," Aranxta said to him, eyes downcast and unfeeling. "If only it were on better terms."

"We heard some thoughts of yours that troubled us greatly and felt the need to interfere."

Gladiolus shared the same look of displeasure that Aranxta wore. "As my possible replacement, I found it *especially* necessary to speak some truth into you. Now, get up, for the love of all that is evil, and face us."

Blackfoot stood and registered pain across his lower face. Gladiolus had stepped forward to clap him on the jaw. If Blackfoot were to fill the next seat in the Demonclaw Court, he would replace Gladiolus. Gladiolus would then ascend into some higher realm, retired of his duties. Blackfoot knew, in time, he'd learn of if he'd won the seat. Since Gladiolus felt Blackfoot his responsibility, he pressed upon him more than the others.

"That's quite enough, Gladiolus." Dart stepped forward, raising an arm between Blackfoot and the old demon. "We have seen your thoughts, and they have disturbed us. Your mind is giving over to human impatience, and we cannot have that. The course that you are on is good. We would not have you alter it in any way."

"I don't know what thoughts you have seen," Blackfoot scoffed, forgetting his lowly place among these Demonclaw. "Have I not been doing as I should, all while not knowing hardly a thing about what exactly I am doing?"

"You know what you are doing." Perpetua stepped forward this time as she spoke. "Don't make it seem like you do not. You know that you have been placed on this map to obliterate the prophecy against you. More than that, the prophecy against *us*! And you do, indeed, know which thoughts Dart speaks of."

"And what of them? Would it not be wise to consider getting in front of her and slaying those cursed beasts one by one before she even has a chance to see them? Without them, she cannot reign, you know this to be true."

"We do, but without her, they do not operate at their best," Aurelias added. "If we can cut off the head of the snake, the body may still writhe in agony. Why do you think piracy itself runs rampant on the high seas right now? They cannot operate at their best unless they have their reigning members. Allowing them to try to work under these conditions is our endgame. Besides, if they cannot serve their purpose without her, we can still overtake them. The world can still be ours with them here. And what better way to pay them back than making them suffer through an eternity of destruction? They will have no reason to continue their fight if their empress does not come to them—"

"Which leads us to this," Aranxta interrupted, scowling at Aurelias. "You must remain where you are. You are a fool to think that standing in front of her means it will stop her. You cannot deny the strength of a Dragon Majestic, especially one who is untrained and more lethal now than she ever will be, unaware of the limits of her power. You don't want to be in her line of fire, if I may say so." The others laughed at her double entendre.

"She is weak," Anders smirked.

"She is weak; thank you for reminding me." Aranxta stepped closer to Blackfoot.

"Belladonna Skylark, as you know, has what she calls a 'black heart.' When your well-despised Starlene breathed her last, Belladonna's heart turned black, and it changed her. It made her stronger; it started the beginning of her transformation. With Starlene dead, she was able to step into the position of power that was needed for her to grow. Now keep in mind, to this day, she has not yet taken to her final form. She still does not know all this, which is why we caution you to stay out from in front of her . . . because her fire could fly directly toward you if you are there. But since her heart turned black, she has only been capable of feelings of malice and violence. That changed when she found a stowaway hiding in the darkness. Captain Skylark has started to *love* again. A feeling she thought too far removed from herself to be found again, yet she has found it. But this love weakens her; love makes her vulnerable. Her mind is not so solely focused on the task at hand. In fact, I have captured thoughts from her that wish to denounce the quest and her family name for this boy. That is the seriousness of her situation."

Jolted by the news, Blackfoot stared deeply into his sister's eyes, wondering if all this was true.

"This, brother, is why you must stay behind her. When she falls backward into the arms of romance, you must catch her before her lover does."

"Aye, I see it very clearly now. It is wise counsel." Blackfoot stroked his chin. So Belladonna had a weakness after all.

Suddenly, a revelation happened upon Blackfoot like an unexpected storm. Everything about it was perfect. What was revealed to him would lure Belladonna Skylark straight to him.

"I see *very* clearly now," he whispered, eyes widening with clarity.

"So you do." Bartholomew, the only one who had not yet spoken, confirmed through his knowing grin.

"This is probably the only thing that you all have made clear to me, and for that I thank you."

"But this is the only time!" Aranxta snapped. "The rest of it is up to you. We simply interfered because you were beginning to grow restive enough to tarry."

Blackfoot kneeled, bowing his head. He tried to reach out to grab his sister's hand. When he tried to kiss her fingers, he felt nothing. The seven Demonclaw seemed so *fleshly* that he forgot they merely presented themselves to him as apparitions.

"Thank you, my Most Highly Regarded, for your trust in me." Before he could look up from his lowly stance, each of the Demonclaw disappeared one by one, leaving with a quiet *poof!* as they vanished. Only Aranxta remained before him when he looked up. Her sagging, pale face looked down upon him in earnest.

"It is a pleasure to see your lovely face again, sister," Blackfoot croaked, grimacing.

Aranxta's face was far from lovely.

"I sense something else unsettles you that you have not mentioned."

"Indeed, there is something that troubles me. I seem to have a voice that speaks to me, one that slips me small, but sometimes useful, bits about the happenings on the *Zodiac.* I can't seem—"

"You scoundrel! You must focus. Let us worry about the voice. For now, think of it like a siren's song. The sea speaks, you well know, as do the sirens deep beneath the surface."

"But something tells me it is not just that."

"We know what it is, and I suppose you would do well to keep listening to it!" Aranxta shouted as her body quaked with rage. She turned, beginning to drift away, then faced him again, more gently this time. Blackfoot's questions seemed to mount with his sister's unwillingness to help him. "You knew that when you took on this quest—that we would not make it easy for you. I will remain true to that; therefore, I cannot answer your question about the voice. You need not worry about such things is the only answer I can offer."

Before another word could escape his lips, Aranxta was turning into mist, becoming more difficult to see.

"Finish it for us, Cornelius. If you do, you know the rich reward that awaits you."

Then, he was alone. The encounter with the Demonclaw Court left him shaken. Never in his life had he seen them pull an act such as they had. If they found it necessary to do so, then maybe he did need to realign himself with the reason he had set out in the first place.

And the next step in his journey was so deliciously appealing to him that he could not help but laugh out loud. A roaring, terrifying fit of laughter escaped him so fiercely, he had to hold his gut for fear he would rupture with glee.

The next move was sure to seal his victory. The Dragon Majestics would not reign supreme after this blow to their beloved kingdom. Belladonna was his prey, and she was sure to fall into the trap he would lay for her.

CHAPTER 10
BETRAYER'S BLOOD

Leagues behind the *Zodiac, The Temptress* followed with fresh hope for the future.

"Curse that wretched man," Belladonna said, more to herself than anyone. She wished Blackfoot would come closer so she could strike. But she was not going to start anything that did not need starting for the time being.

It had been nearly a whole year of searching, and still, Belladonna had not located the Isla del Dragón. Much like Blackfoot, her patience was growing thin—and more heated. The fire-fever inside her continued to blaze, just relentless enough to make her aware it was there. Arimetta attempted a few spells that would ease it. Nevertheless, the burning persisted.

Ephraim, still in awe of who she was, asked her once if it hurt. Until he asked, she never thought about it hurting, but it did. It gnawed at her insides; she was endlessly parched. No one would touch her, for they could feel the heat rising from her skin. She prayed for it to cease.

"I am ready to be rid of this burden that I bear," she said one stormy day to her boatswain. The *Zodiac* pounded its way through the foamy waves, which the sudden storm produced. She remembered the day she met Arimetta, the day she warned Belladonna that she would have to ride out many storms to make it to the Isla del Dragón. They had passed through dozens so far, with no island revealing itself on the other side.

"It is a heavy thing for you," Ephraim agreed. Both watched as the crew fought against the storm, wrestling with the mainsheet and the brace to keep the mainsail from tearing. Rain pattered on the deck and drenched every man in sight.

Fortunately, if the men did not agree with Belladonna's decision to make Ephraim the boatswain, they had not fought her. Some of the men had learned the hard way before and would not dare face her again.

Belladonna always embraced the rain. She frequently stood in it, opening her arms to the heavens, letting it beat down on her body. Though she hoped eventually it would put out her fire, it never did.

In the few months that followed Ephraim's promotion to boatswain, he always made himself available to her. To cover this simple act of longing, he told her he only wished to relieve Snaggletooth of some of the duty on board. Belladonna knew better, for she realized the feelings that blossomed in her black heart resounded in his own. Ephraim noticed her gentle favor for him begin to show through her usual torments. He could only associate her feelings as akin to his, but manifested in her own way, of course. She was used to power and sought control over all things without wavering.

Little did either of them know she would eventually start to waver, and it would cost her mightily.

“Now that we have sailed around the entirety of these islands, I am beginning to believe that the Isla del Dragón is just as false as my hope that I would find it.”

“You must not become discouraged,” Ephraim insisted. Snaggletooth stood nearby on deck, looking out over the sea. In his hands, he whittled a small whale. The shavings fell neatly near his feet in a small pile. Romulus crept to the pile to smell it. When he released air through his nostrils, the shavings blew in all directions. He began to paw at it wildly. No matter how ferocious his kind was, one could not deny that his cat-like characteristics showed every now and then.

“It just makes no blasted sense!” she shouted, stomping her foot.

“Did ye really expect for this to be so easily found?” Snaggletooth asked. “Being the kind of place it is, it can’t simply be at the disposal of any mere man.”

“Time is running out,” Belladonna puffed, “and Blackfoot remains ever watchful. And that cursed witch has been useless. She agreed that if she saw anything, she would report to me immediately. That was our deal. I have grown suspicious of her.”

Ephraim, who always held a soft spot for the Hoodoo woman in his heart after she had helped heal him, wanted to defend her.

“Perhaps you should find her and ask her. I suspect that she has lain deep within her mind for many days and mayhap has not come out enough to speak with you. Maybe she needs waking.”

It still chilled Ephraim to think that a body could remain in an entranced state like Arimetta's could.

"I doubt it. But I suppose it would do good to try to threaten an answer out of her. Arimetta so desperately wants to live and obtain her freedom. Fine by me as long as she talks. Snaggletooth, would you find her?"

"I know not where she hides when the sun is up, Captain, but Romulus may have a good nose for sniffing her out." Romulus raised his head. He looked into Belladonna's eyes, waiting for the command.

"Aye. Romulus, lead Snaggletooth to her."

Romulus lifted his nose high in the air, sifting through the scents of all the bodies on board. When at last he located hers, he twitched his tail at Snaggletooth, looking behind him.

Snaggletooth followed the cat, first down through the quarters, then through the gun deck, all the way to the hold in the belly of the ship. Romulus stopped when he left the final step into the hold, raising his nose and sniffing the stale air. The cat crouched as if ready to strike when Snaggletooth placed a hand around his muzzle. Romulus looked up at Snaggletooth, who raised a finger to his lips. Arimetta, still unseen but definitely smelled, was somewhere toward the aft of the hold.

Faint whispers could be heard from deep within the stores. Snaggletooth could not make out any of it, for she spoke so quickly that it sounded like an ancient language. Perhaps it was the language of her island, he thought. However, the more he turned his ear to her, the more words he could make out.

"*. . . it lie thru deh storm . . . Belladonna meke it thru deh storm soon 'nuff, yes . . . Stay close . . .*"

Snaggletooth could only pick out pieces of what she uttered to herself. But the more he listened, the more he began to think that she was not just speaking to herself. She was speaking to *someone.*

He motioned for Romulus to stay where he was and began to tiptoe toward the voice. He could hear more of her words.

". . . Alauda'll come soon, she has deh boy tuh help 'er. And anodda will come tuh 'er."

Finally, he saw her. She really was as far back in the hold as she could go. A chill ran down his entire body at the sight of her. She faced away from him, speaking to the very bones of the ship. She rocked back and forth furiously, dreadlocks swinging with every movement. Snaggletooth heard the tinkling of the shells around her neck hitting each other every time she rocked back or forth. Arimetta was so curled into herself she looked like a spider in its dying moments, legs furled and stiffening.

". . . T'ank yuh, Highly Regarded, fuh lettin' mah voice serve yuh in deh wey of prophecy . . ."

Snaggletooth knew he needed to grasp her and wake her from her vision. The fear in him made him want to cower from her and leave her be, pretending he had not found her. The prophetess was terrifying to begin with. Now, like a cave creature, she was even more so. He crept to her lightly. As he reached out his hand to grab her shoulder, he realized what was happening.

The someone whom she spoke to was the enemy. Arimetta had been feeding Blackfoot news of Belladonna's quest since they'd found her in Port Royal. It was possible she was feeding him information way before then.

Arimetta is bound to die this day, Snaggletooth thought. Before he had time to cringe from her again, he grasped her shoulder. Arimetta's body appeared to snap in half. Her top half turned toward Snaggletooth, blind eyes wide with shock, while her bottom half remained facing in front of her. To him, she looked like one woken from death, unaware of where she was or maybe even who she was. Snaggletooth assumed she may not have been herself during her trance, her body taken over by a spirit that was not hers. How long had she been in her trance?

Minutes, hours, days, weeks even? After a moment, realization dawned on Arimetta's face and it began to wrinkle in horror.

Arimetta was the reason that Blackfoot followed the *Zodiac.* Though drawn to Belladonna's allure and wishing to follow her even before, Arimetta was the one who had informed him that a Skylark child lived and sailed the seas. If not for Arimetta, perhaps the two would not have even crossed paths yet. And maybe the two would have continued to sail not knowing the other still existed.

The prophetess opened her mouth as if to speak and clutched the shells around her neck.

"I am afraid I have heard too much of yer blatherin', Arimetta." Snaggletooth roared. "Ye will come with me to the captain at once, and ye will pay the price for the weight of yer actions." Snaggletooth grabbed her by one arm, dragged her through the hold, and lifted her up each set of steps to where Belladonna awaited. Her fragile body felt lifeless in his grasp. It shocked him that Arimetta did not fight him as he heard her bones crack. All she did was as she usually did: speak to herself while holding the shells, perhaps praying about the eternal destination that awaited her at the end of Belladonna's pistol.

Romulus trailed behind Arimetta as she was dragged, snarling at her. The very woman who had tamed a tiger for service to a pirate captain now seemed to be broken. Her trance had exhausted her, and she would use no power to stop Romulus and his taunting snarls.

When Belladonna and Ephraim saw him approach with Arimetta being dragged behind him, Belladonna rushed to him.

"What has happened to her?" she gasped. With anger coursing through his veins, Snaggletooth stood her up and raised her arm. The effort to stand was too much for Arimetta. She began to crumble, the pale, useless irises of her eyes rolling back in her skull. Snaggletooth kept her held up by his hand. He turned to address the crew, who was not used to seeing Arimetta when the sun shone.

"I bring this devil woman before ye all now as a betrayer!" he shouted, spit flying from his lips. "I have witnessed this woman in one of her trances speaking to our enemy. This leads me to believe she has done so from the very beginning of her time with us. Mark my words ye dogs, this she-witch is a betrayer and cannot be trusted!"

The men began to murmur among themselves, some saying they predicted she would be trouble. Others were stunned by the news, thinking her a harmless soul.

Belladonna's heart started to beat against her ribs. Arimetta had earned her trust. Now, Snaggletooth was proclaiming to everyone around that she was not worthy of that trust.

"Quartermaster, do you speak true?"

"I swear my life upon it."

Belladonna rushed to look Arimetta in the face. The prophetess hung limply from Snaggletooth's hand. Though she did not display any emotion, tears dripped from her cheeks.

"Explain yourself to me, Arimetta!" Belladonna commanded. "Speak now before I send you to hell." The woman did nothing. The only movement Belladonna could see from her body were the rises and falls of her chest. Belladonna clapped her across the eyes with so much force that she might have become blind if she had not been already. "Will you not speak as your captain commands?" Still nothing. Her eyelids fluttered, and her lips moved with the smallest hint of someone praying. Blood poured from her nose.

With her body guided only by her fury, Belladonna reached out with both hands and clasped them around Arimetta's neck. Snaggletooth let go of her arm as her knees buckled. She fell to the deck and came back to life. Her own hands grabbed Belladonna's wrists and tried to fight back. Belladonna's body burned even brighter than before, her fire fever grew into what felt to Belladonna like complete consummation. Arimetta opened her mouth and tried to scream and even though she could not from the force of Belladonna's hands, she did not have to scream. Belladonna's own screams made up for hers.

Ephraim watched Belladonna's skin change in horror. It took on the appearance of a coal set in a fire, charring from the inside, the fire visible through cracks. Even standing as far back as he was from the fight that ensued, he felt the heat that rose from Bella donna, a heat that singed the hairs on his arms. She was horrifying. The woman that he loved in his heart was a monster, and he had always seemed to allow himself to forget that. His compassion for Arimetta, despite this news of betrayal, led him to interfere. Ephraim remembered that pain on his own flesh.

"Stop!" Ephraim yelled as he grabbed Belladonna's arms. That first feeling of cold burning quickly turned into searing agony. Belladonna jumped back, realizing that her very touch had badly burned Ephraim's hands and coated Arimetta's neck in blisters. She looked down at her hands and expected to see them covered by fire.

Instead, she saw nothing. They looked like the hands she always had.

The men on deck looked at these happenings with more fear than they had ever felt for their captain.

Ephraim panted as he lowered Arimetta. She was not dead, but she was badly hurt and dangerously exhausted from her earlier trance. He looked at Belladonna in warning.

"You should not act upon your every whim, Captain. Just as you need the rest of us, so you need Arimetta to finish this journey. She will pay the price for what she has done, but I think we may be able to rid her of her betrayer's spirit. As an advisor to you, I must caution you to keep her alive for as long as you can."

Taken aback, first by her own power, then by Ephraim's words, she puffed out her breast, attempting to remain unshaken by his actions. Never in her years had anyone told her that she should let someone live when they had wronged her. Belladonna would not have her decisions questioned. Not even Snaggletooth had exposed her hatred such as Ephraim just had. But, as these feelings grew still, she knew Ephraim was right. She believed Ephraim, and not in the same way that she would believe Arimetta.

"And what say you then, since you are so bold? What shall we do with this woman who has exposed us so? I cannot have her continue in the way she has been going."

"I know a way," Ephraim declared. "We will bleed her. I think a spirit possesses her, and I have heard a proper bleeding does one good to get rid of such things. It would also do us well to burn fragrant herbs in her presence. I know she keeps them on her. Those who inhabit the spirit world keep them close."

"And do you think this is a just means to end this cycle?"

"Aye, I do, Captain Skylark. For I have seen it done."

"Aye!" the men shouted, for many of them had seen it done as well.

If any other had suggested such as Ephraim had, she would not have allowed it. Knowing in her heart that she *could* trust Ephraim was the only reason she approved.

"Then what is there to wait for? Have her taken to Cromley immediately."

Belladonna watched as two of the sailors volunteered to carry her to the surgeon. As the chaos of the moment cleared and men returned to work, Belladonna bolted toward Ephraim. No one would try to take command unless she told them to.

"What was that, Master Howell?" she hissed.

"I could not let you kill her. Like I said, I do not think she has any ill intentions toward you."

"Simply because she licked your wounds and sang you a tune in your decrepit state does not make her worthy of all the mercy in the world." Ephraim was awestruck. How had she known that Arimetta took care of him? Before he could ask, she replied: "Do not for a moment think I don't know the happenings around my ship. I know the men call me Dragon Lady, for heaven's sake. I try not to let things get past me, except . . . that prophetess and her mind tricks did. I cannot believe that I trusted her at all."

"You had no way of knowing," Ephraim said softly.

"But I did. Oh, I did. Something about her never felt right, though I tried to let my harsh feelings of her fall to the wayside. It was only a matter of time before someone else took advantage of my blindness." Here she sent Ephraim a stern glance. He tried not to remember his days as a stowaway, but Belladonna would often remind him of where he came from.

"She won't be doing it again, Captain Skylark. This will work." As he stepped away to see to the bleeding, Belladonna whipped him back around and grabbed the front of his shirt in her fist.

"Mind your place, Master Howell. You do not command me." She let go, pushing him as she did, and stomped away, back to her maps. More time had been spent studying them now that they were coming full circle, back to Port Royal.

Ephraim wanted to be angry with Belladonna. She may be comfortable in her rank, but that did not mean she needed to bite at the first drop of blood. And for what it was worth, no one even bothered to check Snaggletooth's claims. Perhaps it was a conspiracy to rid the ship of her, the men thinking her to be a bad omen. He wished he had considered this before Arimetta was sent to the hands of the surgeon. There was a possibility she was harmless, and she was about to be bled for nothing.

In truth, as much as Ephraim wanted to believe the Hoodoo woman had no bad intentions, he knew the claims were likely true. A person who mingled with the spirits usually had a vulnerable mind.

And as he made his way to the surgeon, before he would have to endure the bloodshed brought about by his own recommendation, he thought about Belladonna's remark that he needed to mind his place. Belladonna was a terrible figure, mean to the nth degree, but he saw how lost she was in her eyes. Everything about Belladonna was stunning to him. Even in her anger, he saw her beauty. The force which she had used upon him, though he hated to admit, often filled him with an odd feeling of pleasure. Her attention satisfied him, whether it be positive or negative. Still shaken from the encounter, he brushed his clothing with his hands and entered the surgeon's quarters. His calloused hands still throbbed with the burn of Belladonna's fiery touch. He would need to wrap them before long.

The men who carried her to the surgeon remained in the room, holding Arimetta's arms above her head, making it impossible for her to escape the table she lay upon. Snaggletooth, also present, turned to Cromley and gave him a sympathetic look. It seemed to say that he was sorry for the dramatics. Snaggletooth turned back to the operation getting ready to begin. Cromley saw Ephraim enter and picked up a bucket.

"Master Howell, seeing as you are the one who suggested this be done, I would like to ask you to hold this as I make the incision."

Ephraim felt a lump rise in his throat. *Why do I need to be involved in this treachery?*

Just as Cromley bent to cut the flesh open, Belladonna walked in. She had decided it would satisfy her to watch Arimetta be released of her demons rather than go back to the daunting task of map study.

Cromley took his knife and made a cut down Arimetta's side. At first, still numb from the prior events, Arimetta's body lay still. The blood, thick and red, flowed smoothly out of her side. Ephraim watched the bucket begin to fill at the bottom as he held it to her. Blood did not bother him as it had before. Far too much blood had been shed in front of him for him to still get queasy.

Belladonna, cruel as she was, could not hide the evil smirk on her face. He was not sure if she smirked because it gave her joy to watch Arimetta's punishment or if she knew this would not work. When Ephraim looked back down, he saw Arimetta's hanging fingers, almost touching the ground, begin to tremble. From there, the trembling took over her body like a wave. She convulsed violently. Foam shot out of the sides of her mouth and blood seeped between her teeth. The shaking was so ravaging, she had either nicked her tongue or bitten it off entirely.

"Get a rag for her mouth!" Cromley commanded. Snaggletooth took one from the table that Cromley used to hold his instruments and folded it into her mouth. "She needs to be held still."

Every set of hands in the room except for Ephraim's grasped Arimetta's limbs to keep her from falling off of the table. The men's forearms showed strain; they used all of their force to try to calm her body. Belladonna had both of her hands on either side of Arimetta's head, just as the prophetess had done to her in her tellings, keeping her head from continuing to slam against the table. Anyone could tell it was contrary to Belladonna's nature for her to help in this small way, but Ephraim sensed she was beginning to come around to what he had warned her about. They locked eyes for just a moment.

Harsh, muffled moans left Arimetta as the shaking persisted. The thrashing was sure to break her delicate bones if not kill her entirely.

The bucket in Ephraim's hands, now shaking from the tenseness of the moment, was filling up faster. Blood squirted out of the incision, spraying the men who stood at her side. Then, her body slackened. Had the fight done her in?

Cromley leaned over her breast and placed his ear to it.

"She lives," he confirmed. Her dirt-caked skin showed pale through the dark spots. Now, her eyes were closed, and her mouth was wide open with the rag still balled inside of it. Cromley went to grab his instruments to stitch her side. Enough blood had been let this day. Ephraim pounded the bucket on the ground and knelt, putting his head in his hands. He did not feel weak from the blood but rather from the feeling in the air. Arimetta's body did not fight back simply because of her open side. No, it was not her. Whatever possessed her was fighting its dramatic exit.

But did it work? If there was a spirit in her, had it left?

Belladonna wiped Arimetta's blood from her hands on her trousers. Hatefully, she looked down upon the shrunken, worn-out woman who seemed so lifeless.

"You mentioned something about the herbs she carried." Now, she spoke to Ephraim. "Do as you must with them." With this final command, she left the room. Her bloodstained hands and smeared trousers were bound to raise some eyebrows on deck.

Ephraim had heard tales of incense and sage burning, which was used among native islanders to clean the air of bad spirits. He was certain the bloodletting would cleanse her (if a bad spirit really was the problem) but wanted to see this done as well. *No extra measure taken could hurt,* he thought.

Cromley thought it best to leave Arimetta where she was for fear that moving her would cause another spell of convulsions. As for burning, that would take place in his operating quarters, he seemed to think it wise. Most sailors and pirates were superstitious, and the mention of any sort of spirit dancing in the air raised most men's neck hairs.

Ephraim checked her entire person, looking for the stuff he was certain she carried. Finally, he found it, tucked neatly between her breasts.

What an odd place to hide such a thing, Ephraim thought as he examined the bundle in his hands. The foamy green leaves were sage, that much he could tell from their smell, and wrapped tightly with twine. As he held the bundle to the light of the lantern, he saw Arimetta's hand reach up.

"Yuh must open deh door, chile," she said faintly.

"You will guide me in this, then?"

"Yuh must open a door fuh deh spirits tuh leave." At least she had woken, and Ephraim was thankful she was able to comprehend what his intentions were. She did not try to stop him. Arimetta knew she had been possessed for a long, long time. "But I doan know if it work."

"It is certainly worth trying I believe." Ephraim smiled at her. He nodded for Cromley to crack the door open. The advice only made sense. He reached carefully with the sage bundle in his hand to ignite it with the fire from the lantern. Rolling it around so it ignited all of the leaves at the top, Ephraim caught a whiff of the musty odor rising out of the fire. Arimetta tapped him.

"Get deh fire off it. Yuh need deh smoke." Ephraim dabbed it lightly on the dry wood and watched the ashes fall to the ground. "Now yuh need tuh pray."

Ephraim believed that God existed, but did he believe in the prayer Arimetta wanted him to pray? He would try it.

"May these spirits that torment this poor woman be gone." Smoke drifted around the room as he waved it softly through the air. He did not know what else to say. Arimetta's nostrils flared, letting the incense smoke enter her body to cleanse her.

"Bring me deh captin, Masta Howell."

"You want to see Captain Skylark?" Ephraim asked, taken back. He glimpsed the burns on her neck that evidently had not registered with Arimetta yet. The pulpy raised welts looked like they pulsed with fresh fire every second. What chilled him even more is that the burns looked like permanent hands wrapped around her throat. That choke imprint would scar and leave Arimetta looking like an eternal victim for the remainder of her days.

"Aye, Arimetta must speak tuh deh cap'n. Dere is somet'ing she needa know." Arimetta stroked the cloth wrapped around his hand, the other held above his head like a torch with the smoke rising from it. He handed it to Cromley who looked at it questioningly.

"This is the devil's business," Cromley crowed, "but I suppose we are in over our heads now." The surgeon stood up and proceeded to wave the sage bundle around, cleansing the air.

Ephraim walked out of the surgeon's room to find Belladonna standing at the aft of the ship, most assuredly boiling with resentment. She looked out across the sea to *The Temptress* and its billowy, weathered sails. Her body was rigid. Ephraim thought she would snap if he approached her unannounced.

"Captain Skylark, Arimetta would like a word with you." Belladonna whipped around. The captain was indeed coming out of an internal fit of rage. The heat went out from her many degrees higher than usual.

"I do not see how I can face her at this moment. Do you?" she asked. "You know, she would have been dead by now if it were not for you. Hopefully, I do not regret the decision to listen to your words." She bumped into his shoulder as she stomped past him, sending a bone-chilling glare toward him as she did. He stepped quickly behind her footfalls. No one could guarantee that Belladonna was not on her way to kill her now, even after all this.

"What do you need from me, you witch?" Belladonna inquired. "Are you finally ready to tell me what this madness is? Oh, have you *seen* something? It would be a bloody miracle after all this bloody chaos you have taken upon yourself. Are you feeling penitent now?"

Arimetta looked barely strong enough to open her eyes. Hands outstretched toward Belladonna, she bid her fall into them.

"Now is deh time, Captin Skylark." Belladonna had not gotten any closer to her, but her eyes widened in wonder. She dragged Cromley's stool to Arimetta's side and sat.

"Cromley, leave this room immediately. And give that stinking mess to Master Howell."

The surgeon practically threw the smoking sage at Ephraim's chest and ran out. One could hear him sucking in the ocean air outside. Snaggletooth entered just as he left with Romulus at his side.

"I heard that the prophetess was dead and—" Snaggletooth stopped speaking when he viewed Arimetta, frail and sprawled on the table before him. "So she lives. The crew have gotten it out that her body had been given over completely to the spirits."

“Nah, chile, Arimetta still here.” It was clear that it was taking all Arimetta’s remaining strength to speak.

“Please, back to what you said,” Belladonna interrupted. “Now is the time for what? Is the Isla del Dragón close?”

“Dat come soon, but I ’ave tings dat yuh need tuh see. Arimetta needa tell Captin Skylark about ’er deal wit de devil. Why Arimetta talked tuh dat man behind yuh.” Belladonna gulped and grabbed Arimetta’s hand. The small compassion that she had offered Arimetta before was beginning to reappear.

“Tell me this, I command it. How much have you told him?”

“P’rhaps Arimetta can show yuh? It is hard tuh speak.” Arimetta moved her shaky hand to her neck and pointed at the burns from Belladonna’s hands. She had forgotten what she had done among the chaos that ensued after. She supposed it would hurt to speak, and that her body and soul would indeed be drained from her fight.

“Is it going to be too much for you to show me? I may still need you if this information proves sufficient. I believe your body has been rid of its inhabitants.”

“Aye, it has, fah now. Dat is why Arimetta needa show yuh now.” Reluctantly, Belladonna consented. She placed Arimetta’s hands on the sides of her head and closed her eyes. Arimetta did the same. Belladonna cleared her mind of its distracting rage and looked for Arimetta’s eyes.

In what seemed like a world of darkness, she found Arimetta’s blind eyes. They blinked at her then disappeared. Belladonna could now see.

Belladonna saw a woman, one who greatly resembled Arimetta but with eyes that shone with real sight, not just mental sight. It was difficult to resist staring into those pure blue irises.

Had Arimetta been able to see, Belladonna hoped her eyes would look like this. This woman was Arimetta’s mother, that much was obvious. Her mother cowered in her dwelling place, which looked to be a tent of some kind. Her hands were covered in blood and her stomach looked round and deflating.

Under her bloody hands lay a baby. In fact, the child in the vision *did* seem to share the same bright eyes that its mother possessed. The baby screamed the way that all babies do upon entering the world. The mother's hands began to shake, and loud, deep-bellied sobs came from her. The scene at first was beautiful, a mother and her new child, her hands painted red with the fruits of her labor. The longer Belladonna looked, the scene shifted from beauty to horror. The blood on the mother's hands made her look like she had killed a man in her madness. It was then that Belladonna noticed what stood behind the woman.

Present at the birth stood seven cloudy apparitions. None of them appeared to be celebrating the birth. They seemed to be present only because something was in it for them. They were there out of duty.

The mother crouched over her child and shielded it with her arms. This did not stop the female apparition in the middle of the seven from kicking her aside. Something about the way the mother desperately reached out to her child sparked sadness in Belladonna's heart. She had never known her own mother, nor had she felt the embrace of motherly love.

It appeared that this child never got that chance either.

From their place surrounding Arimetta and Belladonna's vision dance, Ephraim and Snaggletooth looked on. The sage still burned. Ephraim could not believe it when he saw tears sliding down Belladonna's cheeks. It was a sight to behold.

In the vision, Belladonna watched the lady apparition that stepped forward lean into the new mother's face. She saw their lips move but could not hear them speak to each other. Something horrendous must have happened, for the mother now began to curl on the floor, her body racked with cries that could not be heard.

The lady apparition picked up the baby. Her eyes rolled upward to the skies, and she placed her right hand, with long, delicate nails, over the baby's face. The baby stopped its screams and closed its eyes. The apparition appeared to chant, swirling her hand around the child's face. When she pulled her hand away, the stunning blue eyes were now dark, looking beyond the lady apparition into nothingness.

Arimetta.

Belladonna did not know this was what Arimetta would show her. But she needed to know this. She needed to know how it began, if Arimetta truly was possessed and speaking to Blackfoot through visions.

After a quick reprieve, she jumped back into Arimetta's vision. But there was now nothing to see except for sickening blackness.

That was when Arimetta spoke in a harsh whisper to Belladonna through the vision, and this time, without her usual thick accent.

"I was born to a line of cursed women. The curse that ravages my body has lived among the generations of women before me. The Demonclaw enslaved my female ancestors because of their special gifts of foresight and prophecy. My women all prayed to the spirits to give them a boy when they found out they were with child. However, the spirits must have found humor in their prayers, for most often they bore girls. So my mother was also possessed by the Demonclaw spirit. Only when I was born, they took more from me than my freedom. They took my sight as punishment for my mother, who had tried to perform a ritual to flee the spirit from her body while I grew in her womb. Belladonna, I was born to *see*—and not just into the future. I was born to see the world that blossomed in front of my feet, to see the complexities of creation. I should have been able to see you as you sit before me now. But all of it, every good thing, was stripped from me. My women have fallen victim to the Demonclaw's whims. And I fear that even though the spirit has fled my body for now, when it comes back, it will come back to kill me and take over me entirely."

At this point, neither Ephraim nor Snaggletooth, not even Romulus, could know what was being shared between the two women. They stared on, impressed at the bond they seemed to share in their moment of shared thought.

"Belladonna Skylark, you *must* free me from this spirit that they have imposed upon my entire line of women. If not for me, do it for the ones after me. How they would revel in the very idea that a woman of their line would not have to live under the crushing weight of the Demonclaw masters! Those demons have used me, and they have sucked the marrow from my very bones."

Arimetta stopped *speaking* to her very abruptly and flashed to a new vision. Belladonna felt herself blinking, adjusting to the light after dwelling in the darkness of Arimetta's speech.

This was the first time Belladonna would get to see Blackfoot this closely since one of Arimetta's earlier visions. Inevitably one day, perhaps more, she knew she would soon be this close to him, but his image shocked her. She did not remember his person to be so intimidating, so gruesome. He looked very much like a pirate, down to the scraggly beard and the tattered clothing. The light around him in what appeared to be a tavern glowed softly behind him.

Arimetta sat before him, her hand hovering over the shells that regularly hung from her neck. They were sprawled out on the table between them. Belladonna tilted her head and thought how she had never seen Arimetta without these around her neck.

It did not take a fool to know why Arimetta was showing her this. The tavern they sat in happened to be the same tavern that Snaggletooth would visit mere hours later to look for new sailors to come aboard the *Zodiac.*

And Arimetta was doing what she did best: she was glimpsing into the future, picking out useful information about who captained the *Zodiac* he saw at sea. The Demonclaw placed her in Blackfoot's path for the very purpose . . . of finding Belladonna at last.

Much to Belladonna's dismay, Arimetta truly was the reason for Blackfoot's pursuit. But unlike Belladonna's earlier suspicions, she now understood it was not by choice. Arimetta was another soul in the line of prophetesses that was being bound up by the Demonclaw's aim for destruction.

It occurred to Belladonna that some of the greatest tragedies of the modern world might have been aided by Arimetta's bloodline. It made her shudder. The power of the woman that *spoke* to her was far beyond what she ever imagined.

Arimetta's face appeared before Belladonna's eyes. She dabbed at them, not knowing why they were so foggy. When she pulled her fingers away she saw the tears that appeared there.

Arimetta looked to be shedding tears of her own.

"You have been a slave for your entire life and you have never tasted freedom. You are one of many reasons that I must take my place on the Isla del Dragón."

"Arimetta know dat yuh can do't, Captin."

In an act that none ever thought possible after Belladonna's heart had hardened, the two women clasped their hands together and looked lovingly into each other's eyes. No one could mistake the look of total and complete understanding they now shared.

Belladonna could not believe it herself but could not fight the feeling of endearment in her heart.

"I am sorry for your plight, my sister. I am sorry for any and all suffering you have endured because of who you descended from. I have forgiven your trespasses against me."

Belladonna's act of sudden grace moved Arimetta to tears. For once in her life, Arimetta believed it possible to be free. In fact, at that very moment, she was as free as she could be. The Demonclaw spirit had been bled from her side and wandered aimlessly along the surface of the earth looking for her. Arimetta did not know how long she could relish in her momentary freedom. At least she would have a taste of what life could be like once Belladonna became the true Dragon empress.

"Yuh most forgiven, darlin'."

Romulus peered up into Belladonna's eyes as their moment ended. Romulus's gleaming eyes confirmed that Belladonna saw true. Oh, how she wished Romulus could speak to her of the long life she was certain he had lived. Perhaps, one day he would be able to speak of it.

Gathering herself, Belladonna stood. And before another tear could be shed by anyone, her face fell back to its usual look of dissatisfaction.

"Arimetta, you have served me, and you have betrayed me. I have forgiven you for this only because I know that with or without your interference, I would have been forced to face Blackfoot one day, as it is prophesied. I can only guess that your tellings might have sped up his part of the quest in some way. And with the spirit gone from you at the present, none knows yet when it may come back to you. Much like you said, the spirit may come back with a vengeance. That is why you must be detained. Letting you get off at the next port is too risky. You have been with me for long enough that any and all information you have about me and my quest could prove dangerous. That spirit that haunted you seemed able to completely take you over at times, and I know not who the Demonclaw would place in your path for you to give that information to. What I do *not* need are others who are curious about the island thwarting me. Blackfoot is enough. However, if and when the spirit comes back to you, it is out of my control. All we can do is continue to bleed it out of you—if you even live through its next reaping. I hope you understand my reasons for locking you below."

"Aye." Arimetta nodded. The sisterhood that was shared between them had bridged the gap of any misgivings the two might have had with one another before. Arimetta and Belladonna (who would come to find out in time the full extent of the prophetess's power) were both forces to be dealt with. The two together could have made the quest to the Isla del Dragón on their own without the help of any man.

As he thought about it, that very idea made Ephraim's presence in the room feel small. He had joined a quest to restore peace to humanity that was overwhelmingly large compared to what he had resolved was his place in it. Ephraim was only present to bolster Belladonna toward her endgame.

Snaggletooth cleared his throat. In his hands, he held the shackles that Arimetta was to wear on her ankles. He still seemed irate with her for what she had done. But he did not see what Belladonna saw and could not feel that same compassion.

He clasped them around her ankles and propped her up with her feet on the floor. In the days that followed, sleep would overtake her. It took so much of her mental force when the spirit consumed her and made her use her foresight to speak to Blackfoot's mind. It was another thing entirely that she had been choked and bled, along with her *telling* and *showing.* Every aspect of her person had been pushed to the brink. Arimetta would be useless to Belladonna in the days that followed.

As Snaggletooth began to drag her away, back to the cell that she started in on the *Zodiac,* Belladonna made one final command of her: "If you happen to *see* something, call upon Romulus to bring me to you. He will be listening."

Arimetta looked beyond Belladonna but nodded in understanding.

She would not *see* anything for several days.

Ephraim wanted to thank his captain for her compassion toward Arimetta. He had felt that compassion for her in his heart since the moment he realized she was the one who saved him from death's grip. Not to mention, this small act of kindness added to the growing reasons why Ephraim admired Captain Skylark.

Belladonna escaped the surgeon's room just a moment after Snaggletooth left. Ephraim could tell something had popped into her head that had to be tended to at that very moment. When he reached her, in the very spot he'd found her before, when Arimetta wanted to see her, he ran to her.

"Captain Skylark, I wanted—"

Before he could finish speaking, his jaw nearly fell to his feet. The ship that been cruising behind them at its leisurely pace, the ship that had grown to be like an old scar one cannot be rid of, was gone.

Nowhere on the horizon could Ephraim see *The Temptress* as he looked all around. She was not behind, nor next to, nor in front of the *Zodiac.*

Blackfoot had vanished into thin air.

Ephraim expected Belladonna to be furious, to demand that Blackfoot be relocated at once. Instead, she surprised him with what she said.

"Good. It will do us well to have him off our tail, even if just for a while." She spun away, headed back to whatever business needed tending to before the madness with Arimetta had begun.

The calmness he heard in her voice both alarmed him and set him at ease. It was true; this was the first time since setting out from Port Royal that *The Temptress* did not creep behind them. With Blackfoot declared indisposed, at least for now, he had been moved down on her priority list, Ephraim realized.

Now was the perfect time for her to get as far ahead of him as she could and find the Isla del Dragón.

CHAPTER 11
WITLESS LOVERS

With Blackfoot nowhere to be found, just as Ephraim suspected, Belladonna found that it was time to make real progress toward finding the Isla del Dragón. The quest had been long—nearly three years by this time—and it was beginning to drive Belladonna to desperation.

Mortal men—*men* used in the sense of all humanity—all come to a point when their fight seems daunting and then useless. Long wars sometimes end in surrender because armies of men eventually long for home more than victory. Belladonna found herself at the precipice of this very thing. Belladonna's every fiber pulsed for more than herself but for humanity, yet she still had not discovered that side of herself. Her humanity was tearing at her nerves, her will to fight diminishing. Blackfoot's absence did not necessarily motivate her. Out of what felt like an obligation, she decided the best use of her time would be to start searching harder for the Isla del Dragón—if that was even possible.

And not only was the quest drawing itself out, but she found herself becoming increasingly distracted by Ephraim's presence. The feelings that stunned her at first, thinking herself incapable of them anymore, she had now learned to embrace, and not without hope for herself. Never had she admired the heart that had hardened after Starlene left her. It was all so *inhuman.* She felt more like a soulless animal than a young woman. But with Ephraim's presence, her human capacities were returning to her, and this made her smile—often. She was not so totally lost to her roots and her human nature.

In almost a year's time, the *Zodiac* had circled the Caribbean islands once over. She was well-stocked with supplies and ammunition and did not need to stop for any reason, but Belladonna found herself itching to step on dry land again. She could not remember the last time she felt the steady ground beneath her feet. And with Port Royal being one of the leading ports for fellow pirates, she was certain there had to be one or two of those fellows that held secret knowledge of the Isla del Dragón. For a moment, she thought about the vision that Arimetta showed her not long before, of herself and her enemy sitting across from one another at a tavern in the same port, Arimetta searching for visions of a voyager to the Isla del Dragón to feed Blackfoot's curiosity. However, this would be different. She would not recruit anyone to come along. All she wanted was information. Besides, she would just kill whoever she spoke to if they pried too much, so promised the blackness that still held some of her heart. After all, her old ways were not entirely gone.

"Quartermaster," she called to Snaggletooth, who was quietly overseeing the men. "Since we are rounding to Port Royal again, I will be taking one of the longboats with Master Howell into port to search for any knowledge of the Isla del Dragón. I am in dire need of any information I can get my hands on, and I am afraid I must now seek that from outsiders." Snaggletooth raised an eyebrow and crossed his arms.

"Need I remind ye of that sleeping prophetess we have below that has dragged us into a spot of trouble? And found at that very port, for that matter?"

"I understand your concern, but I have already decided that I must do it and what I *will* do to anyone who knows more beyond what they should. I will be presenting myself to them as a weary traveler in need of a good pirate tale. I think that is as good a cover as any."

"Aye, that seems well." Snaggletooth removed his pipe from his mouth and puffed out a few smoke rings. "Ye have done well to not go flaunting yer name about. Some may have heard of ye but, by heavens, I am sure none of them know yer face."

"Precisely. And while we are busy scouring the port for anything we can, I want you to find someplace close by to careen the ship. She undoubtedly needs it."

"It has been quite some time. There should be an estuary nearby, not too far from port. When will ye have us come back to get the two of ye?"

"No longer than a day. Give us the night and come in the morning. And please, keep watch for Blackfoot." She looked out behind the ship, out of habit. He still was not there. "God in Heaven only knows where he is or what he might be doing. Without Arimetta's voice, I am confident he is sailing in circles, that halfwit scum."

"Ye have my word, Captain." Belladonna started to leave to find Ephraim when Snaggletooth thought of another question. "But why Ephraim? Why must he go with ye?"

Snaggletooth's question made her heart pump faster. Yes, why *did* Ephraim need to come with her? She knew the answer but could not voice it, not when her dark reputation preceded her onboard. Her interior was softening, but for now, her exterior needed to remain unchanged. No logical explanation would come to her, no argument as to why Ephraim must be the one to come.

Getting close to Snaggletooth, she simply said: "Much like Arimetta, I am beginning to feel that Ephraim serves a purpose to me. I like the boy. He is a warrior, and because of that, I need him on my side. And whatever his purpose is, perhaps it will reveal itself while at port."

Belladonna regretted what she said as soon as she closed her mouth. How naive she sounded! Ephraim did serve a purpose to her and her quest, but she was not ready to admit what she knew he would mean to her. Especially not aloud. No one, she hoped, had probed her about her generous dealings with Ephraim yet. Even if they did, she would do as she was presently doing: cover it all with lies.

Little did Belladonna know that Snaggletooth had his own growing suspicions about the pair. He had been witness to their happily getting along, and for some of the things that Ephraim said and did, he was surprised she had not yet killed him. Snaggletooth knew his place with Belladonna and found room in his heart to love her still. Ephraim was a fantastic addition to the *Zodiac;* Snaggletooth sensed his love for her, as well, but had prayed that it would not hinder their voyage. However, he was beginning to see that it was. Aware of this and knowing not to peer too much into her personal feelings, he gave no indication that their stopping off would bother him.

"If that be how ye feel, then it must be certain then." Snaggletooth gave her a warm, knowing smile. It set Belladonna on edge.

Of course, Snaggletooth would be the first to discern their kindling romance. Now was not the time for explanation.

Ephraim looked up from where he stood on the starboard side of the ship as if he knew they spoke of him. Belladonna waved him over.

"Master Howell, now that we seem to have some relief from Blackfoot, you and I will be making a stop when we come around to Port Royal to find out anything we can about the Isla del Dragón. Considering Arimetta's incapacitation and my current lack of knowledge, I am in need of any hint a man can give me, even if only a morsel."

Ephraim looked back and forth between Snaggletooth and Belladonna, wiping his hands with a dirty rag, suspicious of his involvement in the task.

"How are we to do that? I thought you wanted to remain as unknown as possible to keep your quest to yourself."

"We have concurred that this is what would be best right now. And we will make it seem as if we are two visitors to the island, simply curious about any tales that are passed around among the pirates. Just two inquisitive souls in search of an adventurous story. It's quite genius, I find. And best not for me to go alone so as to make myself more vulnerable to attack, if any suspicions arise." Snaggletooth saw through Belladonna's words. She wanted Ephraim to be under the notion that it was not her idea alone that he would join her.

She is crafty, so she is, Snaggletooth thought to himself.

"If my captain wills it then I must oblige." Ephraim showed his teeth in a dazzling smile, one that he specifically reserved for Belladonna. She acted as if she did not notice it.

"We will set out when we can see the port on the horizon. Until then, attend to as much of your duties as you can. You will be losing almost a whole day's worth of work by the time we come back to the *Zodiac.*"

Ephraim nodded, not ignoring the rapid beating in his chest. Evidently, Belladonna had come to trust him enough to have him at her side as she sought what she might need on land. This was an opportunity to protect her, show her what she meant to him. The knowledge of what he was about to do for Belladonna puffed up his pride. Now, he was to be the dutiful protector of his beloved captain, the captain that he held secret feelings for in his heart. What bliss this would be! If he could not love her the way he so longed to, at least he could be near her.

After two more nights of sleep, Ephraim awoke early, long before sunrise, to find the night watchmen poised at their various posts around the deck. He stretched and yawned, shaking off the slowness that sleep bestowed upon him. The stars twinkled in the pre-dawn sky with wispy pink and orange clouds hanging lightly, veiling the stars. He trudged to the front of the ship and looked over the bowsprit. Land lay not too far away from where the ship rocked. If Ephraim was not mistaken, it was Port Royal that lie ahead, waiting for Captain Skylark and himself. Memories of his drunken days awaiting the perfect ship to dock there so he might stowaway emerged in his mind as he looked at the line on the horizon. Even today, he never denied that the *Zodiac* had called him. Now, as he was becoming a crucial part of the journey the *Zodiac* had set its course on, he saw why the ship had called him.

It was still early, and they were still not close enough to the island of Jamaica to leave on the longboat. Ephraim felt in his heart that whatever was to be accomplished while they stalked around the port city, disguised as two restless vagabonds looking for a good time, it would certainly draw him and Belladonna closer to each other.

When the time came for them to set out, Ephraim climbed into the longboat and placed himself in the nose of the boat to row. He looked behind him and saw they were not very far from the island. Snaggletooth helped Belladonna down into the longboat, and Ephraim grabbed her extended hand to help her settle herself. Normally, Belladonna alternated between luxurious, silk gowns or fitted trousers with flowing linen shirts. It would have been horrendous to anyone except the crew of the *Zodiac* to see her in the male garb she often wore. When she was in the mood for a silk gown and one saw her leave her quarters in it, every man knew it was best to keep away from her. The silk gowns she had onboard were stolen from Chinese merchant ships during raids on the Pacific side of the globe. Ephraim had not been around for the *Zodiac's* nearly two years of pillaging with her as captain, but he quickly learned that Belladonna's glamorous tastes had been satisfied by the loot that was taken.

Today, she was dressed in a simpler way. Instead of her fanciful silks, she wore plain petticoats that hid her shape. Ephraim could tell that this had a great impact on her mood, for Belladonna only wanted the finest of things or the most practical of things, depending on her daily mood. Despite her forlorn appearance and her very apparent dislike for what she wore, Ephraim could not ignore that she was still, in fact, perfect in every way.

"I see you have dulled down your looks today, Captain Skylark." He greeted her, half in jest. Belladonna did not appear amused.

"Let's make the best use of the time that we have while we have it, shall we?"

"Aye." Ephraim started rowing and looked behind him to gauge the distance while attempting to hide his embarrassment. His efforts to lighten the mood between them were often lost to Belladonna's coldness. He was hopeful that would change.

Even though they rowed a long time and were getting closer to land, Belladonna had not spoken a word. Maybe this time with her would not be so great, after all.

Port Royal was as lively as Ephraim remembered it to be. He marked the parapets that surrounded the port, canons aimed at the sea. Men and women of all sorts bustled about, most of them filthy from their lifestyle or from far too many nights spent in the taverns. Out of the corner of his eye, he could see Belladonna struggle to get even footing. Not since he knew her had she been on land, and according to the others on board, many years had passed before then without enjoying port city pleasures.

Ephraim offered his arm to her, which she willingly took. It probably hurt her pride to do so, but she would not be able to take two steps without his help. As they entered the narrow lane of taverns and inns, Belladonna looked around her anxiously. She kept a low profile at sea by being very strategic about who she attacked and where, and she never left any survivors to warn other pirates of her deeds. Her ears pricked, listening for the sound of her name being whispered among the passersby. All of this was nothing but paranoia, for Belladonna had no reason to fear the drunkards that flounced around her. Ephraim felt her grip tighten increasingly the further they walked into the city. He gently placed his opposite hand on hers.

“You must relax, Captain Skylark. I am quite sure no one knows your face here.”

“I cannot be so certain. Even though I have done well to hide my own tracks, there is no telling how many times Blackfoot has spewed my name out of his mouth when he stops.”

“Do you think Blackfoot so stupid to reveal his quest to humble men, as well?” It was a good question, and one that Belladonna obviously did not think about often. Just as she did not want others thwarting her, so Blackfoot probably wanted the same.

“‘I suppose you are right.” With this, she loosened her grasp on his arm. Tensing herself would only reveal that she was uncomfortable when really, playing the role of a traveler, she must make herself look at home among the revelry.

And so it was. The two were entirely unsuspecting. Their clothes were simple and their appearances even more so. To the men and women that moved about the island, they looked to be normal citizens—or normal pirates at the very least.

Ahead of them was a sign that read “Tavern.” Ephraim remembered it well and knew that it was frequented by a variety of people that claimed the sea as their primary home. He pointed to it and Belladonna nodded. They needed to begin somewhere. A famed tavern would help them blend into the folk around them.

The tavern was roaring with laughter, music, and friendly chatter. Belladonna’s nerves sat on edge. She was not used to this kind of environment, and really, she’d never had the chance to become acquainted with it because of her life hidden on the *Zodiac.*

What things have I missed because of my lot in life? She asked herself with self-pity. A sudden wave of sadness washed over her. She remembered how old she was now—nineteen by this date, she guessed—and that her Skylark name kept her from the world that everyone else lived. She surveyed the merriment around her. Her initial reaction was anger. There was an entire battle ensuing between peace for all and destruction for all, which they did not even know of.

Belladonna herself carried the peace of the people in the tavern on her back, yet none so much as even looked her way. Their fate rested on this young woman that stood among them now as a common traveler. How she loathed the way they lived so freely, without any earth-shattering consequence for their actions.

Ephraim caught the heat that was starting to radiate from her, the temperature rising higher with every minute that passed. He placed a hand on her covered shoulder, for that was the only way he could touch her without feeling the heat on his own hand. Doing so made his hand throb as he remembered the burns he suffered to his palms when saving Arimetta from her fiery clutches.

"Let's sit and get ourselves a drink. Then we can watch the room and see if anyone stands out to us." Belladonna nodded, coming out of her angst for just a moment, and they shoved their way to a table in the corner of the room. Even though she did not spend much time on land or in taverns, she knew that any decent pirate sat with their back to the wall to avoid any sneaking attacks. Ephraim came to the table with two glasses of some strong drink; she knew not what it was. Quickly, she grabbed a mug from him and took a swig. Whatever it was would numb her and that was all that she wanted in this room that she felt so lost in. Ephraim could see her brooding stare as she looked from person to person.

"Something troubles you," he said to her.

"I am absolutely disgusted by everybody in this room who takes their easy life for granted, which I know is every last one of them." After she said this, she picked her mug up and drained it. Ephraim widened his eyes in surprise.

"What do you mean?"

"I know that you know about what it is I am setting out to do. In fact, you serve a purpose to me, which I have not yet identified, but you play a part in it that is vital to who I will become. Surely it has not been hidden from you that I am to become Dragon empress of the Dragon Majestics on the Isla del Dragón."

"Aye, yes, I have heard briefly of your role there. And I knew the tales even before I found you."

"Then you know that the peace of all these forsaken people lies with me? Do you know that the only thing keeping them from a world of hurt is the very woman that sits in this corner? If I were to die here, right now—say someone came to me and rammed me through with their sword—Cornelius Blackfoot and his hideous Demonclaw agents would have the world to do what they wished. Yet, these know not. They live their noisy lives ungrateful for the sacrifices of the ones who have charted the course of their very lives."

"That may be very true indeed but consider this: most of the world thinks your kind to be a myth. Surely, they all have their gods and the ones they believe keep the peace, but they do not know about your kind. Your kind exists as exactly what you called it before: a pirate's tale that passes through the waters. And perhaps they will never know of the Dragon Majestics in their small lives. Do you feel you need recognition in order to fulfill your duty to your family name?"

"I do not expect recognition!" Belladonna barked back. "But it would do for these people to consider that the Dragon Majestics exist outside of tall tales. I can only pray that one day they will know."

"These people here do not think about where their peace comes from. If the world seems in good spirits, then they do not think of it. You have chosen to stop at a place that crawls with pirates. Had you chosen somewhere, like back home in England, you would see that their peace feels threatened by our very kind. You are among those right now who *are* the destruction of this age. Do not expect them to know any different right now. This is their peace for the moment, and they are too full of rum to know any better."

Belladonna reached for Ephraim's mug and tipped it into her mouth. She clearly wished to be among the drunkards at the present.

"I suppose you are right." Belladonna found Ephraim so agreeable. Her nature to argue her point vanished in his presence. Still, that did not mean she felt any better about the people around her. All that she had to accomplish seemed so unfair. This was not the first time she asked, *why me?* Some of what she felt for herself was pity, but mostly, it was a deeper question. Out of all people that would ever roam the earth, what qualified Belladonna to bear the Skylark name? And more than that, why did the Skylark name hold so much meaning? Maybe one day, when she was situated among the Dragon Majestics, she would hear the answers to these philosophical questions.

Why can I not live the lives of these common people? she wondered.

Ephraim would not push Belladonna to do what she did not want to. By dusk, the tavern overflowed with nighttime guests, and the noise was far beyond that which Belladonna was used to. Partially overwhelmed and partially fearful of giving too much away about herself, she never once moved from her seat, her back pressed against the corner of the tavern. Ephraim constantly looked at her, expecting her to make a move toward any of the guests. She drowned herself in drink after drink, yet she never seemed phased by its effects. He thought about what time it must be by now and decided that they had wasted many, many hours sitting in the tavern. Had Belladonna lost all motivation in those long-gone hours?

Finally, she looked at Ephraim after finishing off another drink, appearing glassy-eyed. "There must be an inn somewhere near here, or someplace we can sleep for the night." Ephraim looked deeply into her eyes, trying to see from what trance she must have just woken from. Did she not realize that many hours were wasted? How many of those hours had Blackfoot been able to get ahead of her, if at all?

"I thought we came here to find out about the Isla del Dragón?" He asked. "You have not moved at all and you have not inquired of any of these people. There have been plenty of them here for you to ask!"

"Well, it was in that time that I decided that every man and woman here is far too drunk to be asking such things."

"But there are plenty more taverns here that we can go to, surely some more sophisticated than this. I would hate for you to have wasted your day doing damn near nothing but indulging yourself." Belladonna cast her eyes on Ephraim and glared. She did not approve of his words.

"Watch yourself, Master Howell. Do I need to remind you once again that you do not speak to me thus?"

"My apologies, Captain Skylark. It was not my place to reprimand you." He glanced down at his hands wrapped around his mug and looked into it. He did not know if he was truly sorry. He was beginning to toy with the idea that Belladonna was not whiling away the hours without purpose. There was a chance, in his mind, that she was enjoying the welcome distraction of the lives around her, and maybe of his company as well. "But I would prefer that you call me by my Christian name."

"And what is that name again?"

"Ephraim." Belladonna had never forgotten his name like she made it seem she had. She relished the name, held it very close to her. She simply wanted to hear him say it.

"Now I remember. Ephraim." It felt even better to say the name herself. She had wanted to say that name aloud so many times before but had kept it locked in the back of her throat. Joy spread over her, and she allowed him to see her smile. For the first time in many, many moons, Belladonna began to laugh.

Ephraim laughed with her. The sound of her laughter surprised him just as much as it surprised her. "What is so laughable about my name?" he asked through his smile.

"I don't know. I have always wanted to say it. Now that I have, it feels odd." This made her laugh even more. There was humanity left in her. Her rough shell cracked a little when she unleashed her laughter. Ephraim could see her shoulders relaxing and her jaw unclenching. So much of Belladonna's demeanor, though most of it entirely true to her character, was put on. He had seen this immediately, from the time he met her. The insecurities that he saw before still existed. But he was beginning to do his job. He was cracking Belladonna enough for her to accept herself—to become Alauda. One day, she would shed the skin she wore in front of him and flourish into the magnificent empress she was predestined to become.

"It is an odd name, isn't it? It's from the Bible, but many think it sounds funny. Many pronounce it wrong as well."

"At least your name is not Belladonna," she blurted out. This sent both of them into roaring laughter, not too far removed from the cheer around them. "And for heaven's sake, look at poor Snaggletooth. He does not even have a real name!"

"He doesn't?"

"He did, he supposes, once upon a time, but he has been called Snaggletooth so long he has forgotten it!" Soon, they were both roaring with laughter until their sides ached. Neither of them had shared that much laughter with anyone for far too many years.

"My gosh, it feels good to laugh every once in a while!" Ephraim heaved as he wiped tears from his cheeks. "Thank you for that, Captain Skylark."

"You think it has been so long since you laughed? Imagine me! Stuck with those dull sea dogs on my ship. Snaggletooth provides me a laugh every so often but not nearly this hard." Without warning, Belladonna placed her hand lightly over Ephraim's. She turned to him. Her eyes seemed different. And her skin was not so consumed with its usual heat. "And please, if you would have me call you Ephraim, please call me Belladonna. If not just for tonight."

Her gaze stunned him. Her luscious green eyes spoke to his very soul. They said to him that they admired him, that they wanted him. Gooseflesh broke over Ephraim's skin.

"Aye," he agreed. She removed her hand from his and stood, ready to find a place to stay for the night. Quite honestly, Belladonna had not given the night much thought. What started as searching for clues to the Isla del Dragón had turned into an escape from her reality.

They fled into the street, pushing through the throng of festivities. Ephraim, encouraged by her hand over his in the tavern, grabbed the same hand and pulled her along behind him. He knew the city better than she and knew where they could stay for the night. In fact, he had spent many nights in the very place just a year before.

The greatest part about their walk to the inn was that not once did Belladonna object to his hand in hers. She clung tight, not letting go for a second. Ephraim's heart fluttered happily, allowing himself to be grateful for it. When they arrived before the inn, "The Resting Place," as it was so aptly named, Ephraim turned to her.

"Shall I put us in for two rooms then?" he asked.

"It might be more practical if we were to have one. It would help our cause, though no one seems to be onto us. Two lovers roaming the earth together would share a room, would they not?" Ephraim's cheeks flushed.

"I was not aware that part of our cover involved being two *lovers* that were traveling. I thought we were merely traveling together." He grinned at her, watching the stars in the night sky reflect in her eyes. Not a more lovely woman existed. "That makes sense then. I am curious to see how you will continue to alter our cover while we are here. Will we seek any counsel from anyone tonight or tomorrow on the island?"

"No, I have entirely rid myself of the notion that we will learn anything that is of importance to us."

"Don't you think you might be giving up too soon?" He furrowed his brow. What Ephraim really wanted to ask was, "What was your real reason for wanting to stop here?" He did not desire to probe too much into her mind. They had the night left still. Perhaps she would open up to him.

"Who knows? Maybe someone will stumble upon us that has seen the island for themselves? The night is young." Belladonna winked at him. Her simple gesture spoke volumes. From what Ephraim could tell, she had entirely given up tonight, overwhelmed by the goings-on around the island. A vast number of people ferried around, and none looked too bright to make their way to the Isla del Dragón, not even if they put forth a real effort. If someone like Belladonna, who earnestly sought the island, had trouble finding it, none of these simpletons could either.

Ephraim paid for one room—captain's orders—and they made their way to the room they would share for the night. When Belladonna opened the door, she was greeted by the musty stench of weary and forlorn sailors. In fact, the room did not smell much different than the men's quarters on the *Zodiac*. The smell was familiar to her and almost welcome; it made her think of the ship she called home. The small bed, covers folded down nicely after being freshly made, beckoned her. She was not sure she had ever slept in a bed that did not roll along with the waves, not that she could remember anyway. The features of the room were dim and dull. It was a place to rest one's head and nothing more. She plodded to the single window, just next to the bed in the middle of the room. Any man who laid upon that bed would open his eyes and be welcomed by the view of the port city. Though by no means a friendly or welcoming place, certainly not one for sophisticated travelers, one could never deny that it was still an island. The drawn curtains revealed the moonlit sea, its movement calm from the night, and the palm trees that decorated the coastline. Ships of all sizes bounced along the edge of the coastline while their anchors kept them in place. No matter how nasty this famed port city may be, she was willing to overlook it enough to soak in the exquisite view.

Quietly, Ephraim snuck behind her and looked over her shoulder. "It is a remarkable place, isn't it?" he asked. "I remember this view quite well from my time here."

"So this is where you called home before you stowed away on my ship?" For just a moment, Ephraim could hear the old Belladonna, the evil one, creep through her words. Her normal heat did not rise, though, meaning she was not angered. It was difficult to tell when Belladonna was speaking in jest, but her warmth often told someone everyone all they needed to know. It was one of her quirks that Ephraim was familiar with.

"You could say I haunted these very walls before I decided to haunt the *Zodiac,*" Ephraim laughed. "After I left the Navy, of course."

"Have they tried to find you?" she asked, still not looking at him. She was immersed in the bustling of the town outside the window. Ephraim sat on the edge of the bed.

"Presumably so. If they were to ever find me, they would undoubtedly punish me. Abandoning your post is forbidden."

"I think you did the right thing." Belladonna now turned to him. "To leave the Navy, that is. Your freedom was not your own there. Pirates create their own freedom. Ones that are not me, anyway. I do not have the freedom the others have. I am bound to my name and the duty it holds. But you—you have the seas at your fingertips. You could make a life of that freedom. I cannot say that I do not envy you."

"You love the sea."

"Oh, it is much more than that." She turned back to the open window, and Ephraim saw her hair blow in the slight breeze. "The one thing I have been able to love despite my black-stone heart is the sea. She has held me when I thought all I could do was fall. She has been the constant guardian in my life, protecting me from nature's forces and follies. We are kindred, she and I. Because even though she may roll and heave and move every which way, she does not change. She is always the sea. I am grateful to her for that."

Ephraim thought about this profound relationship. "And your captain before you? She showed you a glimpse of this freedom?"

"I do not speak of her." There was no anger in Belladonna's voice when she said this, which surprised Ephraim. From what he'd heard, her old captain proved to be a soft spot for her. "She was supposed to stay and never change, just like the sea, but she did. She, like all living things, passed on into the next life. I cannot say that I will ever forgive her for it; though, that is such a foolish thing to say. I know that mortal beings must die, but she did not feel mortal. She was freedom incarnate in my eyes. Starlene defied so much in life. And with her passing, my freedom passed as well, and I was made to know about the life I was bound to. Starlene was my freedom. Now, it is no more."

Her words were filled with sorrow. Ephraim felt that sorrow in his heart. Never had he felt such sympathy toward her situation. It was true; her life was not her own. Belladonna's life belonged to every living soul that would depend upon her for tranquility.

"I'm sorry," Ephraim whispered. At this, Belladonna scoffed.

"No one needs to be sorry for me. It is my burden to bear, and I must bear it to the end."

"You have more love in your heart than you realize, Belladonna. If you were truly as anger-stricken as you claim to be, you would not have made it this far in your quest. Clearly, you must feel some passion about your family, for neither would you do this if you did not think your parents deserved justice."

What he said was true. Belladonna did have more feelings in her heart that were *not* anger. However, little did Ephraim know at the time that her stirrings for justice and revenge and duty were slackening. The quest was so *heavy,* so difficult and lonely. What would happen if she threw up her hands in surrender?

But she would not tell him this. She would not tell anyone this.

"I hope you are right," Belladonna muttered. She felt the weight of his rough, scarred hands on her shoulders. Slowly, she reached up and turned one of them over and looked at it.

The palm was red and raised, pink flesh outlining old burns. "What happened to your hands?"

"You happened," Ephraim laughed. "When I stepped in to save Arimetta from you, I grabbed your wrists and burned the insides of both hands. It hurt to do my job for a few days after, but they healed nicely."

"It is still so difficult for me to remember that my very flesh burns those whom I touch. There is so much about myself now that I do not know. I'm sorry for hurting you."

"You should never be sorry for something you have no control over." Ephraim wanted to embrace her, to let her know he did not hold anything against her. Instead, she twirled around and made her way to the other side of the room. With her back facing the wall, she started unlacing the back of her gown. Not knowing what he should say or do, Ephraim blurted out: "Oh, uh, I can leave the room if you need a moment."

"No, it's no matter to me." Before slipping out of her gown entirely she brushed her hair behind her neck. Ephraim would not look in her direction but heard the gown billow to the ground. Clearly, within a matter of hours, the walls Belladonna had built around herself were falling. What was causing this to happen? He was sure that before tonight, she would never have done this in his company. However, he could not remain as he was all night. At some point, he would need to look at her. Seeming as she did not care, he carefully lifted his eyes from the ground.

Belladonna now sat on the edge of the bed that they would share. Her back was to him and he looked at the knots of her delicate spine. She was bent at the waist, removing her shoes. Locks of her scarlet hair hid the parts of her body that he longed to see the most. Then he noticed her thigh.

The Mark was horrific. Not in the way that darkness is horrifying to a small child but horrific in the sense that it told many tales without a word spoken. Her Mark, the green, reptilian thing, twisted up her thigh, looking up at its wearer. Ephraim could now fully believe in the dragon that was imprisoned in Belladonna's body. The horrifying part of it was that here she was, a human, yet underneath, she was the fiercest, vilest creature known to man. Who could ever say they slew a dragon, apart from the men in fairy tales?

Since its first mention, Ephraim had erased the Mark from his mind. He doubted he would ever see it with his own eyes. More than that, he did not imagine himself living long enough under Belladonna to see it. Snaggletooth warned him that he would believe in her majesty when he could glimpse and lay his hand on the Mark. And here it was, in the flesh, before his very eyes.

Alauda, he thought to himself. *She wears Alauda on her skin and that is what she will soon become.*

The very thought sent shivers down Ephraim's back. He backed against the wall as far away from Belladonna as he could. To be so close to someone—*something*—that possessed so much power and strength was frightening.

Belladonna heard him strike the wall with the back of his heel as he cowered from her. It did not take her long to realize why he had reacted to her this way. Looking down at her thigh, she traced the lines of the dragon on her leg.

"I used to despise her," she said quietly, "but I have grown to love her. She and I are one and the same. Besides that, she is so very unique. Who else can say they wear this on their skin?" She looked back at him inquisitively, clearly waiting for Ephraim to lower his defenses.

"That thing, that Mark, it frightens me. I can't say that I ever believed in what you were until I saw it just now. Snaggletooth told me I would not believe fully until I saw it and touched it. Its power is unimaginable!"

Ephraim almost seemed ready to bow down at her feet and beg for his very life. And even though Belladonna knew she would one day transform into the dragon that graced her thigh, she did not truly know her dragon-self yet. So much of her power was still hidden deep within her, without the knowledge to release it. Both of them, she and the dragon, could not be as powerful as they one day would be together.

His weakness plucked at her heart. She hated to see him afraid of her. Never had she cared so much for someone who looked at her and felt fear. All she wanted was for Ephraim to let go of his fear and come to her.

"Then you must come to me and touch it." Belladonna stood up from the bed and turned to him. Deftly, she stepped his way with her hand outstretched. Ephraim, still very much afraid, took in as much of her body as he could. Her curved hips swayed gracefully as she walked toward him. Her breasts seemed to shine in the moonlight. He could not move closer for fear that the dragon would strike him.

"She is not awake. She sleeps within me." Belladonna stepped slightly closer, her hand extended toward him. "You do not need to fear me. Only love me instead."

Ephraim felt in an ambivalent haze. All he ever truly wanted was to love her. Belladonna had done so much to prevent him from trusting her. Yet, he was willing to forget every stone she had cast his way, to overlook the monster that peeked through her eyes every now and then. He would accept Belladonna Skylark for who she was and who she would become.

The fear began to melt from him, and he placed his hand in hers. She backed toward the bed, never taking her eyes from his. When she sat, he sat down beside her. The hand that held his own guided him to the Mark. For just a moment he braced himself for the searing pain that so often unleashed itself from her skin. When he finally laid his hand upon it, he only felt the low, pulsating warmth that rose from her when she was at ease. The touch sparked an awakening in his mind. Without any doubt, now that Ephraim had seen and touched the dragon, he knew he beheld the next Dragon empress. The very idea of touching it just moments before drove him to quaking terror. Now, he regaled her, awestruck by this woman who wanted his love. His fingers gently traced every line of the dragon: the curves of the eyes, the bends of its scales, the points of its tail. At once he agreed; Belladonna was correct. What was once so horrendous that it was difficult to look at was now beautiful. His heart beat for her.

"If you want me to love you, does this mean that you would love me as well?" Ephraim asked. Belladonna did not say anything. She leaned into him, breathing him in, and placed her lips on his. Ephraim wrapped his arms around her and kissed her back. His right hand moved to her hair, and he twisted it around his fingers. Belladonna pulled away and pressed her forehead against his with her eyes closed.

"I have loved you for a long time, Ephraim, and haven't had the courage to face it until today."

"Why do you speak that way?" he asked, taking her face in his hands.

"I have not been courageous enough to let you in, to realize that I can still love someone who can leave me."

Ephraim frowned and brushed her hair away from her face, tucked it behind her ear.

"I will not leave you. I will stay to see you take your place as Dragon empress and love you through every part of your journey." Ephraim kissed her forehead. Belladonna did something she had not done in many years now.

Belladonna let tears fall from her eyes.

Ephraim wiped her tears away and smiled at her. He brought her face back to his and kissed her again. She climbed on his lap and unbuttoned his shirt. He slipped it off his arms and threw it on the floor. Still kissing her, he lay her down on the bed and lowered himself over her.

With her permission, and knowing that she wanted him, he would love her this very night as the Caribbean breeze drifted through the room around them.

Why is the ship not moving?

Belladonna's eyes fluttered open after she'd spent some time in her half-awake state. The world around her did not sway as it usually did. It was not until she rolled over that she remembered that she was far from her quarters on the *Zodiac.* She propped herself up on her elbows and looked around her. The sun shone through the window and lit the morning outside with a yellow hue. Next to her, Ephraim breathed steadily, still asleep on his stomach. As she lay back down, she ran her fingers over the striped scars that covered his back. Terrible memories of the day he received them came to the forefront of her mind. Ephraim did not appear to hold anything against her, but she could not help but feel an onslaught of guilt. One day in the past, not very far in the past, she grinned as she watched him grit his teeth through lashings from every man on her ship. It pleased her to watch him suffer. Now, here she was after a night of giving herself over to him completely. The tables had certainly turned, that much was true.

Arimetta saw Ephraim's importance early on when Belladonna herself had not. The prophetess had a hunch that she should let him live, that he would serve her journey in some capacity. Now, she was confident she understood Arimetta's cautioning.

Was Ephraim to stand beside her on the Isla del Dragón? Now that they had shared their bodies and souls with one another, did that somehow create an ability for him to become the Dragon emperor? Belladonna desperately wished she had someone to ask these questions to, but no one around her knew anything about the Dragon Majestics and their inner workings. She was alone in that regard.

But other thoughts, thoughts that lingered the night before, began to stir her. She thought about what she said to Ephraim the previous night about his freedom. He possessed a freedom that she would never even be able to taste. How common he was, so unlike herself. Her heart ached for the freedom that she was sure Ephraim took for granted.

What if I could have that freedom as well?

This idea penetrated all others. Her quest was long and tiresome. It would not get easier. In fact, it had never truly been easy. With so little to go on and so few resources, Belladonna was lost. The oceans she sailed were overwhelmingly expansive and new islands seemed to pop up out of nowhere almost every day. Her quest had started in the Pacific, went around the horn of Africa, then through the Atlantic, and into the Caribbean islands, and still, she had not found the Isla del Dragón. Her earlier doubts of its existence came to her again. What would happen if she gave all of it up after the course of one night?

Hardly any of her sufferings seemed worth it any longer. She was spending years of her life avenging the family she never even knew. There were certainly aspects of her quest that made it seem real and worthwhile, like the Mark and Arimetta's small bits of information, but it was far too great a task. Belladonna thought about what it would be like if she and Ephraim never went back to the *Zodiac.* Never in her life had she lain with a man, and now that she had, she felt the importance of the bond they shared. If they ran away together, far from where the *Zodiac* sailed, could they start a life together and forget the whole prophecy ever happened?

Belladonna found herself thinking of what a normal life would look like. She imagined them living somewhere remote, hidden from the dangers of the Royal Navy and her abandoned quest, maybe even with children. She thought about Romulus and wondered if there was any way she could free him. If she wanted to keep him, it could not be as a pet, for she would make sure he did not possess his magic—in case she could be located through him. Most of all, she thought about a life filled with love, love the way that it was meant to be shared between two people. Not at sea doing the devil's work, but in a home built with their own hands. As she continued to finger the scars on Ephraim's back, he stirred in his sleep.

These were such silly thoughts, she knew, but she could not keep her mind from wandering. For the first time in her role as captain, she did not care about what she was supposed to do. Her heart was empty of its passionate need for revenge and bloodshed.

All she wanted was to live free from the crushing weight she currently bore. And if she gave up her quest, would the burden follow her? Could the dragon-side of her stay suppressed forever, without showing itself?

By the time Ephraim started to awaken, she had it all figured out. They would get back on the *Zodiac,* acting naturally, of course. Belladonna felt her heart's rough exterior crack the more she let Ephraim's love wrap around her, but she was still capable of her usual cruelties. Not much changed on that front; her heart was still black for heaven's sake. Then, when the timing was right—perhaps at night—they would escape on one of the longboats, not too far from shore. Port Royal was not the place to escape to or else she would suggest staying. But for now, she would show that she was still entirely devoted to her cause. It was all she could do at the present.

Ephraim turned his head to look at her and smiled sleepily.

"Good morning, Captain." He muttered.

"I told you to call me by my real name," Belladonna laughed.

"Good morning, Belladonna." He rolled the name off his tongue sensuously. The way he said her name caused her heart to skip a beat. Her name had never sounded so sweet as it did when Ephraim said it.

"We must be getting back to my beloved *Zodiac* this morning." She began to sit up and brushed his hair behind his ears.

"Do we have to? Can we not just stay here forever?" Now, he sat up and planted a kiss on her forehead. If only Ephraim knew how badly she wished they could.

"Yes, we must. We still have an island to find."

"And what do we tell of our little stop-off for the night?" He clutched her hand and brought her knuckles to his lips and kissed each of them.

"I am the captain; they do not need to know anything. Being in charge has its benefits."

"Aye, you speak true. They do not have to know a thing about this then." Ephraim stood, wobbling on his sea legs still, and searched the floor for his clothes. Belladonna admired his slender hips and long arms. He was by no means the strongest man she knew, but she liked his lankiness. Belladonna slid gracefully from the bed and slipped her gown on. Before Ephraim opened the door to leave, she grabbed his wrist.

"For now, our romance will not be spoken of among the men." She did not mean to sound so stern, but finding herself caught between being captain and lover, she needed Ephraim to understand her. He bit his lower lip and nodded. A relieved sigh escaped Belladonna. Despite having to stay true to her post, she was pleased simply knowing that her love was returned. No fanciful displays of admiration were needed, just the knowing was enough to sustain Belladonna until they could run away.

Anchored along the eastern wall of the port was the *Zodiac.* Snaggletooth had stayed true to the task she had given him and now, the ship was marvelous to behold. Her careening was much needed. When the waves washed away from near her underside, Belladonna could see freshly scrubbed wood, not the usual barnacles and filth that clung there. Belladonna closed her eyes long enough to thank God that none of the sea's authorities had scoped her out while tucked into whatever hiding place Snaggletooth had found. Ephraim did not have to row the longboat very far before they reached her beloved ship. Snaggletooth stood hovering over the stairs as she made her way up and grabbed her hand to help her the rest of the way.

"She be a sight to behold, don't ye say so?" Snaggletooth shouted cheerfully.

"Aye, she is a work of art if I have ever seen one," Belladonna agreed, matching his cheer. "I am proud that you were not caught."

"Ye know that ol' faithful Snaggletooth is far too tricksy to get caught by any man." He was in an exceedingly jolly mood, and for once, Belladonna could match it. The time she spent with Ephraim had left her in good spirits. "Did ye learn anything useful about yer island, Captain?"

"Oh, lots," she lied. Ephraim smirked behind her. "I feel much better equipped to move forward."

"I will be glad to hear everything ye have to tell." Snaggletooth brought himself lower to her level and held her elbow, getting closer to her ear. "And I hate to be such a bother with ye just gettin' back and all, but yer prophetess be awake, and she has *seen* something of high importance."

CHAPTER 12
OUT OF THE DOLDRUMS

The voice that spoke in Blackfoot's mind came back. It struck like lightning, quick and unexpected. Blackfoot rested on every word once again filling him. For, far too much time had passed since the last words he'd heard.

He'd heard the voice frequently in the weeks before it had stopped speaking to him. Whoever it was that spoke had made his pursuit much easier. In fact, he had nearly felt as if he'd been cheating by allowing the voice to feed him the crucial information about the happenings on the *Zodiac.* However, Aranxta had known about the voice and had told him not to concern himself with its origin, which clearly meant it was all part of their grand plan for him.

Since the time the voice had then ceased to entice him with its words, Blackfoot had *lost* Belladonna Skylark. It happened within the time it takes one to blink. One moment, he'd been steadily charting his course behind the *Zodiac,* and the next moment, it was gone entirely from his sight. Blackfoot frantically searched the sea around him in all directions . . . but nothing. He was desperate enough to have his crew search the near horizons, but they could not find the ship either. It relieved him to know his mind, or the voice even, was not playing tricks on him by masking the *Zodiac.*

Her disappearance had been a mystery, but Blackfoot worried more that he could *hear* and *feel* the empty void in his head, free from the constant, lurking presence of the voice. That feeling of being watched faded, though he learned to deeply appreciate the feeling. It had been guiding him after all, and that guidance had been welcomed.

But after the silence came the doldrums. They began first in the center of his mind, where the voice had resided, and crept into his entire demeanor. Irritability was a trait of Blackfoot's no matter what day it was, but he sunk further into his misery with every minute of each passing day in which he did not hear the voice. His thoughts were empty and meaningless; he was unable to even think about how he would move forward from here. Utter hopelessness filled his heart. Some days, he thought that his moody sister had disowned him because of something he might have said to her at their last meeting; though, he could not think of anything that had been *that* offensive. The more he tried to think, the more he realized he could not think at all. Was he cast out forever from the Demonclaw that promised him so much? Was this his punishment for not killing the girl sooner?

The doldrums that brought Blackfoot's thoughts to a standstill were not just in his mind. *The Temptress* entered a short season of her own doldrums. Endless, tiring days were spent willing her to move out of the still waters that seemed to grab and hold her. The ship's goal was aimless. Nothing waited on the horizon as far as the eye could see. The crew, already restless to take part in pillaging, started to fall ill to the effects of cabin fever. When the ship would not move, there was no work that could be done. And no other ships had been seen for far too many days. Wherever *The Temptress* was, it was not the real world. Blackfoot's conscience slipped into darkness.

Is this purgatory? Is this what it is like to be rejected by both heaven and hell?

Then suddenly, in another blink of an eye—after what felt like an eternity—*The Temptress* moved with an alacrity that it had not possessed just a moment prior. And when she moved, the voice came to him.

"She has made berth off Port Royal with her lover. If you hurry, you will catch her. Now is your time."

As soon as the words filled his mind and settled in his heart, Blackfoot showed all his crooked, stinking teeth in a wide grin. The crewmembers around him who saw shivered, for Captain Blackfoot did not smile often, but when he did, mayhem was afoot.

Praise be, it calls to me again! he shouted in his head. Maximus, his first mate, approached him when he saw the evil smile spread across Blackfoot's face.

"I suspect it's back then?" Maximus inquired. Instantly upon hearing Maximus's high voice, the smile disappeared from his face.

"Aye, it is, but I don't see why you must concern yourself with it." Blackfoot reached for his scabbard, which he kept faithfully at his side, and Maximus cringed away. The captain was full of empty threats, too cowardly to make any sudden moves. Maximus knew these things, but his threats still dismayed him.

"You are right, sir, but now that we can move, I wanted to see if you had any commands for us, seeing as we have made it out of the doldrums."

"You can say that again," Blackfoot scoffed, removing his hand from the scabbard and resting it on the brass rail of the main deck.

"Where are we headed, Captain?" Maximus asked, more demanding this time. Much like everyone else on *The Temptress*, Maximus was eager for orders.

"How many of our men have been decommissioned for the moment?" Most of the men had been put on opium by the ship's surgeon to cure the cabin fever.

"They are starting to return to normal, sir."

"Good," Blackfoot snarled, "because I need every man on deck." All at once, the captain began to stomp on the main deck, summoning the men below from their hammocks, shouting: "I need every man to me now—all of you, even you half-wits and crazy lowlifes!" The men started coming out of the woodwork, some clambering while others strode confidently. "Lads, we are close upon her, and we will attack her at once! That girl has made a fool of herself and has weakened herself to love." At this, the men laughed. Was that not typical for a girl of her age? "The voice has come back and has told me exactly where she lies. We must chart a course to Port Royal and locate her. Then, we fight. And when we destroy her, the Isla del Dragón is ours for the taking!"

All of the men cheered, even the ones doped up on opium. Much like the Demonclaw did for him, Blackfoot promised a hearty reward for his men if they assisted him. Little did they know that he planned on slaughtering every single one of them before they could even catch a glimpse of the island. For now, he only needed them to help him get there. He could handle the rest of the quest, dragons and all, by himself. Satisfied with the unification of his crew for his cause, he removed his sword from its scabbard and raised it high above his head.

"We have made it out of the doldrums, and now, we seek paradise!" he roared, and the men cheered and raised their weapons along with him. Pride swelled in Blackfoot's heart. He had not forgotten his master plan for Belladonna, the one revealed to him when the Demonclaw assembled with him. Captain Skylark would be his to destroy once he enacted his genius plan, and the Isla del Dragón would lose its crowned victors once and for all.

Meanwhile, on the *Zodiac,* Arimetta was slowly moving out of the doldrums that had ensnared her. By the time she felt her mind clear enough, she felt the spirit that had lived within her for her entire life repossess her. She was alone when it happened, tucked away in the dark, damp crevice below the boat's life. As it had always been for her, not a soul was nearby to calm her rapidly beating heart as the spirit toiled with her. However tragic it was, she could at least be grateful that it had not killed her. Instead, it fought with her. Just as before, she could still *see* if she tried, and not with the spirit's eyes. When she tried too hard to *see,* it felt like arms were tightening around her, squeezing her until she felt her eyes would bulge. In her visions' place, the spirit would speak to Blackfoot, and she was powerless to stop it.

While Ephraim and Belladonna spent the night in each other's loving arms on Port Royal, Snaggletooth came to check on Arimetta as he was accustomed to doing while she was impaired. What he saw frightened him, and what he heard was even worse. Arimetta was clawing at herself with her disgusting fingernails. Her arms dripped with blood, which her hands then smeared all over her body. To an outsider, it looked as if she had killed an animal in the cell and then eaten it with her bare hands. The *voices* were unnerving. He could make out her own voice, pleading with someone.

Then he would hear the voice of something not of this world, something completely inhuman.

"Arimetta, stop! Stop yer scratching!" Snaggletooth went for the keys he kept at his side to open the cell to restrain the prophetess. He swung the door open with a loud clang and struggled to find her arms, all while the voices kept at their duel. Arimetta began to scream. She knew she was being grabbed but not by whom, the arms that tried to hold her felt like those of the spirit.

"Yuh hands offa me, ye spirit!" She begged.

"Shut up, you whore!" The unearthly thing said back.

Snaggletooth thought he had her tightly enough to keep her from cutting herself any longer, his clothes now covered in her blood as well. Just when he felt she would calm, her face turned to him and growled at him. Superhuman strength overcame Arimetta, and she nearly leapt from his grasp. He could feel her body tighten and spasm.

"I need a man down here! Any man!" Snaggletooth shouted. "And bring something for me to bind her with!" Several of Belladonna's crew raced down from above. Romulus followed, growling and groaning at the disturbance. When he saw Arimetta, the Hoodoo woman responsible for the cat he was, convulsing and scratching, he crouched into a defensive position and hissed. Snaggletooth took the rope from the men.

"Ye, grab her arm, and whoever else grab her other arm. We are tying her to the cell." Two of the men stepped forward, worried for their lives. Arimetta was frightening without trying, but this only added to their fear. Snaggletooth bound her left arm to one of the bars of the cell and then the other. Arimetta's head hung limply between her shoulders. Her chest heaved with great effort, exhausted yet again. Snaggletooth bit his lip. "It's back, ain't it?" he asked.

"Aye, deh spirit back," she responded breathlessly. Blood dripped from her arms. The version of Arimetta that was found among the taverns at Port Royal could have been considered clean compared to the Arimetta that stood before them now, bound and bloodied. "But Arimetta need deh captin. She gonna pass thru many storm. 'N deh spirit—it done told Blackfoot where she be. He comin' fuh her, 'n he comin' tuh finish her."

Belladonna quickly came down from the clouds after her night with Ephraim when Snaggletooth told her she needed to see Arimetta. *So she had lived.* Belladonna guessed she should be grateful for that. And she certainly hoped the spirit had not come back for her.

When she shone a lantern near the cell, she was forlorn. Arimetta was a wounded animal trapped in a cage, her torso thrust forward from where her arms hung.

"Why is she like this?" Belladonna asked. No one would answer her. A few of the men had been below to keep watch over her to make sure she did not break free. Belladonna's anger slowly seeped back into her veins, and her memories of the previous night were pushed aside. "What is the matter with her?" she demanded.

"The spirit has come back for her, and it wrestles with her greatly, much more than before," Snaggletooth replied sorrowfully. Romulus stood when he saw his master enter the room and brushed his head against her hand. Belladonna looked at the prophetess pitifully. Selfishly, she was sorrier for herself than Arimetta. Any clear-headedness that she might have had while the spirit was banished could have been useful to her, but instead, she'd left her down here to struggle. Belladonna wondered why she had not forced Arimetta for visions when she'd had the chance.

"Come closa, my chile," Arimetta wheezed. Belladonna snatched the key from Snaggletooth's belt and unbolted it. The men that stood around backed away, ready for the prophetess to come flying out. Instead, Arimetta remained suspended in her place. "Deh spirit gone and tell ol' Blackfoot where yuh is right now, 'n he means tuh come tuh yuh, ready tuh fight." She stopped to cough. "Deh demon have a plan, miss."

Dread washed over Belladonna. *Why did I not stay in Port Royal? Why did I not insist upon hiding?* Her motivation to continue was practically non-existent, especially after concluding she would abandon her post. Allowing herself to stop in Port Royal had been a mistake. She had let herself fall prey to distraction while simultaneously giving Blackfoot the upper hand. Now, everything she wanted before was coming to a head. And seemingly at the wrong time.

"He mean tuh take from yuh," Arimetta continued, "dat demon mean tuh wrap yuh 'round his bony finga."

"I will not let that happen. I will fight him until he is dead."

"Nevertheless, he come fuh yuh. Beware o' him." Her head lulled to the side, and she appeared to have dozed off. She came to again in an instant. This time, her nostrils flared, and she opened her mouth wide, inhaling some invisible cloud. Arimetta's eyes chilled Belladonna to her core; she could not see with her eyes, yet she was staring directly into Belladonna's.

"Yuh will pass thru many storms, Belladonna Skylark. Dis deh vision Arimetta alway had 'bout yuh. Pass thru deh storm, chile!" Arimetta was shouting. Her body shook and her bones rattled inside her. "Pass thru deh storm!"

"I remember you said this to me before. What does this mean?" She grabbed Arimetta's shell necklace and pulled her toward her. "We have passed through many storms, and none of them have led me anywhere. Speak clearly, devil woman!" Belladonna slapped her. Frustration had taken over her, and she did not have the control to suppress it. Arimetta never spoke directly and Belladonna could only assume her lack of clarity had led the *Zodiac* in circles. "What storm have we been through that has meant anything at all to this quest? Have we passed the damn island countless times?"

"Deh map. Go to deh map."

"I swear on my life that if you don't stop your empty prophecies and—" A hand fell on Belladonna's shoulder. Ephraim stood behind her when she spun. Her skin was fuming. Ephraim felt it through her clothes and pulled his hand away quickly before the burn spread to his skin again.

"You should do as she says. I think she is trying to tell you something," he cautioned her. "If she has made mention of a storm before and is now telling you to look at the map, then you might find an answer." Ephraim was the only one who could get her to think rationally, like he had done at other times when she was beyond rage.

"Come, Romulus, let us have a look at this map." She strode to the stairs and stomped up them, one by one, Romulus noiselessly slinking along behind her. Ephraim and Snaggletooth stepped out not too far behind her. She abruptly swung open the doors of her cabin and nearly ran to her desk. The map was still there, untouched unless Arimetta had performed some secret magic on it. Both men stooped over her shoulder and looked with her. Even Romulus rested his snout on the desk, eyes downcast and scanning the map. Belladonna sighed.

"Just as I suspected: nothing. Nothing has magically appeared. Arimetta is nothing to me until she puts forth an effort."

"No, Belladonna—" Ephraim stopped, looking at Snaggletooth to see if he heard him say her name. Snaggletooth had, indeed, picked up on it, and he gave Ephraim a knowing grin. ". . . listen to me. You are too blinded by your anger toward her to think clearly about this. What she said may be like a riddle or something with a double meaning. Have you ever thought about her sayings that way?"

"Why should she continue to waste my time with that nonsense? If she means to tell me what she sees in the future, she must tell me without playing silly games."

"Belladonna . . ." Ephraim came around to the front of the desk. He jabbed his finger at the map.

"What are ye doing, boy?" Snaggletooth wondered aloud. He was already thinking about what Ephraim said about riddles and double meanings.

"Look at the map hard. Every feature, take all of it in. You will find the meaning of her words." After Ephraim spoke, Belladonna took a deep breath. Meditating on bringing her flame back down, she closed her eyes. Between her angry burning and her burning anger, she could not think straight. Bringing her body temperature back down to its normal, steady heat would help her. Slowly, she felt herself simmering. The map was spread before her when she opened her eyes again.

She scanned the islands. Every port city she read aloud, she tallied on her fingers every island she named. Nothing showed the Isla del Dragón. All of these places the *Zodiac* had passed once or twice before.

But surely, the island would not be that easy to find if no man could go there. *Why have I not thought this way until now? I have always known this but never thought about it.* Now, she started to take in the little details of the map. Whales and narwhals marked the map in certain spots while thunder clouds hung over other parts. The cartographer had placed many things on this map, apparently in very specific locations. She started to wonder who the cartographer was when she saw it.

You will pass through many storms before you get there.

In the middle of the Caribbean Sea lay the illustration of a gigantic whirlpool. Coming out of its center was the head of what looked to be a great serpent, a massive sea creature residing within it. Upon closer examination, Belladonna's eyes widened, and she placed her hand over her mouth. It was not a serpent that twisted its way out of the whirlpool.

It was a dragon.

"I have been so blind and stupid," Belladonna said quietly to herself.

"Well, I'll be damned! The answer to yer most burning desire has been in front of ye this whole time." Belladonna cast an evil glance on Snaggletooth. "How have we missed that? The *Zodiac* has sailed those waters over many times, and we never seen it."

"Perhaps because you were not looking for it," Ephraim chimed in. "Ships usually stay well away from a monstrous thing like that."

"We have to get to this place, Snaggletooth!" Belladonna grabbed the map and jumped up. "I think it has hidden itself from us. That is how all of this works. No man has ever been there because it is hidden. Something opens it up to sailors that so wish to fall into it. Do you think Arimetta knows what it is?"

"I think Arimetta could be the key," Ephraim declared.

"You suppose that is why the Demonclaw cast such a burden on her family line? They knew part of the prophecy of it all was that a woman of her line would unlock it?"

"We have no way of knowing until we arrive at the spot." Snaggletooth sighed. "But me thinks we shall soon find out."

"I do not know that we have any evidence to support this. Just as so much of this quest has been, only time will tell." Belladonna paused here, thinking about Arimetta. Boldly, she offered herself as a guide to the *Zodiac.* In her tellings to Belladonna, she had emphasized her desire for freedom from the Demonclaw. If Arimetta really *was* the key, did she know that she was? Or worse yet, did she know she may never taste the freedom she so longed for? Belladonna started to feel sorry for Arimetta. If she was the one who could open the maelstrom and send her to the Isla del Dragón, she might have to die before freedom would ever be seen. These thoughts were unsettling; Belladonna did not want to believe what she was thinking. She hoped they were merely thoughts and nothing beyond that.

Ephraim sensed Belladonna's unease and leaned down close to her ear and brushed her cheek with his lips.

"It might not have to be that way," he whispered. "I pray it is simpler than that."

How is it that he already seems to know my thoughts? Their bond was growing stronger. Snaggletooth cleared his throat. Ephraim and Belladonna had both momentarily forgotten about his presence behind them.

"Shall we ask the prophetess what she knows of opening the maelstrom?" he asked.

"Not yet. I will not have her thinking about such things at the moment. For now, we must detain Blackfoot before we can get to the whirlpool. I will not allow him to ride my coattails as he has been doing for so long now. Besides that, we do not know if Arimetta is the key yet."

"Ye don't want to lose her, do ye?"

"Nevermind what I want!" Belladonna shouted, slamming her fists on the table before her. "This is the first we have made sense of the island's whereabouts, and we must get there immediately. We will worry about opening it when we find it. Tell the men to raise the sails and make haste toward the whirlpool. Let Alistair know he must start rationing, for by the time we reach that whirlpool, we will be far from land. And if Blackfoot runs into us along the way, I will kill him with my bare hands."

"Aye, Captain Skylark." Snaggletooth left the room, his mission clear. In his head, he had already marked the exact location they would need to be to find the maelstrom. Ephraim looked at Belladonna while her eyes remained fixed on the map.

"Are you confident this is where you must go?"

"Out of all of my wanderings in my time as captain, I have never felt more confident. How was I so thoughtless of these things?" She pointed out objects on the map that now stood out to her: the squid with tangled tentacles and the circle of sharks. "Have we passed through all of these spectacles and not even seen them all? I now feel confident of the island's location, but I have also never doubted myself such as I am now." Her hands began to shake. "This task is so great, and I am not prepared to finish it."

"But you are, my darling," Ephraim grabbed her hand, only mildly warm now. "You were born for a time such as this. It is in your very blood. You have learned much, and you will continue to learn. You were not born with all of the knowledge in the world. This is all part of your growth into who you will become."

Belladonna looked up into his eyes, full of love and hope. "Do you believe so? Truly?"

"More than anything." He bent to kiss her forehead. She closed her eyes, taking in his affections. It was true; Ephraim did encourage her. It was as if she was sailing to the far reaches of the map for him alone. Then she remembered her desire to flee. If she could get ahead of Blackfoot, or better yet never find him at all, then she would get away with him while she could.

Belladonna's heart was encouraged, but it was not still entirely willing to give all of itself to her inescapable future. Running from it was still an option. But she would have to act quickly.

CHAPTER 13
THE HEAT OF BATTLE

The thought that Captain Blackfoot may soon be out of her way was enough to fill Belladonna with a small degree of motivation. If killing him meant being one step closer to the freedom she so desired, then a fight would be worth every moment.

Belladonna left her quarters with Ephraim after their cartographic discovery to rally the men. Battle was just another part of pirating that the men were prepared for at all times. Unbound by any national laws, the men were willing to sacrifice their lives for sea-bound freedom. In fact, the adrenaline of battle was what brought many to the *Zodiac.* They would not hesitate to fight, even though they did not fully comprehend their reason for doing so. Belladonna kept her fair share of secrets concealed from her crew. About all they knew of their mission was that Cornelius Blackfoot, a notorious pirate in his own name, was following the *Zodiac* to the Isla del Dragón for some very important reason. Comparable to many who had crossed Belladonna's path so far in this tale, they sensed an importance to the task at hand; their bravery and fortitude pushed them to take part in something far larger than they could wrap their minds around. Such as it was, the crew never asked many questions or objected too much: they were pawns in a crucial game, yet they did not know how to play the game.

"Gentlemen!" Belladonna bellowed from her high place on the quarter deck. "Soon, if not today, we will fight. That bilge-sucking Captain Blackfoot will be ours, and we will reach the Isla del Dragón unhindered. He has found us once again through the spirit's voice that has so tragically fallen back upon our prophetess. But we need not worry; we need only to thrust our enemy through his heart and be done with him." Here she paused to share a glance with Ephraim. *Soon we will be free.*

"I need all my gunners at the ready and every able-bodied man on board to fight. Even those of you who do not normally fight, you must fight. *The Temptress* will come alongside us, and she must be met with cannon fire. No negotiations will take place between Blackfoot and myself. I am not willing to negotiate with a man who wishes for my life to end at the tip of his sword. Defend your fellow man, all of you! Save yourself as well as any others! We cannot afford to lose anyone. And if you should happen to face Blackfoot, do not engage him. I would so desire the opportunity to kill him myself. He will not know what to think when a Skylark slits his throat end to end. Down with *The Temptress*; down with her minions, and down with Cornelius Blackfoot!"

"Down with Blackfoot!" All of the men shouted. The buzz that circulated among the crew was evident. The chance to pilfer and pillage was enticing enough, but to kill one of the sea's most well-renowned captains was another.

"Hoist the colors, lads!" Snaggletooth shouted. The crew began to scurry around the main deck, prepping their weapons, hauling cannonballs and barrels of powder. Belladonna watched as two of them began to raise the flag that Starlene so proudly designed. Watching the flag ascend the mast and into the sky never failed to thrill her. In her career as captain, and in her life aboard the *Zodiac,* anticipation kept her motivated. The fight ahead was one of her sole motivations now as she hoped Blackfoot would soon be no more. Then she could break loose from the debt she previously thought she owed.

She moved to the aft of the quarter deck and leaned on the brass rail. It struck her that she should try to seek Arimetta's counsel. Maybe Arimetta had good news about the battle ahead. Then she remembered that Arimetta could lose control of herself now at the drop of a pin. Arimetta was practically useless now. Hopefully, she could protect herself if it came down to that.

Or maybe the Demonclaw will keep her alive so they can continue to use her as their puppet.

The bustling on the main deck pulled her away from her thoughts of Arimetta and she noticed Ephraim standing beside her, hand resting on the hilt of his sword at his side.

"Shall I man the swivel gun above?" he asked.

"Yes, I want you and you alone on the swivel gun. Have any other men you have trained on the gun deck with the cannons. As soon as Blackfoot comes alongside us, command the men to fire a broadside at my command."

"Aye," Ephraim looked at her longingly, seeing that his love was lost to her thoughts. "What troubles you so? I can see it on your face."

Belladonna was not ready to tell Ephraim her plan to snatch him and run into a world that was entirely different from the one they were in. Would he think less of her for wanting to give up her pursuit of the Isla del Dragón? Or would he be relieved because he wanted the same? Now was not the time to discuss the matter.

"I just want to send Blackfoot back to the hell that spat him out into this cruel world." She leaned on the railing again, rocking as she did. Her nerves were building.

"You know the prophecy: you are meant to crush him with your own foot."

"But I wonder if that will be what happens today. I feel in this black heart of mine that it won't be so easy as engaging in one battle. Besides Arimetta's vision that she shared with me when I stood directly in front of Blackfoot, I have never faced him in the flesh, which is why I feel like this may be a fight to begin the rest of our fights. That this fight is only the beginning."

Ephraim gave her a sorrowful look, unsure what to say. He could not deny that out of all of them, what Belladonna felt mattered most.

"We will find out by the time the sun sets. You are stronger than you want to believe." Ephraim took her hand and kissed her fingers. Belladonna drew him close and kissed him with a passion that frightened him. He did not know why the kiss left such an uneasy taste in his mouth, but he accepted it all the same.

"Ephraim," she whispered, "I love you. And thank you for being who you are." There they stood in each other's arms, foreheads pressed together. Ephraim's heart fluttered upon hearing her soft words. This would be their last quiet moment before tragedy struck.

"I love you, Belladonna." Both felt a nudge at their waists. Romulus butted his head between them and rubbed against Belladonna's legs, a low purr rumbling through his body. When he peeked through the rails, he bared his teeth and his purr turned into a growl. The pair looked out over the rail into the vast sea that fanned behind the *Zodiac.*

In the mist that lurked over the deep, still far enough away to seem like a menacing mirage, a ship hove forward. Its colors were raised, but they were still too far to be seen.

Belladonna's stomach churned. She did not have to see the colors to know that it was *The Temptress* that crept toward them.

"Is that him?" Ephraim asked, moving away from Belladonna to look closer.

"It can be no one but him," Belladonna grunted. "And I pray this may be the last time I see that bloody ship on my tail." She turned and dashed across the quarterdeck to find Snaggletooth. Snaggletooth was already looking at her, prepared for what she was going to say.

"She is moving in on us."

"*The Temptress* comes forth, ye men of the sea! Ready yer positions and prepare yer weapons! We fight as soon as she be alongside us!" Snaggletooth grinned. The love of a fight had not left him yet in his older years.

When Belladonna came back to the railing with Ephraim, he squinted at her.

"What do we do now?" he asked.

"We wait. We wait for the fight to come to us."

The *Zodiac* bobbed along the water in the dreadful silence that filled their waiting. The crew, some nervous and some anxious, held their positions, ready to fight or fire. Ephraim had made his way to the single swivel gun on the port side of the deck. The plan was a simple one, one that many pirates had used before. As soon as *The Temptress* got within firing distance, and at Belladonna's command, they would fire a broadside at her. Belladonna did not concern herself with Blackfoot's plan. She only cared that the men of the *Zodiac* defended her well enough to keep her unharmed. This meant pounding Blackfoot's ship with as much cannon fire as possible. Quite honestly, Belladonna did not care so much about destroying the ship itself. She wanted Cornelius Blackfoot in her clutches at whatever cost. If that meant killing every man in his crew or sinking his ship, then that is what would be done. If this were to go the way she wanted it to, none of those things would have to happen. She would make her way to Blackfoot quickly and slice his throat, reveling in the blood that would spray on her as his life ended. Blackfoot had killed every person, known or unknown, that would matter in her life. She did not remember her parents and had never met her long-begotten brother. Starlene was wrenched from her life by his doing. Not another soul would she lose to him. And it was time for him to pay for the blood he had shed.

An eye for an eye, a life for many lives.

As *The Temptress* churned toward Belladonna and her crew, silence permeated the air. Belladonna's hair whipped around in the ocean air. The only noise that could be heard was the slapping of the full-masted sails and the creaking of the wood. From a distance, the *Zodiac* would have seemed to be a ghost ship, floating along in the Caribbean without a soul aboard. But Blackfoot was wise enough to know the *Zodiac* was full of life. Life that he meant to annihilate.

Belladonna's heart pounded in the waiting. Many merchant ships were conquered under her flag, yet none of her encounters with the merchant ships would be like the one that awaited her in mere moments. The merchant ships were almost always ready to surrender upon seeing her Jolly Roger fly, knowing they would undoubtedly lose against a pirate ship.

Unlike those situations, Belladonna was currently a sitting duck. The *Zodiac* tread lightly on the surface of the ocean, waiting for her fight. It was foolish to fight this way, she knew, but she was more than ready to conquer *The Temptress* and be done with the miserable business.

Ephraim stood beside her and would remain there, along with Romulus, until the ship got within shooting distance. Part of Belladonna's plan was to appear willing to negotiate before any blows could be exchanged. The captain could not hide the smirk on her face. With the way that Blackfoot moved so seamlessly into this fight, it was almost like he wanted the affront. But what tricks did he have up his sleeve? It could not be so simple as it seemed.

When *The Temptress* seemed about a league away, Belladonna grabbed Ephraim's hand and gave it an affectionate squeeze. Ephraim hoped that she would look into his eyes before he left her side, but she would not. Her gaze was fixed upon her enemy. Ephraim could not be angry about that. He tromped back to the swivel gun that would face *The Temptress* when she came alongside. Just as he told the men he would, he stomped a tune with his foot, the gun deck directly below him, telling the other gunners to be at the ready. This is how he would communicate with them from his place above them.

Snaggletooth looked through his telescope to see if Blackfoot had hoisted his flag. When he saw it, he cringed. The Jolly Roger that stood out on the black flag had a long, slithering tongue that jutted out of its mouth. He thought about the serpent that tempted Adam and Eve in the garden of Eden. That serpent had been full of deception and sin. Those qualities seemed fitting for Cornelius Blackfoot. Snaggletooth burned now with a rage akin to Belladonna's as he thought about the man—the thing—that had killed his beloved Starlene. *Down with Blackfoot,* he said to himself.

The rest of the crew urgently said their last rites among themselves. Belladonna did not like that they seemed so doubtful of their survival. She needed them to be courageous warriors, not dead men walking. Quickly, she pushed her worries about them aside and focused on Blackfoot's approach.

Finally, the man that she so hated came into sight. He stood about where she did on the quarterdeck of his ship, arms outspread, seeming to welcome her. From Arimetta's vision, Belladonna remembered his ugliness. Blackfoot's black hair blew behind him and he smiled, showing his disgusting, pointed teeth. The captain was tall and lumbering over the rest of his crew and appeared rawboned. His crew seemed weak and fragile but that meant nothing. They could have been Trojan warriors, and she would not have known. Blackfoot opened his mouth and stepped closer to the railing of his ship, meeting her gaze. Ephraim looked at her waiting for her signal for the broadside, but she held her hand out at her side letting him know to wait just a little longer. Belladonna wanted to know what he had to say.

"At long last, here is the unknown child of Jade and Abraham Skylark, emperor and empress of the Dragon Majestics, who were once gloriously seated as such on the Isla del Dragón. How lovely it is to finally behold thee." Blackfoot spoke in a raspy, theatrical voice and bowed to her. Belladonna responded only with silence.

Even the demons believe.

"Now, now child, there is no reason to be so silent. Such a chance as this does not happen often in one's lifetime. Perhaps we could talk this out, make it work for both of us." The Demonclaw accomplice laughed as he spoke, and his crew laughed with him.

Now they mock me.

"You are a beautiful lass, maybe you would like to come a little closer for me to lay my eyes upon? I am sure you are a real treat underneath those sailors' pants." Now Blackfoot roared with laughter. Belladonna felt the hatred brew; her skin was reaching an unbearable temperature. Oddly, she felt the need to rupture, to break free from her own skin. That power lay within her but she did not know how to use it, not yet at least. Something much larger than herself had awoken from its slumber in her heart.

"What do you want, you old goat?" she yelled, spit flying from her mouth. "Have you come to mock me? I know that is not all you wish to do with me this day."

"Show me the Mark on your leg. That way I know that you are one of the true Dragon Majestics and not just some hopeful admirer."

"You want to see the Mark, eh?" she smirked. "Are you sure of that? I would not want you to suddenly fear me before a fight." This time, her own crew laughed—all except Ephraim. He did not take too kindly to the idea of her revealing the dragon when it had been such an intimate experience to him before. Now she would bare it all before her crew, finally showing them what she was and confirming to her enemy that his hunt was real.

"Let's see it and be done with it," Blackfoot raged, "then we can get to the good part. The Isla del Dragón, that is."

Belladonna looked around her, the crew boggling at her. The Mark had been part of the tales passed around among pirates when speaking of the Dragon Majestics. But now, they would see that it was, indeed, no myth. One of the Dragon Majestics was their captain.

Ever so slowly, Belladonna began to roll up her pant leg from her leather boot. She took care to do this seductively, serving as a distraction from the broadside that would soon be fired. From

The Temptress, she heard whistling and hooting laughter. A playful smile spread across her face, beckoning Blackfoot's crew to watch closely. The dragon started to reveal itself, first its tail, then its scaled body, all the way up to its head and ever-watchful eyes. Now Blackfoot's crew gasped and jumped away from the railing, petrified of the proof that lay before their eyes.

Blackfoot remained unmoved, arms crossed over his body.

"See men, you have no reason to fear her," Blackfoot cried. "Look how she is quick to show her legs like a whore."

A mixture of anger and eagerness swirled in her. This was what she wanted from Blackfoot. Steadily, she flicked her wrist at Ephraim. He readied himself behind the gun, prepared to fire. He stomped his foot once to the gunmen below.

"It is such a pity," Belladonna clicked her tongue, "for you will soon see that I am no whore."

"*FIRE!*" Ephraim shouted.

A boom, loud enough to shake the earth, fired from the port side of the *Zodiac.* Belladonna felt her ship sway from the heat she unleashed on her victims. When the ship settled again, she removed her hands from her face and looked toward *The Temptress* but saw that the air before her was filled with only smoke and ash. Across the water, the other ship was silent. Out of the smoke and after just a moment of ear-ringing silence, grappling hooks flew upon the railing before her. The silence broke with the loud and sudden roar of men on the move.

"Here they come, men!" she yelled. "Brace yourselves!"

Blackfoot's men scurried across the lines and climbed onto the *Zodiac,* screaming and snarling with their knives between their teeth. Belladonna and Snaggletooth pulled their pistols from their left sides and their swords from their right. The chink of the unsheathing metal overjoyed the captain. The *Zodiac* had gone far too long without combat.

Swords clanged as the men of the *Zodiac* advanced to the fight. Bullets whizzed through the air, close enough to their ears that they felt as if they had been grazed. Romulus roared loudly, leaping into the air to attack his welcome prey, seeking to shred them apart with his massive claws.

Side by side, Belladonna and Snaggletooth fired their pistols at the base of the mainmast, their backs against it to cover themselves on one side. Sailors ran at them with their swords drawn, ready to run them through. Effortlessly, the captain and quartermaster blasted or dashed through everyone that came their way. The *Zodiac* rocked again when the gunners unleashed another round of cannon fire. Ephraim swiveled around to the deck and removed his sword from its hilt, slashing any of Blackfoot's men that came near enough to try to remove him from his place.

Amid the uproar and chaos that ensued around her, Belladonna noticed that their cannon fire was not being returned.

That man is an imbecile. He must want to perish.

The smoke around them was choking them, but the men fought hard. After each man that she destroyed who came her way, she made an effort to check her surroundings. What she saw reminded her of the battle that Starlene engaged in on the day she died. Belladonna had grown so much stronger since then. The only difference was that now, she was unmoved by the violence that was settling in around her. Blood squelched under her feet as she moved away from the mainmast. Taking turns between her pistol and her sword, she cut down anyone that stepped in her way. In the heat of battle, she had forgotten about her sole aim in the fight. Belladonna looked for Blackfoot. She wanted his blood to paint her deck next.

"Shall we keep firing?" Ephraim yelled to her. "They have not returned anything!"

"Is she disabled?" Belladonna asked back as she thrust her sword through a small, staggering man that jumped in front of her. He fell on her, the sword sticking out of the backside of his body, and she shoved him off. Blood sprayed her face.

"Just enough to slow her down."

"Fire off two more rounds then leave it be. His ship is not our enemy. It's him we are after!"

"Ready your guns, men!" Ephraim shouted and stomped on the wood beneath him. He loaded his gun and aimed it at what he assumed to be Blackfoot's quarters. Pulling back on the gun, he watched the cannonball fly toward *The Temptress* and shatter through the windows of Blackfoot's quarters. He cheered, loving every moment of this fight. "To hell with Blackfoot!"

Belladonna moved away from Ephraim, past the foremast, and stood in the middle of the main deck. From what she could tell, Blackfoot had more men than she. However, most of the bodies that sprawled on the deck around her were not any she recognized. Her crew was doing fine at the moment. Her efforts needed to be concentrated on Blackfoot.

Still with his back against the mainmast, Snaggletooth was firing off round after round, hardly missing. Belladonna came near him and asked him: "Quartermaster, have you seen the captain?"

"No, I have seen no trace of him. Maybe ye should advance on *The Temptress.* I feel he is hidden." Snaggletooth blew off the head of the man that ran at him with a single shot. The body staggered and fell to its knees as if in worship to Snaggletooth.

Harsh buzzing broke the air above and fell upon them.

"Powder flasks!" someone shouted. Small iron grenades dropped on the *Zodiac* and hummed before exploding. Any man that stood near one was blown back. Belladonna watched one of her men get blown back and stabbed through his middle with the sword of the man that stood behind him.

"Why does he not fight back with cannon fire?" She asked aloud to no one in particular. *The Temptress* was suffering much damage at the hands of Ephraim and his gunmen. What would the powder flasks do in comparison to cannon fire?

He does not want to engage, she said to herself. *He has a strategy of his own. As thoughtless as it may be.*

She would not risk boarding *The Temptress.* Blackfoot could have many things planned.

Right now, it seemed his plan was to lure her onto his ship as he hid from her, waiting for her to cross his hidden path to attack her without prior notice. No, she would not fall into his arms. Not that easily.

But to kill him would be such sweet victory. After all, that is why she fought in the first place. Maybe wiping out his entire crew and destroying his ship would be enough to disable him for good.

She wondered how far he could make it without these two vital aspects of his journey. Unnoticed by anyone around her, Belladonna slipped belowdecks. First, she came to the gun deck. The men appeared to be preparing for their next shot, bustling with cannonballs hung low between their arms, ready to be loaded. She descended deeper into the ship. Blackfoot would not hide anywhere that was occupied by her own men. She wound her way deeper into the ship, passing through the sleeping quarters and down to the hold. Belladonna heard screaming in the damp darkness. *Arimetta.* The prophetess wrestled with the spirit more than she ever had now that her two masters were within close proximity to her. The cell rattled wildly. For a brief moment, she thought to ask Arimetta if Blackfoot was with her, caressing the face of his guide like she was his loving pet.

"Him do not know it is Arimetta dat speak tuh 'im!" Arimetta cried. The Hoodoo woman felt Belladonna's presence from the excruciating heat that rose from her body and sought to answer her internal questions. Belladonna trusted the voice that spoke, for it was Arimetta's and not that of the spirit. It was the same voice that had spoken to her through her *tellings*. Blackfoot was not hidden on the *Zodiac*. Where was that wretched thing?

As she came back on deck, the number of men piled in their own blood had grown. The *Zodiac* still seemed to have the advantage. Not one spot on the deck was free of blood. In fact, it had started to trickle down the sides of the ship, making the *Zodiac* appear to be a mobile battleground. Belladonna was sure *The Temptress* looked worse with its gaping holes and torn sails from her gunners.

Ephraim popped into her thoughts as she looked away from the blood that soaked beneath her. The stand behind the swivel gun was empty. Now that she had a moment to realize this, she wondered why she had not heard cannon fire in a while. She pictured the men below, fuses ready to light the cannon and blast Blackfoot's ship, waiting for Ephraim's signal. Ephraim was knowledgeable about combat, and she assumed he had a plan. Perhaps now, it was necessary for the gunners to fight with their hands and abandon the destruction of *The Temptress*. After all, Belladonna had re-emphasized that destroying the ship was not the primary focus.

Her sword continued to fly, injuring and killing Blackfoot's men. Her strength was fading and she was seeing double. Every move she made felt pointless if Blackfoot himself was not the one suffering. Belladonna was filled with bloodlust, and her skin smoldered from the fire in her bones. How desperately she wished she could peel the skin from her bones and break free from her fleshly bondage. The dragon wanted to spread its papery wings and soar high in the sky, spraying fire down on *The Temptress* and in turn, on Blackfoot.

I am far too underequipped for this fight, she admitted to herself.

When she willed herself to muster more strength, a shrill whistle pierced through the atmosphere. At the sound of the whistle, any man of Blackfoot's that still stood paused. Ones injured and lying on deck began to crawl toward the grappling hooks that still held to the railing. The others that could use their legs scampered quickly to the lines they had cast and jumped on them. The last man to climb on one of the lines would cut it, leaving the grappling hook attached to the *Zodiac, and* drop to the water while those who stayed behind on *The Temptress* pulled them back. Dumbfounded by the quickness with which Blackfoot's men moved, Belladonna's crew froze. In less than one minute, every last man that could still move had made their way back to Blackfoot's ship with militant timeliness.

Anyone left on the *Zodiac* peered around the deck. Bodies of still-bleeding men slumped over the rails, over loose barrels. Much like the battle that took Starlene's life, limbs lay strewn all around. Dead eyes from severed heads looked up into their murderers' eyes. But the blood, the blood was insufferable. Snaggletooth felt himself wading in it, sliding with each step to look over the side. The *Zodiac* was painted all down her sides with it. Death's stench permeated the nostrils of every man still alive.

The crew began to cheer when they realized their victory. Considering the bodies that lay dead were not their own, they had essentially immobilized their opponent. It sickened Belladonna to listen to them cheer. In her mind, this was far from victory. Not once had she lain eyes on Blackfoot during the scrimmage. More than that, she had not killed him herself. The thought that maybe one of her men took that responsibility upon himself engulfed her with even more internal flame. Blackfoot was hers and hers alone to destroy.

"Shut your mouths, all of you!" she called out. Her men fell silent. Before she had a chance to ask if any of them had slain Blackfoot, one of her sailors, John-Boy, cried: "She sails away! *The Temptress,* she sails away!" He pointed frantically in the direction of Blackfoot's battered ship. Astonished by his words, Belladonna ran to the railing and watched.

As sure as the turning of the tide, *The Temptress* began to steadily advance forward.

Unlike the *Zodiac,* she was not bloodied, but she was badly damaged.

"Angels in heaven!" Snaggletooth gasped beside her.

Belladonna could not believe what she saw. Blackfoot's ship had withstood enough damage to sink her. Yet she cruised forward and away from the fight, smoke trailing behind her. The colors had been lowered, and no flag of surrender had been raised. *The Temptress* would continue on her quest, and her captain along with it.

"It is impossible," Belladonna murmured. "How does she still float?" Her men buzzed. No matter how closely Belladonna tried to look, there was no trace of Blackfoot. But she knew that he was not dead. Her stomach tightened with rage. Blackfoot was still breathing, and now he was getting ahead.

Their fight was not yet finished.

CHAPTER 14
AFTERMATH

"I did not kill him," Belladonna said aloud, turning to Snaggletooth, who stood behind her now, watching their enemy flee.

"Not a soul saw him, Captain. He kept himself locked away it seems."

"What a coward," She said between gritted teeth. "Cannot even face his own enemy. Did he not do the same with Starlene? He did not kill her himself. That creature is as helpless as they come. Yet, I still did not kill him."

"Something tells me we will be crossing paths with him once again." Snaggletooth's chest heaved with the effort of battle, his age revealing itself in his struggle to slow his breathing.

He still stood, and that was enough for Belladonna.

"Oh, we will certainly be crossing paths with him. More than a handful of times, I fear. I seem to believe that I am not meant to finish this fight until we reach the shores of the Isla del Dragón." Belladonna noticed a sickness swirling in her gut. The longing to escape from her task tugged at her. With Blackfoot still on the move, her escape was further away than before. How badly she wished she and Ephraim had stayed at Port Royal! None of this would have happened if she had stayed. *Let Blackfoot have what he so searches for,* she thought. *Let him have it and let my miserable part in this be finished.*

No matter how she wished for that, her furiously black heart told her otherwise. All she wanted was for that heart of hers to be ripped from her breast. It told her things she did not want to hear: that she must finish her mission to completion, that she must bring justice to the Skylark family. It also told her that she would face Blackfoot again. A small, quaint corner of her mind wondered if Blackfoot would end up killing her. She knew the prophecy, that much was true, but what if such things were not meant to happen? What if the prophecy was created to destroy her and every Skylark after her, once and for all?

But no, she must carry on. She must do what she set out to do at whatever cost. No matter how much she longed to live a quiet life with Ephraim.

"We must assess the damages to the ship, Captain," Snaggletooth said, taking her away from her conflicting thoughts.

"He searches for the maelstrom." Belladonna turned back to the railing and watched *The Temptress* grow smaller ahead of them. Romulus approached her now, swaying with exhaustion, his snout bloodied. She stroked his ears. "He knows just as well as I where it lies. Do you suppose Arimetta told him? That spirit in her needs to be silenced again."

"Me thinks he always knew where it was. He wanted to follow ye. I believe him to be drawn to ye."

"Only because he is my sole enemy. Blackfoot lures me along with him. It is all part of his grand scheme." Belladonna turned and examined the bloodshed around her. She noticed the abrasive tear in her foresail, the damaged teak from the powder flasks underneath her. Then there were the bodies—and the blood. Vast quantities of blood. The crew would have to make repairs on the move. The *Zodiac* could not afford to stop now, not when Cornelius Blackfoot had the advantage.

Belladonna walked away from the railing. The shrouds that attached to the sails were slashed, some of the rope burnt. Thankfully none of the sails beside the foresail needed repair.

All of the bodies, and the parts of bodies, would need to be tossed overboard to the sharks.

Countless man-hours would be spent swabbing the deck of the blood and other body matter that soaked the wood. As she looked at the faces of the dead men she tried to identify which belonged to her and which to Blackfoot. Fortunately, she did not see very many familiar faces.

"How many have we lost?" she asked Snaggletooth.

"I have counted nine, at least. Others are injured and need to be looked after. But we were lucky to not lose more than we did."

"That is because those men were not ready for a fight. Blackfoot had one plan. He sought to board my ship and negotiate the way some captains do. Whatever that plan was, I cannot figure it. And I still am not sure if he stepped foot on this ship to see his plan through." Now, she stopped to look at the men surrounding her. Every one of them looked startled. She still needed to address the fact that every man on board now knew that she was one of the Dragon Majestics and their purpose in sailing for the Isla del Dragón. "Gentlemen, all of you have gained some helpful insight into your role on my ship. Your captain is a Dragon Majestic, and I seek the Isla del Dragón to take my rightful place there. I cannot guarantee your safety, or your life, from this point forward. However, that is a risk you took when you signed the articles. All of you know that your life is not guaranteed in this business. I hope that each one of you will stick with me to the end. Whether you die or live, I am sure that the Dragon Majestics will reward you handsomely, in the afterlife or in this life. Do you understand me?"

"Aye!" Many of them yelled, some feeling disgruntled and others filled with excitement. They would have to process what they now witnessed on their own. Belladonna did not have time to explain any more than she did.

"Now, where is my boatswain? I must speak with him about the work that must be done while we chart a course toward our destination." Here she stopped, glancing at each man. None spoke and none stepped forward. She could not see Ephraim anywhere. "Is he down below with the guns?"

Mace, who had taken a liking to Ephraim since he first appeared on deck many months ago, stepped forward. He was the only witness to what happened during the fast-paced battle. He sighed, his heart grieved by what he would have to say. Mace cared for the boy and did not want to speak about what he'd seen. In fact, he still did not want to believe it. Not one of the crew besides Snaggletooth knew what the boy meant to their captain. They would soon find out.

"Captain Skylark," his voice broke as he spoke, "I saw Captain Blackfoot take Master Howell to his ship." The other men gasped. Belladonna's face melted in unhidden horror.

"Were you the only man who saw this?" she wanted to know. Her voice wavered.

"Aye, I believe so. Blackfoot came over the rail when Master Howell's back was turned away from his gun, and he smothered him with something. I am not sure what he used. But Master Howell struggled for only a moment before he appeared to be unconscious. Then Captain Blackfoot dragged him away to his ship. Master Howell is on *The Temptress* with that devil!"

Belladonna's breath caught in her throat, and she felt her heart stop. This news was far beyond anything she could stand. Slowly, she sank to her knees on the deck before her crew. Never had the crew seen their captain in such a vulnerable position. She had put on such a powerful front since Starlene's death that she seemed impenetrable. Devastation swept over her for the first time since that dreadful day.

Before she could attempt to speak, she looked up at the hazy afternoon sky. The sun was creeping toward its rest, and the clouds sprawled before her. Against the sky, she saw the flag that she'd adopted from Starlene after she became captain of the *Zodiac.* Even in that moment that she found herself in, she stopped to truly take in the details of the flag that she never paid much notice to before. On the flag stood a skeleton, a spear in one hand and a heart in the other. The skeleton appeared to be triumphant, the winner of some unknown battle. Beneath the heel of the skeleton's right foot lie a snake, twisted and bleeding underneath the skeleton's weight. The prophecy that Belladonna Skylark was to fulfill was emblazoned upon the colors of her ship. In her numbness, she watched the flag flutter in the wind. It whipped furiously around, distorting the image.

Belladonna found herself now in a place that resembled much of what she had endured in her life so far. Cornelius Blackfoot, the cause of her family's demise, had taken from her yet again. All that *thing* knew how to do was take. Blackfoot knew that love stirred in the crevices of her heart and sought to pluck that love from her. The demon so badly tried to weaken her by stealing every ounce of love she'd ever felt. Such was the cause of her rotten black heart.

Her enemy held too much power over her, tried to manipulate who she would become by damaging her heart.

Ephraim was now a prisoner of Blackfoot's, and thus, Belladonna was as well. As long as he held Ephraim captive, he also held her heart captive.

Every thought of a life of freedom was forgotten. Her destiny would never allow her to be free. But her destiny would allow her to save those who had to suffer simply because she loved them. And it would allow her to annihilate the destroyer of all she loved. Belladonna would coexist with the dragon within her and allow it to carry her to her rightful place as Dragon empress.

ACKNOWLEDGMENTS

It doesn't feel real that I get to hold this story in my hands. When I was eight years old, my dad sat me down in front of our television, and I watched *Pirates of the Caribbean: The Curse of the Black Pearl* for the first time. Little did anyone know that that film would spark a lifelong love of pirates and satisfy my need for an adventure tale. Belladonna's story has lived in my head since I was nine. Now, here it is, printed and available to the world.

I would like to thank my father and mother, the two who encouraged my creativity from the beginning. My father passed on his love of pirates and all of their adventures to me, certainly unknowingly. My mother recently told me of a time when I was in third grade and I wrote a story about a man in prison who cursed like a sailor. She wanted to be angry with me for knowing such profanities at that age, but she said she couldn't because, after all, wasn't that how prisoners usually spoke? It was the combination of my father's love of pirates and my mother's encouragement of my creativity that I was able to write as a child. For that, I am eternally grateful.

Thank you to my husband, Justin, my best friend and steadfast supporter. He was one of my first readers and spent many, many nights with me on the couch dialoguing back and forth about how I could make this story work. Not only that, but he is one of my biggest cheerleaders and hypes *Skylark* up to anyone he can. I love you, and I am thankful to have you by my side through all things.

Thank you to my cousin, Lydia Gentry, who provided the illustrations for the front cover and interior of this work. I told her my vision, and she ran with it. I am pleased that she got to share in this journey with me, as I am proud that her artwork is now on and in a book that someone can touch and feel. Lydia, your art deserves to be seen by the multitudes.

For everyone who read *Skylark* in its early days, whether that be family, friends, or fellow Morgan James authors, thank you. I appreciated every ounce of feedback you gave, positive or constructive, and am grateful for the supportive community that has backed my writing. All of you are precious to me and my journey.

Lastly, I'd like to thank my Morgan James Publishing family, who I have the pleasure of both publishing through and working for. Thank you to David Hancock, who knew I was a first-time author yet took a chance on me and believed that I had a story worth telling. Thank you to my editor, Cortney Donelson, for encouraging my voice in my writing and helping me perfect it at the same time. Additionally, thank you to Jim Howard, Heidi Nickerson, Amber Parrott, Karen Dimmick, Chris Treccani, and Shannon Peters; all of you played an integral part in *Skylark* coming to life.

ABOUT THE AUTHOR

Emily N. Madison has been a lover of pirates, dragons, and fantasy since the first time her father showed her *Pirates of the Caribbean* at eight years old. Since then, she has read countless books and immersed herself in many worlds. She holds a Bachelor's in English Literature and American History from Regent University. When not working on her other hundreds of book ideas, Emily can be found with her nose buried in a book or at a heavy metal concert. She resides in Virginia with her husband, Justin, and her shelties, Appa and Arwen.

To keep up with what Emily is up to next, see what she is reading, or to get in touch, please visit:
WWW.ENMWRITES.COM
or follow her on Instagram
@EMILYNMADISON_AUTHOR

CPSIA information can be obtained
at www.ICGtesting.com
Printed in the USA
JSHW020206250622
27478JS00002B/2

9 781631 958366